Mr Hendricks swore aloud then said in a more moderate tone, 'The upper classes are all quite mad. I had hoped for a time that you were proving to be otherwise, for your request to go to Scotland was within the bounds of possibility. But you are blessed with a stubbornness that is well outside the bounds of sanity, and a single-mindedness that could wear reason down to a nub.'

'At least I am consistent, Mr Hendricks.'

'You are that, My Lady.'

And then Dru tried something that had not occurred to her before, and dipped her head slightly, doing her best at a shy smile, as her sister would have done when trying to charm a man. Then she looked up at him through her long dark lashes. 'I am sorry to have been such a bother. You have done your best to keep me safe, and I have much to be grateful for. If you can help me in this one last thing, I will see to it that you are properly rewarded for the inconvenience of it.'

He laughed. 'So it has come to this, has it? You mean to use your wiles on me now that all else has failed.' There was a strange pause before his response, as he stared boldly back at her in challenge. 'And how might you reward me if I risk my neck for you?'

AUTHOR NOTE

When I sat down to write LADY FOLBROKE'S DELICIOUS DECEPTION I had a pretty good idea of the communication problem between the two main characters. But beyond that there was nothing but a grey area, and a lot of silence. If Emily had friends, she wasn't telling me. And, other than drinking and fighting, Adrian didn't seem to have much of a social life. The more people I added, the more likely these two were to come to an understanding before I could start their story. It was a conundrum.

And then John Hendricks arrived and sorted out my plot for me. As always, he was timely and efficient, hovering just on the edge of the plot, stepping forward when I needed him and disappearing when I didn't.

It was a thankless job. But I had birthed him into an era when he had no reason to expect anything more than being a secondary character. And yet I liked him. I thought he deserved better. When he decided to storm off at the end of my last book I was eager to know where he'd end up.

And then I met Drusilla. And that explained everything.

LADY DRUSILLA'S ROAD TO RUIN

Christine Merrill

First published in Great Britain 2011
by Mills & Boon, an imprint of Harlequin (UK) Limited,
Eton House, 18-24 Paradise Road, Richmond, Surrey TW9 1SR

ISBN: 978 0 263 21821 3

Harlequin (UK) policy is to use papers that are natural,
renewable and recyclable products and made from wood grown in
sustainable forests. The logging and manufacturing process conform
to the legal environmental regulations of the country of origin.

Printed and bound in Great Britain
by CPI Antony Rowe, Chippenham, Wiltshire

Christine Merrill lives on a farm in Wisconsin, USA, with her husband, two sons and too many pets—all of whom would like her to get off the computer so they can check their e-mail. She has worked by turns in theatre costuming, where she was paid to play with period ballgowns, and as a librarian, where she spent the day surrounded by books. Writing historical romance combines her love of good stories and fancy dress with her ability to stare out of the window and make stuff up.

Previous novels by Christine Merrill:

THE INCONVENIENT DUCHESS
AN UNLADYLIKE OFFER
A WICKED LIAISON
MISS WINTHORPE'S ELOPEMENT
THE MISTLETOE WAGER
   (part of *A Yuletide Invitation*)
DANGEROUS LORD, INNOCENT GOVERNESS
PAYING THE VIRGIN'S PRICE*
TAKEN BY THE WICKED RAKE*
MASTER OF PENLOWEN
   (part of *Halloween Temptations*)
LADY FOLBROKE'S DELICIOUS DECEPTION†

And in Mills & Boon® Historical *Undone!* eBooks:

SEDUCING A STRANGER
TAMING HER GYPSY LOVER*

Regency Silk & Scandal mini-series
†linked to LADY DRUSILLA'S ROAD TO RUIN

To Jim, James and Sean:
for holding down the fort.

Chapter One

John Hendricks took a sip from his flask and leaned back into his corner of the northbound mail coach, stretching his legs in an effort to take up as much space as he could before another passenger encroached on his person. After the week he'd had, he was in no mood or condition to be packed cheek to jowl with strangers.

Mr Hendricks, if there is something else you have to say on your hopes for my future, know that I decided on the matter from the first moment I laid eyes on Adrian Longesley. Nothing said by another is likely to change me on the subject.

The words were still ringing in his ears, three days later. And with each repetition of them the heat of his embarrassment flared anew. The woman was married, for God's sake, and above his station. She'd made her uninterest in him plain enough. If he'd suffered in silence, as he had for three years, he could have kept his job and his pride. Instead, he'd been so obvious in his infatuation that he'd forced her to speak the truth aloud.

He took another swig from the flask. If the blush on his cheeks was visible in the darkness, better to let the others think it was from drunkenness and not the shame of unrequited love.

Adrian had known all along, of course. And would have allowed him to continue as a part of the household, if he'd not made such an ass of himself. But once it was out in the open, there was nothing to do but give up his position and slink away from London.

John's feelings for his old friend rose in a tangle of jealousy, pity and embarrassment at his own behaviour. Despite all that had happened, he liked and respected Adrian, and had enjoyed working for him. But what did it say of his own character that he'd even consider stealing the wife of a man who would need her support and unwavering love as the last of his vision faded?

And how foolish did it make him to think that Emily would leave a blind earl for an unacknowledged natural son? He might have been an equal to Lord Folbroke in looks and temperament, but he had no rank, no fortune. And though his sight was better than Adrian's, he could hardly call it perfect.

John slipped the flask into his pocket and removed his spectacles to give them a vigorous wipe. There was not a woman alive who would leave her husband for a man whose only asset was marginally better vision.

He stared sullenly through the cleared lenses at the two people on the seat opposite as though daring them to comment about his earlier drinking. When he had bought the ticket, he'd had some hazy idea that travelling to Scotland would be like venturing into the wilderness. It would be a place to heal the soul and the nerves in quiet and solitude. He had not allowed for the fact that, to arrive at this hermit's paradise, he would be crammed into a small enclosure with the very humanity he despised. They had been rattling about the interior of the conveyance like three beans in a bottle for hours already. He felt the impact of each bump and rut in his bones, his teeth and his aching brain. The swaying of the coach was made even worse by the gusting winds and the rain that hammered the sides and tried to creep in at the poorly sealed window on his right, wetting the sleeve of his coat when he tried to relax against the curtain.

He thought of the coaching schedule, forgotten in his pocket. It was over thirty hours to Edinburgh and he suspected that, with the wet roads and the gathering darkness, it would take even longer than normal. Not that it mattered to him. He was his own man now, with no schedule to keep.

He wished that the thought cheered him. Thank God that he was still half-drunk. When the last effects of the alcohol had gone from his system, they would be replaced by the panic of a man who had destroyed his old life.

Hung over was no way to start a new one. But when he'd gone to the Swan with Two Necks, trying to buy a ticket out of London, he had been several gins past the point of making that decision and would now have to live with the consequences.

'Beastly weather we are having.' The man across from him seemed to think that stating the obvious was a witty opening gambit.

John ignored him. He'd been forced to leave London because he had said far too much to his employer. That did not mean he wished to blurt every thought to strangers.

The woman that shared the coach with them seemed to have similar sentiments. At the sound of the man's voice, her skirts rustled and she clutched the book of sermons she had been reading, bringing it closer to her face to catch the flickering light of the reading lamp in her corner.

John saw her give the slightest flinch as the other man turned his attention to her. 'Travelling alone, miss?'

She looked up long enough to give the man next to her the frosty glare of someone who did not answer to those to whom she had not been properly introduced. Then she returned to her book.

But the man who addressed her was undeterred. 'Because I would be happy to escort you to your destination.' Although there was plenty of room in the body of the coach, he'd made a point of choosing the seat next to the young lady and tended to use each swerve and jostle as an excuse to crowd her. Now, he was definitely leering.

John had a moment's concern that she might be naïve enough to accept the man's offer out of hand. Then he dismissed it as none of his business.

Her skirts gave another rustle as she drew them tightly to her legs, as though trying to shrink herself enough to minimise contact with the stranger. But that would be near to impossible, for she was of an uncommon height. She did not seem to realise that the movement of the cloth over her legs outlined areas of her body that the man accosting her found most interesting.

As did John, come to that. They were long legs, to match the length of her body. If they matched the small amount of ankle he glimpsed beneath her skirts, they were well shaped. A pity the girl was so Friday-faced. If she'd smiled, she might have been quite pretty.

Though her expression hinted that she was travelling to a funeral, her clothing did not. Bright colours suited her fair skin and the deep blue of her gown made her brown eyes seem even darker. The fabric was expensive, but the cut was conservative, as though she renounced fashion when it impinged on movement or modesty. Her long, black hair was dressed severely away from her face and hidden under a poke bonnet.

If John had to guess, he'd have said *spinster*. Clearly, this was a girl with money, but no prospects. It was a very unusual combination, for the former often created the latter. But reading sermons in public hinted at a moral propriety that would make her unpleasant company, should she deign to open her mouth.

Her dark eyes caught his, just for a moment. In the dim light they seemed to glitter sharp and dark, like the eyes of a hawk.

Do something.

Had she spoken? Or had he just imagined the words, planted firmly in his brain? Surely, if they had come from her, there would have been some softness in them, some urgent courtesy in their appeal to a stranger for help. The command was an invention of his own drunken mind.

'It is quite lonely,' the other man announced, 'to travel without a companion of some kind.'

A merchant, thought John, for he could not seem to resist speculating about the other passengers. And a prosperous one as well. The man could afford his extra weight, for the fabric of the vest stretched across the bulging stomach was a fine brocade. But his head seemed to be outgrowing his hair, which struggled to conceal an expanding forehead that the man now mopped in the early summer heat. He spoke again, addressing the girl, who had not responded to his earlier comment.

'Is there someone waiting to join you at the next stop?'

He was eyeing her carefully to see if there was some small acknowledgement that she was not as alone as she appeared.

John looked as well and saw no such response. The mystery deepened.

Her eyes flicked to him again, and then away, sharp and quick as a knife cut.

Well?

Well, indeed. The only advantage of being a gentleman of leisure was that he did not have to be at the beck and call of anyone. Not even young ladies with large dark eyes and forbidding expressions. It was ungentlemanly of him, but so be it. If nothing else, the last few weeks should have taught him not to become embroiled in the schemes of beautiful women who, in the end, would offer nothing more than dismissive thanks as they rushed past him to the object of their desire.

Very deliberately, he yawned and closed his eyes, pretending to sleep. Then he opened them just enough so that he could continue to watch his companions.

There was a flash of lightning, followed close by a crack of thunder loud enough to make the other man jump in his seat. But the woman was unmoved and the cold white light threw the annoyance on her features into sudden sharp relief.

Do you mean to allow this?

When John did not respond, she turned to look at the man next to her. The merchant was impervious to whatever messages she was sending or he'd have turned to dust in his seat before speaking again. This time, he was louder, as though he thought she might not have heard him before. 'I said, is there someone to greet you at your destination?' John watched the flicker of truth on the face of the girl that admitted she had no one.

Their companion saw it as well. 'I noticed, at the last stop, that you did not eat. If you lack funds, you needn't fear. The Cap and Bells does a fine joint. I would be only too happy to share my portion with you. And perhaps a brandy and hot water, to keep away the chill.'

Then he'd offer to share his room as well, John had no doubt. The fine example of London citizenry across the coach from him was on the make for a bedmate. Without someone to aid her, the man would grow more predatory the farther they got from town.

John offered a silent plea to the sense of duty that pushed him to become involved in the business of others, begging it to lie still, just this one time.

Without warning, the girl announced, 'I am not alone. I am travelling with my brother.' And then she kicked John smartly in the ankle.

It was rather like a nightmare he'd once had, of being an actor forced on stage in a play that he had not learned. The girl opposite him seemed to think him obliged to rescue her, though she had no way of knowing whether his intentions were any more gentlemanly then their companion's.

Very well, then. And be damned to his own sense of honour for participating in this farce. He gave a garumphing, snuffling cough, as someone awakening after a long sleep, opened his eyes with a start and shouted, 'What is it? What? Have we arrived already?' He looked straight into the eyes of the girl across from him, shocked at the feeling of sudden connection between them, as though she could manage to relay the whole of her situation with just a glance. Then he stared at the man beside them, as though just noticing him. 'Is this man bothering you, dear heart?'

'I most certainly am not,' the other man replied. 'And I doubt that you know any more of this girl than I do, for you have been travelling with us for some time and have said not a word to her.'

'I did not feel the need to speak to someone I have known since birth,' John said with some asperity.

'And you—' the man glared at the girl '—I'll wager you do not even know this man's name.'

Come on, he thought, in her general direction. *Choose anything and I will answer to it.*

'It is John,' she said.

He tried to contain his surprise, for she had chosen the single most common name in the world. There was something disappointing about the fact that it fit him so well. He glared at the insolent cit. 'And if I were to give you leave, you would call her Miss Hendricks. But I do not. My dear?' He held out a hand to her, and when she took it without hesitation, he pulled her across the body of the carriage into the seat beside him.

The carriage gave a sudden jolt and she landed half in his lap. The sudden contact was most pleasant, and, for a second, his thoughts were in no way filial. But not a hint of answering blush tinted her pale skin and she grabbed the strap beside the door and sorted herself into the seat between him and the opposite window without further assistance.

To hide his momentary confusion, he removed his spectacles and wiped the lenses on the corner of his handkerchief. When he replaced them, he could see that the woman next to him was bristling in outrage. But she was directing it at the other passenger, glaring in triumph across the coach at her adversary.

You are beautiful when you are angry. It was a foolish sentiment, even when true. Knowing the trouble that they could cause, what sane man wanted to make a woman angry? But in her case, there was a strength and energy in her that was accented by her indignation. John had a moment's desire to reach out and touch her, running a hand lightly over her back as one might, when soothing the feathers of a flustered falcon.

'My apologies,' the man muttered, giving John a wary look. 'If that was the way of it, you'd have best spoken sooner.'

'Or you could have found your manners before speaking at all,' John said back, annoyed at the cheek of the man and at himself for his foolish thoughts. Then he settled back into his seat, pretending to doze again.

Beside him, the woman removed a small watch from her reticule, and looked uneasily from it to the shadows of the landscape passing by their window. In the flashes of lightning, he saw violent movement, as though the trees and hedges were being whipped about by the wind. The swaying of the coach increased. Though it was barely midnight, it appeared that their journey was about to take an unfortunate turn.

Chapter Two

The rain had been falling steadily for hours, and Drusilla Rudney fought the desire to remove the coaching schedule from her reticule to try to catch a glimpse of the stops in the guttering lamplight. They had been forced on several occasions already to get out of the coach and walk in the pouring rain as the horses navigated difficult stretches of wet road. That last time, as they'd stumbled in the dark and the gale, she had managed to raise her head to look and she'd seen the difficulty the coachman had in controlling the frightened animals, who rolled their eyes behind their blinders, trying to watch the storm. But he had managed to calm them again and shouted to the passengers to hurry and take their seats so that they could start again. And now the three of them sat, damp and unhappy in their clothes, waiting for the next stop and hoping that there would be enough time for a hot drink.

Since the fat man who had bothered her could not manage to keep quiet, he had speculated briefly with the other man about the likelihood of a delay. But her pretend brother had said not a word to her since pulling her down to sit beside him.

She remembered the way the fat man beside her had pressed his leg against her skirts, and then imagined how much worse it might have got, had Mr Hendricks not intervened. She had never been this far from home without some kind of chaperon. And although she had known the risks to her reputation, she had not thought that they might involve actual harm to her person. Leaving in haste had been foolish. But common sense had been overcome by her fears for Priscilla. Even now, her sister might be experiencing similar dangers.

She did her best to disguise the involuntary shudder that had passed through her at the thought, hoping that the two men would think it a reaction to sitting in rain-dampened clothing. It would be unwise to reveal her fear in front of a man who had already showed himself willing to prey upon a vulnerable woman. She glared at the merchant across the coach.

She should consider herself lucky that all men were not like him. If they were forced to spend a few hours at the next coaching inn, she would try to pull Mr Hendricks aside and thank him for his aid. Maybe she could even explain some portion of her story, although there was nothing about him that made her think he wished to know her reasons for travelling alone. He had been rather slow to take an interest when she'd needed his help. But now that he had given it, she wished to know if she could call on him again.

She'd heard the slur in his speech when he'd bought his ticket. But his tone had been mild enough. And the spectacles he wore gave a scholarly cast to his features. She'd decided he was a man of letters, perhaps studying for holy orders. Although he was clearly lost to drink, there was something in his face and his mannerisms that made him seem kind and trustworthy. Thus, he would be easily manipulated, even by one as inexperienced with men as she. Of course, Priscilla would have had the man dancing like a puppet by now. But Dru had assumed that his sense of chivalry would bring him promptly to heel in defence of any lady. Instead, it had taken an actual, physical goad.

Of course, now that she could see him from close up, there was a touch of the disapproving schoolmaster about the set of his mouth. She wondered if he thought her fast for travelling alone. Not that he had any right to cast aspersions. When he had first entered the carriage, he had brought with him a cloud of gin and had fallen rather heavily into his seat as though his legs would be taking him no farther for quite some time. But he had been nipping regularly from his flask and had refilled it with brandy at the last stop.

She held the book of sermons before her, wondering if he was more in need of it than she. If he was a clergyman of some kind as she'd suspected, then he had best see to his own weaknesses before correcting others. He had fallen in with her lie quickly enough, when he could just as easily have defended her with the truth. A liar and a drunkard, then. But compared to the coarseness of the other man, he seemed quite harmless.

Yet when she'd almost fallen to the floor of the coach, his response had proved that his reflexes were excellent and his arm strong. He had sorted her back into the other seat as though she weighed nothing. And the thighs on which she'd accidently sat had been hard from riding.

It was a conundrum. She'd have expected him to forgo the saddle for a pony cart, as would befit someone of his nature. The physical prowess he seemed to possess was wasted on a man of letters. And there was something about his eyes, when he had removed his glasses in that moment when he'd cleaned them. The clarity of the colour in them was quite handsome. They were a strange, light brown that shimmered protean gold in the lamp-light. They were the eyes of a man who had seen much, balked at little and feared nothing.

But the man of action she'd imagined, who would ride like a centaur and fight like a demon, was just a trick of the light. He was gone with the return of the spectacles, leaving a drunken cleric in the seat beside her.

At the next inn, the guard shouted for them to leave the vehicle. And they alighted, meaning to stretch their legs and twist the kinks from their backs, only to step down ankle deep into the puddles in the courtyard. The wings of the inn sheltered them from the worst of the wind, but gusts of it still tore at their clothes, making the short scurry to the front door a difficult trip. But her unwilling protector raised his topcoat over their heads to offer some shelter from the worst of it and shepherded her quickly into the public room. In the doorway behind them, the driver was deep in conversation with the innkeeper. When she glanced out of the window, the team was being unhitched from the coach and led away, but there were no replacements stamping eagerly on the flags, waiting to be harnessed.

'What—?' she said to the man who might be called Hendricks.

He held up a hand to silence her, clearly eavesdropping on the conversation of the guard with some other drivers who were gathered at a table by the bar. Then he turned to her. 'It is too bad to go on. I might have known, for it has been growing worse by the hour. Our driver fears that there may be downed trees ahead of us, and does not want to come upon them in darkness.

If the mail gets through at all, I am afraid it will be without us, at least until the morning. We will set out again, at first light, if the storm has abated.'

'That cannot be,' she said firmly, even though she recognised the futility of it.

He gave her a disgusted look. 'Unless you have some arcane power that allows you to change the weather, you are stuck here, as we all are.'

Glancing around the room, she could see that the place was crowded even though the hour was late, for many other coaches on the road had used this town as safe haven. She scanned the faces for the only two she wished to find. But they were not there, probably farther up the road, clear of the storm and still travelling north. 'Never mind a little rain. I must get to Gretna Green before—' Then she shut her mouth again, not wanting to reveal too much of the truth.

He gave her an odd look and said, very clearly 'Nonsense, Sister. You are going to Edinburgh.' He glanced at the fat merchant who had bothered her, then gave her a significant look. 'With me.'

'Not on this coach we are not,' she answered. 'If you notice, we are in Newport, headed for Manchester. If you wish to travel to Scotland on this route, a more logical destination would be Dumfries.'

The man next to her narrowed his eyes and pulled the coaching schedule out of his pocket, paging hurriedly through it. Then he cursed softly, turned and threw the thing out the door and into the rain, glaring at her, as though geography were somehow her fault. 'Dumfries it is then.'

'You do not care about your destination?'

'There are many reasons to go to Scotland,' he said cryptically. 'And for some of them, one destination is as good as the next. But in my experience, there can be only one reason that a young lady would be rushing to such a rakehell destination as Gretna.' He looked at her sharply, the schoolmaster expression returning. 'And what kind of brother would I be, if I encouraged that?'

True enough. She knew from experience that when one's sister had chosen to rush off for the border, one must do their best to put a stop to it. And to share as little of the story as possible with curious strangers. So she looked at the man beside her, doing her best at an expression of wide-eyed innocence. 'Do we have family in Dumfries, Brother?' she asked. 'For suddenly I cannot seem to recall.'

He gave a snort of derision at her inept play-acting and said, 'No family at all. That is why I chose it. But perhaps I am wrong. I did not know until today that I had a sister.'

'And you took that well enough,' she said, unwilling to offer further thanks, lest they be overheard. 'In case anyone enquires, would it be too much trouble for you to have a sick aunt in Dumfries?'

'I suppose not.' He gestured to a table at the fireside. 'As long as you do not mind sitting in comfort, while we have the chance, instead of hanging about in the doorway.'

When she hesitated, she noticed that behind his lenses, there was a twinkle in his eyes that might almost have been amusement. 'It is marginally closer to Scotland on the other side of the room,' he said, as though that would be enough to pacify her. After he had seated her, he procured a dinner for her, adding, in a perfectly reasonable voice, that there was no reason not to take nourishment while they had the chance.

There was one perfectly good reason, she thought to herself. The contents of her purse would not stand for many stops such as this. She thought of Priss, halfway to Gretna by now, and carrying her allowance for the month, because, as the note had said, she had *greater need of it than you, Silly.*

Without thinking, she sighed aloud and then came back to herself, relieved that her new, false sibling had gone back across the room to get himself a tankard of ale. Now that she could compare him to other men, she found him taller than she had estimated, but powerfully built. The timidity of his demeanour did not carry to his body when in motion, nor did the liquor he'd drunk seem to affect him. There was strength and surety in his gait, as though a change in circumstances did not bother him a bit. He navigated easily back to her through the crowded room without spilling a drop of his drink, then slid easily on to the chair on the other side of the small table they shared.

She looked at him apprehensively and wet her lips. And then she stared down into the plate that had been placed before her, as though she had not used his absence to make a detailed examination of his person. She really had no reason to be so curious. While she might tell herself that it was a natural wariness on her part, and an attempt to guard herself against possible dishonour, she was the one who had come on this journey alone and then sought the protection of this stranger, based on necessity and assumptions of good character.

She took the first bite of dinner though she had no appetite for it, and found it plain fare, but good. She vowed that she would finish it all, hungry or no, for who knew when she might eat again? As long as he showed no signs of troubling her as the other man had, she would allow Mr Hendricks to pay as well. If he complained, she would inform him that she had not requested to be fed and that it was sinful to waste the food.

But the man across the table from her was not eating, simply staring back at her, waiting. 'Well?' he said at last, arms folded in front of him. He was looking rather like a schoolmaster again, ready to administer punishment once a confession was gained. 'Do not think you can sit with me, well out of earshot of our companion, and give nothing in return.'

She swallowed. 'Thank you for coming to my aid, when we were in the coach.'

'You left me little choice in the matter,' he said with reproof, shifting his leg as though his ankle still pained him from the kick. 'But even without your request for help, I could not very well sit silent and let the man accost you for the whole of the journey. It was an unpleasant enough ride.' He glanced around him at the rain streaking the window of the inn. 'And not likely to become more pleasant in the immediate future.'

That was good, for it sounded almost as though he would have helped her without her asking. That made him better than the other man in the carriage who would surely have pressed any advantage he had gained over her from her lie. 'I am sorry that circumstances forced me to trouble you, Mr...' And now she would see if he had given the correct name before.

'Hendricks,' he supplied. 'Just as I said in the coach. And you guessed my given name correctly. While I do not overly object to the loan of mine, I suspect you have a surname of your own.' He stared at her, waiting.

Should she tell him the truth? If the whole point of this journey was to avoid embarrassment to the family, it did no good to go trumpeting the story to near strangers.

'Come now,' he said, adjusting the fold of his arms. 'Surely you can be more open with me. We are kin, after all.' He leaned forwards on the table, so that their heads were close together and he could whisper the next words. 'Or how else do we explain our proximity?'

The obvious reason, she supposed. On this route, anyone seeing a couple in a tête-à-tête would think them eloping for Scotland, just as Priscilla had done. She took a breath, wondering if she should she tell him of her father's title, and then decided against it. 'I am Lady Drusilla Rudney.' Then, hoping there would be a way to gloss over the rest of it, she fluttered her eyelashes at him and attempted a smile. 'But to my friends, I am Silly.'

And then, she waited for one of the obvious responses.

I expect you are.

Did they give you cause to be?

Apparently, Mr Hendricks had no sense of humour. 'An unfortunate family nickname, I assume.' And one he would not be using, judging by the pained look in his eye. 'And given to you by the Duke of Benbridge, who is your uncle. No...your father.'

He'd read her as easily as the sermon book in her pocket. She must learn to be quicker or he'd have all the facts out of her, before long. 'Actually, it was my sister who gave me the name. A difficulty in pronunciation, when we were children...' Her explanation trailed off. It surprised her, for rarely did conversation with a stranger leave her at a loss for words.

'Well then, Lady Drusilla, what brings you to be travelling alone? You can afford a maid, or some sort of companion. And to travel in the family carriage, instead of stuck in the mail coach with the likes of me.'

'It is a matter of some delicacy and I do not wish to share the details.'

'If you are going to Gretna, then you are clearly eloping, travelling alone so that your father does not discover you. Little else is needed to tell the tale, other than to ascertain the name of the man involved.'

'I beg your pardon,' she said sharply, insulted that he would think her so foolish. 'I am not eloping. And how dare you think such a thing.'

'Then, what are you doing?' he shot back, just as quickly. The alcohol had not dulled his wits a bit, and the speed of his questioning left her with her mouth hanging open, ready to announce the truth to a room full of strangers.

She took a breath to regain her calm. 'I wish to go to Gretna and stop an elopement,' she whispered urgently. 'And I do not want anyone to know. Once my end has been achieved, there must be no hint of gossip. Not a breath of scandal. No evidence that the trip was ever made.'

Mr Hendricks paused as though considering her story. Then he said, 'You realise, of course, that the trip may be futile.'

'And why would you think that?' Other than that it was probably true. But it was better to appear obtuse in the face of probable defeat, than to be talked into giving up.

He tried again in a much gentler tone. 'Should the couple involved be determined, they will not listen to you. And if they had much of a start on you, they are miles ahead already.'

'Quite possibly,' she agreed.

'The honour of the girl in question is most assuredly breached.'

'That does not matter in the least.' After a day and a night with her lover, allowing the wedding to occur would be the logical solution. But if Priss disgraced herself by marrying Gervaise, she disgraced the family as well. And Dru would get the blame for it, for it had been her job to chaperon the girl and prevent such foolishness. Father would announce that, no matter how unlikely it might be that his awkward daughter Silly could find a man to haul her to Gretna, he was unwilling to risk a second embarrassment. There would be no Season, no suitors and no inevitable proposal. She would spend the rest of her life in penance for Priss's mistake, on the unfashionable edge of society, with the wallflowers and the spinsters.

Was it so very selfish if, just this once, she ignored what was right for Priscilla and looked to her own future? 'I will not let him marry her.' If she had to, she would grab Priss from the very blacksmith's stone and push Gervaise under a dray horse. But there would be no wedding. Dru narrowed her eyes and glared at Mr Hendricks.

He glared back at her, his patience for her wearing thin. 'By travelling alone and in secret, you have compromised your reputation, and are just as likely to end in the soup as the couple you seek to stop.'

'With the need for speed and secrecy, there was little else I could do.' The Benbridge carriage was already tearing up the road between London and the Scottish border, and Priss had left her barely enough to buy a ticket on the mail coach, much less rent a post-chaise. But the scandal of it would work to her advantage in one way: in comparison with Priss's elopement, a solo journey by her ape-leading older sister would hardly raise an eyebrow.

Mr Hendricks saw her dark expression and amended, 'Perhaps

you will be fortunate. The rain that traps us might trap them as well.'

This was hardly good news. Until now, she had been imagining her sister and Gervaise travelling night and day in a mad rush to reach their destination. But if they were held up in an inn somewhere, the chance for recognition and disgrace multiplied by a thousandfold. And in the time they spent alone together, unchaperoned…

She decided firmly that she would not think about the details of that at all. There was nothing she could do about the truth of that, especially if she was already too late. She gave her new brother a look that told him his opinions were unwelcome and said, 'Knowing Mr Gervaise as I do, they are likely to dawdle, for he will not wish to spoil his tailoring in the rain.'

'You do not know the man as well as you think if he has taken some other girl to Scotland.' Mr Hendricks's gaze was direct, and surprisingly clear, as though he were trying to impart some bit of important information. But what it might be was lost upon her.

'It does not matter that I do not know his character. It only matters that I know his destination. He is going to Gretna. We had an understanding.' She had paid him well enough to leave Priss alone. He had taken her money, then he had taken her sister as well. And she was not exactly sure how, but when she found him, she would make him suffer for tricking her and dishonouring the family. She glared at the man across the table. 'The marriage must not occur.'

Mr Hendricks was watching her uneasily, as though he did not quite know what to make of such illogical stubbornness. In the end, he seemed to decide that the best response was none at all, and focused his attention upon his meal, offering no further words of advice or censure.

But watching his enthusiasm for the food, she could not contain a comment of her own. 'After the amount you have been drinking, it is a wonder you can eat at all.'

He glanced up at her, and said, around another bite of meat, 'If you are shocked by it, then you had best stick to your sermons, little sister. What you have seen me drink is nothing, compared to what I imbibed before.'

'That is hardly a point of pride,' she said with a sniff.

'Nor is it any of your business,' he added, taking a large drink of ale. He thought for a moment, and then said, 'Although if it hadn't been for my level of inebriation, I might be riding, right now, in the coach that I intended to take, and not have collapsed into the first one I found. With an excess of blue ruin, I have found my long-lost sister.' He toasted her with his tankard. 'Fate works in mysterious ways.'

'Do you often drink so much that you cannot tell one route from another?' For though he was somewhat rumpled now, when she looked closely at him, she doubted that the behaviour was habitual.

He stared down into his glass, as though wishing it would refill itself. 'My life, of late, has taken an unusual turn.' Then he looked at her, thoughtfully. 'It involves a woman. Given the circumstances, an excessive amount of alcohol and impromptu coach travel made perfect sense.'

'And is this woman in Edinburgh?' she asked, remembering his original destination.

'She is in London. My plan was to take a coach to Orkney.'

'You cannot take a coach to an island,' she said, as patiently as possible.

'I planned to ride as far as John O' Groats and then walk the rest of the way.' The glint in his eyes was feverish, and a little mad. 'The woman in question was married. And not interested in me.' The sentences fell from his mouth, flat and heavy, like pig-iron bars.

For a moment, Drusilla considered offering her sympathy. Though he was inebriated, Mr Hendricks had come to her aid, and gone so far as to buy the food she was eating. But the recent changes in her own life had put her quite out of charity with young lovers, either star-crossed or triumphant. 'If your goal is no more specific than that, you might just as well drown yourself by the Hebrides. Once we reach Scotland, they will be closer.'

'Thank you for your kind words of advice, Sister.' He gave her a strange, direct look, as though he were equally tired of the likes of her.

They would have fallen into silence again had not the innkeeper appeared at their table, followed close behind by the fat merchant, who was shifting eagerly from foot to foot as though he had heard some bit of gossip that he could not wait to share. 'It has been decided that the coach will not continue until morning, if then,' he said, with a satisfied smile.

'I am aware of that,' Mr Hendricks said. His eyes never left hers, as though he thought it possible to ignore the other man out of existence.

'I assume you will be seeking accommodations?' the innkeeper added.

'Obviously.'

'Then there is a small problem,' the innkeeper responded. 'There are three of you, and I have but two rooms left.'

From behind him, the merchant gave an inappropriate giggle, although why he found the prospect of further discomfort to be amusing, she could not imagine.

The innkeeper continued. 'One of the rooms will go to the lady, of course. But you gentlemen must work out between you what is to be done with the remaining space. You can share the other bed, or draw lots for it. The loser can take his chances in the parlour, once the bar is closed. But you had best decide quickly, or I shall give the space to someone else. I suspect we will be seeing more like you with coaches stalled here, or turning back because of the rain.'

'And I see that as no problem at all,' the merchant responded before Hendricks could speak. 'My companions are brother and sister. Since they are such close family, a single room will suffice for them and I will take the other.' He shot her a leer, as though pleased to have caught her in her own trap, and waited for her to admit the truth.

'That will be all right, I am sure,' Mr Hendricks answered before she could so much as gather her breath. She wanted to argue that it would most certainly *not* be all right. She was the Duke of Benbridge's daughter and had no intention of sharing a room with any stranger, much less a strange man.

But there was something calming about the tone of Mr Hendricks's voice, like a hand resting on her shoulder.

It will be all right. Although why she was certain of that, she could not say.

In her silence, he continued as though he was accustomed to speaking for her, and it mattered not, one way or the other whether or not she was in his bed. 'Drusilla shall have the mattress, of course. But if you could spare another blanket for me, I would be most grateful.'

The merchant looked vaguely disappointed, like a dog that had not managed to flush a bird. Then he turned his scrutiny on her, waiting for the weak link to break and the truth to come tumbling out of her.

She stared back at him, showing what she hoped was the correct amount of annoyance at having her plans changed by nature and an overfull inn, but without the outrage that she should be feeling.

Beside her, Mr Hendricks was haggling with the hosteller, who allowed that there might be enough bedding. But there would, of course, be an extra charge for it. Apparently it was at least twice the rate that Mr Hendricks found appropriate.

As the innkeeper argued about supply and demand and reminded her *faux* sibling that the same blanket could be let at triple the price to the next passenger who would be forced to sleep on the floor, the sounds of the room seemed to diminish. All Drusilla heard was the sound of imaginary coins clinking from her reticule into the hand of the innkeeper. She had taken all the loose money she could find when setting out after Priss, without picking the pockets of the servants or going to her father and explaining the predicament. There had been scant little available. She suspected Priss had seen to that, specifically to prevent her following.

When Dru had counted her funds, it had seemed enough to mount a rescue. There was enough for the ticket, her food and perhaps one stop along the way. But she had not allowed for tipping the guard, emergencies, or the exorbitant rates that she might find in places where travellers were at the mercy of innkeepers and would pay what the market might bear. At this rate, she would be penniless by tomorrow's lunch. She would be forced to turn back and admit everything to Father, or to put herself at the mercy of strangers and hope for the best.

She glanced at Mr Hendricks, who was still arguing with the innkeeper. 'I will do without the blanket. But for that price, I expect we will have space to continue this meal in our room. Give us the larger of the two, and send the bags up so that we might be comfortable. Drusilla?' His tone was that of an older brother, used to controlling his family.

But the sound of her own name, said in that smooth male voice, and without any polite preamble or foolish nicknames, made her skin prickle. 'Yes, John,' she answered, ducking her head in submission and grabbing her plate to follow him.

Chapter Three

When the door of the room closed behind them, Mr Hendricks released a string of curses directed at no one in particular. And although she should have been shocked, Drusilla had to admit that they effectively described her own feelings on the latest turn of events. He turned to glare at her. 'Do not think to complain about what has occurred, for it is completely your own fault. If you had not forced me to lie for you, you would have the room to yourself.'

'And at the prices they are charging, I would not have been able to pay for it,' she responded, just as cross.

'You are a duke's daughter. And you do not have enough blunt in your pocket to stay in an inn?' He laughed. 'Call the innkeeper back, mention your father's name and not only will he extend you credit, he will turn out one of the other guests so that we may have two beds and a private sitting room, instead of this squalid hole he has given us.'

'If I wished to bandy my father's name in every inn between here and Gretna, I would be travelling escorted in a private carriage. And you would be sleeping on the floor of the taproom.' She narrowed her eyes. 'Where you belong.'

Her unwilling companion bowed in response. 'Thank you so much for you kind opinion of me, Lady Drusilla. It is particularly welcome coming from one who cannot pay for her own bed.'

Though she was used to being the brunt of sarcasm at home, somehow it hurt more coming from Mr Hendricks. And she had brought it upon herself by taunting him.

But before she could apologise, he continued. 'I suppose the next thing you will do is request that I loan you sufficient to cover your dinner, the room and tomorrow's breakfast as well.' When she did not correct him, he laughed bitterly. 'Why am I not surprised at this? Is it not typical that a member of your class should be relying on me, yet again, to rescue them from their own folly at the expense of my own needs?' He was gesticulating wildly now, pacing the little space available in their room. 'Mr Hendricks, write my letters for me. Mr Hendricks, rent me a room. Mr Hendricks, lie to my wife. Not a word of this to my husband, Hendricks. As if I have no other goal in life than to run hither and yon, propping up the outlandish falsehoods of people too foolish to predict their outcome.' He stopped suddenly, as though just noticing that he was speaking the words aloud. Then he dropped his hands to his sides and examined her closely. 'You are not about to cry, are you?'

'Certainly not.' She reached up and touched her own cheek to make sure. She was not normally given to bouts of tears, but it would be most embarrassing to succumb without warning.

'That is good,' he said. 'I am not normally so transparent in my feelings. But it has been a trying week. And as you pointed out earlier, I am somewhat the worse for drink and ranting about things that are no fault of yours.'

'But you are right in your displeasure,' she allowed. 'It was unfair of me to request your help in a situation you had no part in creating.'

He sat down next to her suddenly. 'I almost wish you were crying. I'd have been much more able to resist you had that been the case.'

Resist me? She had hardly brought the force of her personality to bear on the man, other than the kick on the ankle. And although she was often described by men as formidable, it was usually said in a tone of annoyance, or occasionally awe. Though it meant nearly the same, it felt much nicer to be irresistible.

He looked at her thoughtfully, pushing his spectacles up the bridge of his nose as though trying to get a clear view of the situation before speaking again. Then he said, 'Leaving London with no chaperon and no money was very foolish of you. But since I was equally foolish to leave the city drunk and on the wrong coach, I have no right to upbraid you.'

Comparing the two situations, she could hardly call them equal. His was probably the worse. But he was the one with the fatter purse and she was in no position to make enemies. 'Thank you,' she said as mildly as possible.

He frowned for a moment, as though trying to remember something, then added, 'Did I mention earlier that I am currently without a position?'

'No, you did not.' Although why it should matter, she had no idea.

'Then, my lady, I see a solution to both our problems.' His previous insolence evaporated in a single sentence. In its place was a natural deference, with no hint of the obsequious servility she'd seen in some servants. 'I have some experience in dealing with situations rather like yours. Until several days ago, I was personal secretary to the Earl of Folbroke.'

That would explain it, then. He wasn't a preacher or a teacher. He had been a confidential employee of a peer. 'And under what circumstances did you leave this position?' she asked, trying to decide where the conversation was likely to lead them.

'Nothing that would prevent him from giving a positive reference, were he here now.'

Drusilla was glad he was not. The room was hardly big enough for the two of them, without adding former employers into the mix.

'I have letters to that effect,' Mr Hendricks said.

'Which are?'

'In London.'

'I see.'

He removed his spectacles to polish them before continuing. 'But that job gave me experience in dealing with the sort of delicate situations that sometimes occur in families such as yours.'

Utterly mad ones, you mean. The way he'd been raving before, she was sure that he had interesting stories to tell, were he the sort of man to share confidences about his employers. Which he was not.

'Handling matters with discretion is a personal strong point of mine,' he confirmed, as though reading her mind. 'And if you could ensure me of repayment when we return to London, a bit more for my troubles, and perhaps a letter of reference?'

'More than that. My father will write the letter himself. And he will see to it that you are generously rewarded at the end of the affair.'

Behind his glasses, Mr Hendricks's amber eyes glittered. References from an earl were no small thing. But if he could win the favour of a duke, he would be seen as nearly invaluable by his next employer.

'The Duke of Benbridge will be most grateful to hear that the matter was handled with discretion.' After he got used to the idea, at any rate.

'He will not mind that you are travelling alone?' Hendricks asked, searching for a flaw in her story.

Her father would be livid when he learned that Priss had run, and even angrier to know that Dru had not caught her before she'd left the house. In comparison to that, travelling alone or hiring a stranger would be as nothing. 'He will not be happy,' she admitted. 'But it is not as if I am the one eloping with Mr Gervaise. I am trying to prevent his elopement…with another.' If it was possible, she would keep Priss out of the story a while longer. If Hendricks knew of her father, then it was possible he'd heard gossip of Benbridge's wilful younger daughter and would realise that the girl might need to be dragged kicking and screaming back home. 'Just a trip to Scotland and back. It will be very little trouble at all.' At least Drusilla meant to be no trouble. Her sister was likely to be trouble enough for two people. 'Once I find the couple, I will be able to handle the rest of it. But if you could clear the way for me, paying bills, handling luggage and protecting me from men such as our companion?'

'And keep my mouth shut at the end of it?' For a moment, the candid Mr Hendricks had returned and was grinning at her.

She returned a small, polite smile. 'Precisely.'

'Very well, then. I am at your disposal.' He offered his hand to her. She accepted it and was given a manly shake. His palm was warm and dry against hers and the feeling of carefully contained power in his arm gave her a strange feeling in the pit of her stomach.

When he released her hand, he had an odd look on his face, as though he'd felt something as well. Perhaps it had to do with the quality of the cooking, for they had shared the same food.

And now they shared a room.

Her stomach gave the same little flip. It was probably nothing more than nerves. Because Mr Hendricks showed no signs of quitting the place and leaving her in privacy. To speed him on his way, she asked, 'And this evening?' She glanced around the room, and then significantly at the door. 'Where do you intend to sleep?'

'Right here, of course.'

'You most certainly will not—'

He cut her off before she could object and the firmness returned to his voice. 'There was nothing in the agreement we have made that would lead me to believe I must sleep in the stable.'

'Nor was there anything about it that implied that I wish to share a room with you.'

'The implication was tacit,' he said. 'If not, you could have announced in the tavern that our relationship was an illusion.'

'I never expected things to progress as quickly as they did,' she said. 'Nor did I expect you to be stubborn on the point.'

'I see,' he said. 'You think my wishing to sleep in a bed when one presents itself is a sign of stubbornness and not common sense.'

'I expect you to behave as a gentleman,' she said. 'And as one who is in my employ.'

'It is late. And it is not in my ability to aid you until the morning,' he said. 'My service to you will begin at first light. I expect, at that time, that I will need all my wits to keep ahead of you. And for that, I will need adequate sleep. If you were seeking a dogsbody who would lie in the hall just to ensure your modesty, then you must seek him elsewhere. In my last position, I was treated almost as a member of the family and well paid.'

'And yet you left it,' she pointed out and saw the tiny twitch of his eye at her reminder.

'But even dead drunk, I had the sense to leave London with enough money for accommodations,' he countered. 'You did not. I have paid for this room and mean to stay in it.' He smiled benevolently. 'Since you are my employer, I will hardly deny you the space, if you wish to remain with me.'

Perfectly true and annoyingly rational. 'Then it is I who must sleep in the stable,' she said, doing her best to look pathetic and elicit his sympathy.

'Or on the floor,' he offered. 'Although it does not look very comfortable. Or you can take your half of the mattress, if you will leave me in peace.'

'If I leave *you* in peace?' she said, outraged.

'I have no intention of accosting you in the night, nor do I mean to tell anyone of the close quarters,' he said. 'I know my own nature and feel quite able to resist your charms.'

'Thank you,' she said, a little annoyed that at the first sign of conflict she had gone back to being her easily resistible self.

He glanced at her, as though speculating. 'But I cannot vouch for your motives. In our first meeting, you were the aggressor.

For all I know, you are the sort of woman who forces herself on to unwary travellers and robs them of their purses, or murders them in their beds.'

'How dare you.'

Then she saw the twinkle in his eye. 'I am properly convinced. Only a lady of the bluest blood can raise that level of outrage over so small a jest. Your honour is safe from me. And as for my honour?' He shrugged. 'I doubt you would know what to do with it, should you find it.' He sat down on the edge of the bed and pulled off his boots, then stripped off his coat and waistcoat and loosened his cravat.

There was no reason that his words should hurt her, for they were true. They were not even an insult. No decent girl should have any idea how to approach a strange man in her bed. But she hated to be reminded of her ignorance and to feel that he was amusing himself with her *naïveté*. But it was late and she was tired, and could think of no alternative sleeping arrangements if he was unwilling to move. She stared at the bed, then at him. 'If it is only for the few hours until dawn, I think I can manage to control myself.'

'Unless you are driven wild by the appearance of a man's bare feet,' he said, not bothering a glance in her direction. 'I will retain my shirt in deference to your modesty. But I mean to remove my socks and dry them by the fire.'

'Is there any reason that I would be inflamed at the sight of them?' she asked, suddenly rather curious. For other than in paintings, she could not remember ever seeing any male feet.

'None that I know of. But if you wish, you may assure yourself that they are not cloven hooves.' He pulled back the covers and she caught a glimpse of them as he rolled easily into his side of the bed. They were quite ordinary, although there was something distinctly masculine about the size.

But being able to travel with dry toes tomorrow would be rather pleasant. So she went to her side of the bed, with her back to him, and as discretely as possible removed her boots, undid her garters and rolled her own stockings down.

Then she glanced at the bed again, trying not to look at the body already in it. To lie down beside it would be more than a careless disregard for modesty. But she was very tired, and there might not be another chance to sleep in a bed, not even part of one, between here and the end of her journey. 'I have, in the past, been forced to share a mattress with my sister. That did not upset my sleep.' But Mr Hendricks seemed much larger than Priscilla. And he was occupying slightly more than half of the available space. She wondered, uneasily, how much room she was likely to need.

He rolled so that he could look at her again as she arranged her stockings next to his. His eyes flicked briefly to her feet, bare on the cold floor of the inn, and then just as quickly back to her face. He gave her a strange, tight smile. 'But I am not really your brother.' Then he removed his spectacles, folded them and placed them on a stool next to the bed. 'We will manage the best we can.' He rolled so that his back was to her again. 'When you are ready to retire, please extinguish the candle.'

Once she was sure that his eyes were truly closed, Dru dropped the front of her gown and loosened the stays built into it to make sleeping a little easier. She feared that the shortness of breath she was experiencing was more the sign of rising panic. She was not even a day from home, but it was farther than she had ever travelled without escort. And on the very first night, she had fallen into what the map maker might label *terra incognita*, a place where the rules as she understood them did not apply. She was in bed with a strange man and both of them were barefoot. Although no governess had lectured her on this particular circumstance, she was sure that the forecast would have been dire.

She suspected that Priss would have managed the situation much better, for the girl had been so unwilling to follow the dictates of convention that she would not feel their absence.

But Dru missed them sorely. She must hope that the man she had hired to aid her was as honest and dependable as he managed to look, in some lights at least. Once he was rested and sober, and wearing his spectacles again, everything would be all right. She remembered the flash of gold in his eyes, after he'd removed his glasses, but just before he'd closed them. Strange, deep, unfathomable eyes. Eyes that had been places and seen things. And they had been looking at her.

'Here there be dragons,' she whispered, blew out the candle and lay down beside him.

From somewhere on the other side of the mattress, she heard a groan, and the muttered, 'I will slay them in the morning.' And then, there was nothing but silence.

Chapter Four

When she woke the next morning, she was stiff with discomfort and not all the pain she felt could be blamed on the stress of travelling. She had slept with her arms folded tightly across her chest, fearing that the least movement would rouse her companion.

But he had not seemed at all bothered by her presence. His even snoring was a demonstration of that. It had roused her several times during the night. Of course, he was quiet enough now that it was almost light and time to be getting up again. She grumbled to herself at the unfairness of it, tossing to lie on her other side.

He was silent because he was awake. Only inches from her nose he lay facing her, watching.

And why she had thought him a parson on the previous day she had no idea. So close like this, his eyes were reminiscent of some great cat. His body reminded her of that as well, for there was a stillness in it now that did not seem so much immobility, as the gathering of energy that came, right before the pounce.

And that attention was focused on her. Like a rabbit, she responded to it by freezing. Unable to turn away from him, she lay there, paralysed, waiting for the eventual assault, yet was unable to fear it. While she'd not thought further than the desperate effort to save her sister's reputation, she'd put her own honour at stake. And that particular commodity was so shelf worn as to be practically useless. While it was foolish to put it at risk, she sometimes wondered if anyone even cared that she possessed it.

But in this moment, she was sure that Mr Hendricks had noticed, was giving the matter some thought and would divest her of it with efficiency and discretion, should she ask him to.

Then the man next to her sat up, yawned, stretched and reached for his glasses. He put them on; when he looked at her again, it was as if the great cat she feared was safely encased behind a thick, protective window. It watched her for a moment, then lost interest, retreating slowly back into its cage and out of sight, leaving the somewhat owlish parson she had noted on the previous day.

'You slept well, I trust?' he asked.

'As well as can be expected,' she admitted.

'Very good.' He swung his legs out of the bed and to the floor, reaching for his socks and boots. 'I will leave you to prepare yourself for the day, and will be returning in…' he reached for his watch and checked the time '…approximately fifteen minutes. Will that be sufficient?'

'Certainly. I will go down to the common room for breakfast, so that you will know when the room is empty.'

He nodded, then left her.

In his place was a strange feeling, almost of bereavement. It was hardly appropriate. She had only just met the man and should be relieved that he was allowing her some privacy so that she could have a wash. And she had best get about it, for she was willing to wager that when he'd said fifteen minutes, he had meant exactly that and would be measuring it on a watch that was both properly maintained and more than usually accurate. He would be an efficient task master, well aware of the schedule and the need to adhere to it, if she wished to reach her goal.

She should be pleased. Had this not been exactly what she needed? But as she sat up and reached for her valise and prepared to refresh herself, she sighed.

Less than an hour later, they were side by side again in the carriage and travelling north. The man who had bothered her yesterday was there again today, watching her closely from the other seat. He eyed Mr Hendricks as well, as though looking for some resemblance between them or some sign that the night had been spent in more than sleep.

Mr Hendricks noticed it as well and gave the man a dark look. 'I trust *you* slept well, sir.'

Drusilla smiled to herself as the man coloured from guilt.

'I expect the day's travel to be equally uncomfortable,' he said, this time to Dru. 'The driver was in the parlour when I took my breakfast; he has got word that the roads grow more difficult the farther north we travel. They may become impassable.'

'I prefer not to invoke disaster by discussing it,' she said uneasily.

Mr Hendricks shrugged. 'It is better to be prepared against the eventuality of it. Then one can posit likely alternatives, should the worst occur and the coach fail us. Now, if you will forgive me, Sister, I mean to rest. It was a beastly night and I got little sleep.' He glared at the man opposite them, making it clear who was to blame for his bad humour.

The merchant answered with a similar glare, as though to say, even if they were siblings, he did not care.

'But if you need anything, my dear, do not hesitate to wake me.' Although he said it mildly, there was an underlying tone of menace in the words. Yesterday's troubles would not be repeated. If her harasser gave so much as a glance in her direction, he would pay dearly for it. Then Mr Hendricks closed his eyes and tipped his hat forwards to shield his face as he napped.

Drusilla reached for the book in her reticule and tried to hide the strange thrill that it gave her to be protected. When Priss was in attendance, Dru's life was largely without such courtesies. If required to, the men who flocked around her sister might come to her aid, but it would be done as an afterthought, in an effort to curry favour with the daughter that actually interested them.

Of course, Mr Hendricks was doing so because she had agreed to pay him—and he was worth every penny. At each change of horses, he was up and out the door in one smooth movement, even if the coach was not fully stopped. It was strange to think of his movements as graceful, but there was a kind of economy to them that rivalled anything Mr Gervaise could demonstrate on the dance floor. And the sun glinting off his short blond hair was every bit as attractive as Gervaise's dark handsomeness.

He would ignore the coachman's cautions to 'Have a care!' and the shouts from the guard that there would be no time for passengers to alight, then go straight to the innkeeper. She could watch from the window as he described their quarry in succinct terms: a tall dark man, nattily dressed, travelling with a petite blonde in a black carriage with a crest upon the door. He would take in the innkeeper's response, toss the man a coin for his troubles and be back in his seat before the horses were fully harnessed.

He was organised, efficient, left nothing to chance and seemed totally focused on her comfort. He would adjust curtains to make sure her seat was shaded from the sun, but not too gloomy to read. He got her food and refreshments almost before she could request them.

If she was the sort of woman prone to flights of fancy, she would come to enjoy it all a bit too much and imagine that it was anything other than a job to him.

A particularly vicious bump sent her sliding across the seat into him. Without waking, he reached out an arm to steady her.

To maintain their fictional relationship, she tried to take the sudden contact without flinching, but his hand on her arm was strangely unsettling. And for that, she had only herself to blame. She had been too much out of the society, if she could not even manage to accept a little help without reading things into it. Though it was hardly gentlemanly to touch a lady without permission, he could not very well let her slide off the seat.

Yet this felt like somewhat more. Almost as if he had been her brother, or a very close friend, and cared what happened to her, even without opening his eyes.

Because you employ him, said a voice in her head that was as cold and rational as her father would have been. *It is in his best interest to keep you intact, if he wishes the favour of the Duke of Benbridge.*

But more than that, his touch had been innocent, yet strangely familiar. Sure of itself. And sure of her. It had made her want to reach out and clasp his hand in thanks.

She took a firmer grip on the binding of her book, to make sure that the temptation was not acted upon.

It appeared, as they travelled, that Mr Hendricks would be proven right about the difficulties that lay before them. The carriage had been slowing for the better part of the morning, and Mr Hendricks had removed his watch from his pocket on several occasions, glancing at the time, comparing it to the schedule and making little tutting noises of disapproval. When she raised a questioning eyebrow, he said, 'The recent rains have spoiled the roads. I doubt we will be able to go much farther today.'

'Oh dear.' There was little more to be said, other than to voice her disappointment. It was not as if arguing with Mr Hendricks would change the quality of the road, after all.

Half an hour later, the coach gave a final lurch and ground to a stop in the mud. The drivers called to the passengers to exit and for any men strong enough to assist in pushing.

As Mr Hendricks shrugged out of his coat and rolled up his sleeves, Drusilla looked in dismay at the puddle in front of the door. As she started down the steps, her companion held up a hand to stay her. 'Allow me.' Then he hopped lightly to the ground, and held out his arms to her.

'You cannot mean to carry me,' she said, taking a half-step back.

'Why not?'

'I am too heavy for you.'

He gave her an odd look. 'I hardly think it will be a problem. Now hurry. My feet are getting wet.'

Gingerly, she sat on the edge and lowered herself towards him. Then he took her in his arms, turned and walked a little way up the hill to a dry place. He proved himself right, for he carried her easily. His body was warm against hers; suddenly and unreasonably, she regretted that she had not lain closer to him in the night. It felt delightful to have his arms about her and she allowed her own arms to creep about his neck, pretending it was only to aid in balance and had nothing to do with the desire to touch him.

Too soon he arrived at the safe place and set her down on the ground. 'Wait for me here, Sister.'

Was the last word a reminder of her role? she wondered. As he laboured behind the coach, she could not manage to think of him thus. His broad shoulders strained, outlining themselves against the linen of his shirt. She could see muscle, bone and sinew in the strength of his arms and his legs as well, his lower anatomy well defined by the tightness of his mud-splattered trousers.

It made her feel strange, rather like she had first thing in the morning, when he had been staring at her. She put a hand to her forehead, wondering if she had taken ill, and then let it fall to her side in defeat. It was getting harder and harder to pretend that her reactions to Mr Hendricks were related to heat or indigestion. It excited her to have his attention, if she fluttered at every glance and touch.

Perhaps her sister's foolishness was contagious. She was normally far too sensible to be looking at a man and thinking the things she was. More importantly, she should not be looking at this particular man. She had hired him, for heaven's sake. He was her inferior. Not a suitor. Not a lover. Not even a friend. It was no different than Priscilla and her dancing master.

Except in one thing. Mr Hendricks had shown no interest in seducing her. Last night, with the candour brought on by too much alcohol, he had admitted that his heart was already bruised. He had been eager to withdraw from civilisation, particularly the company of women. If he had even the slightest idea what was going on in her head, he would depart from her at the first opportunity, leaving her to face this calamity alone.

As if to punish her for her lapse, the horses gave a tug and the body of the coach overbalanced still further. And then, with a horrible splintering, the mired wheel gave way. She covered her eyes with her hands, wishing she could reject the reality of the destroyed transport and the attractiveness of her companion. It was all ruined, as was her Priss.

And she could not help but think that it was all her fault. If she had behaved with more foresight while they were still in London, been more strict… Or perhaps less so… If she had been a better example, or listened with more compassion to her sister's problems…then Priss would not have run away. And she would not be sitting beside a broken coach, staring at a man's shoulders and thinking nonsense.

She felt the shadow of him cross her face, before he spoke. 'Well, then. That's done for.'

'It's over.' Because it was. She could not walk to Scotland. By the time they could find another carriage, the couple would be even farther ahead of them. She might as well adjust to the idea of Mr Gervaise for a brother-in-law, and a father so angry that she would never see polite society again, lest she follow the path of her younger sister and humiliate him.

He gave a short laugh. 'Then you will be glad that I am here. For while the coach is done, the journey is hardly over. If you wish to continue, that is.'

'Continue? Of course.' Her eyes flew to the coach. 'Can they get us a post-chaise?'

'They'll do it for two passengers, but not for three.'

'There are only two of us,' she said.

Mr Hendricks cocked his head in the direction of their companion who was leaning against the broken axle. 'After the way we have treated him, it is unlikely that he will yield his place to us. And do not think for a moment that you will change partners as though you were waltzing at Almack's and go on with him instead,' Hendricks said firmly. 'I hesitate to think what might happen to you if he gets you alone.'

A variety of responses occurred to her. She should have told him that she was not that foolish, that he had no right to talk to her in that tone. Instead, she announced, 'I have never been waltzing at Almack's, and, if I had, I certainly would not leave you in the middle of a dance.' It was true. She had procured the vouchers with Priss in mind. She had not needed Father to tell her that the girl would not show to best advantage if both of them were on the floor. But it made her look like a looby to announce the fact now. It was bad enough to be thought foolish, but worse to be seen as exactly what she was: a wallflower spinster, too busy watching over the virtue of others to get the benefit of a Season.

Mr Hendricks was staring at her as though she has sprouted feathers. 'Go and speak to the driver. See what else can be done,' she commanded in her most aristocratic tone. 'I wish to be in Scotland before tomorrow, Hendricks. There is no time to waste.'

He did not need to be told his job. She hated people who solved their problems by tongue-lashing the nearest servant, but at least it made him turn from her so she could no longer see his look of pity.

He came back a short time later, holding out a hand to her as though there was nothing strange between them. 'The coachman tells me that southbound drivers claim it is this bad and worse for quite some way. Not fit for coach or wagon even if we could get one. But two horses, keeping to dry ground and travelling cross country, will have more success. I've bribed the driver to give us the wheelers and let us go on alone.'

'You want us to continue on horseback?' As though that was not obvious, without her chattering like a parrot at the poor man.

He answered with a nod; if he thought her dull witted, he was kind enough to ignore it. He produced a compass from his pocket, glancing up at the sun for confirmation. 'We will travel north and hope for drier roads when we reach Lancashire.' Then, as though remembering that it was not he who led, said, 'Does this meet with your approval, my lady?'

She blinked, wondering if she would have managed to snatch victory from the jaws of defeat in such a handy way had she not found him. 'I think I am most fortunate to have taken you on, Mr Hendricks.'

'Thank you, Lady Drusilla.'

Chapter Five

*T*hank you, Lady Drusilla. *As you please, my lady.* Even as John walked back to help unhitch the horses from the coach, the voice in his head mocked him. In taking this trip, hadn't he been planning to get out from under the thumbs of attractive and unattainable women? He'd only just got clear of Emily. And now, this.

When he'd realised that there was no space at the inn, he should have offered to pig up with the cit instead of carrying the farce any further. But he'd been drunk and querulous and the man annoyed him more than the girl.

Of course, it had been fortunate that he'd got time alone with Lady Drusilla Rudney and found a way to make himself invaluable. The Duke of Benbridge was terribly high in the instep; a letter of thanks from him would be a welcome addition to his references. But there would be no glowing recommendations if he was caught playing chamber games with the duke's lovely daughter.

Only moments after he'd accepted her offer of employment, he'd got a look at those shapely calves bared as the stockings came off and begun to regret the whole plan. When he'd managed to sleep, he'd dreamt of her. And he'd woken with a morning's desire, hurrying from the room before she could notice and enquire.

He had avoided her at breakfast, drinking strong black coffee to dull the after-effects of the gin and keeping busy with the plans for their departure. Then he had taken his place beside her to prevent the other man from encroaching upon her space. The carriage rocked her against his body in a way that would have been pleasant had not his role as her brother prevented any enjoyment. To curb the effect her nearness had on his nerves and body, he'd been forced to close his eyes and sink into the headache still plaguing him.

It disgusted him that his resolve to forswear all women and live in solitude had not even lasted as long as his inebriation. But he could hardly be blamed; the cit in the carriage had been panting after her as well and he had not been forced to share a bed with her. Lady Drusilla was a damned attractive woman, but seemed unaware of the effect she had on the men around her, wandering about alone and putting her virtue at risk. Any feelings John had for her were not a symptom of fickleness. They were proof that he was male.

But when she'd said she had an 'understanding' with the gentleman they were chasing, his first thought had been, *At least you are not yet married.* As if that would matter. Even if she was unattached, she was a duke's daughter and he was the bastard of who knew who.

Of course, she had said her Gervaise was a plain mister and not the Marquis of Gretna Green. It seemed that if the lady's heart was engaged, a title was not required. And John knew himself to be a better man in one respect. No matter what the circumstances of his birth, at least he was not the sort who made promises to one lady and ran for the border with another.

He had half a mind to thrash sense into this Gervaise fellow for running off on her. Though Lady Dru's tongue was sharp, she deserved better. That John would find himself rushing her north and into the arms of such a lacklustre lover was an even sharper irony. It was too like the part he'd played in the reconciliation of Emily and her husband.

He'd told himself often enough that his own parentage was not a reflection of his worth as a man. But when given a chance to test the theory, society always proved the opposite. And if Lady Dru was eager enough for her Mr Gervaise to set off cross country without a feather to fly on, hoping to win him back, then she would not be interested in some itinerant gentleman she met in the coach, even if that man was unwise enough to take a fancy to her.

Which he did not mean to do. John thought of a certain amiable widow who lived near the Folbroke country estate. It had been some months since his last visit to her. The extended period of celibacy must be addling his brain. Though he never seemed to be the target of it, the haze of feminine lust around his recent employers had raised something in him that was nothing more than envy disguised as infatuation and a desire to take care of natural and unmet needs.

When the carriage had got stuck, as he'd known it would, it had been almost a relief to exercise some of demons from his brain with pushing on the thing. Of course, to do it he had taken his employer in his arms and taken her to high ground, which had only made things worse. She was curvy under the simple gown she wore. And she had clung to his neck as though she'd enjoyed it, her red lips parted in surprise at how easily he'd carried her. He'd set her down quickly, out of the mud, before she could notice her lapse and his impropriety. If she spotted it, she would scold him for it, putting up barriers of rank and bad temper that were not the least bit threatening, once one knew her.

Strangely, he felt he did know her. Perhaps he was reading too much into the intent way she looked at him, or how easy it had been to talk to her on the previous evening, when they had been alone and no one could hear.

Then there had been that moment of awkwardness she'd displayed earlier, when she'd said she had not danced at Almack's. She must have meant that she had no permission to waltz and that she would not have been so rude as to slight any partner. For a moment, it had almost sounded as though she was woefully inexperienced in the arts of society and had some personal reason not to give him up when he'd held her.

He shook his head. He was dreaming again. If he was fortunate, at the end of the journey he would find a Scottish widow sympathetic to his plight, and he would regain his equilibrium.

As he led the horses back to Lady Dru, he put on his most proper and deferential air, getting clear in his own mind the distance between them and the relationship they must have: respectful courtesy on his part and complete indifference on hers.

She looked dubiously at the horses, which were probably not the fine bloods to which she was accustomed.

'You have experience enough to ride, do you not?' he asked.

'Yes,' she answered, although her tone did not make her sound the least bit sure. 'But I did not pack a habit.'

He almost sighed in relief to hear the sort of clothes-obsessed response he'd expected from a smart young lady of the *ton*, foolish and easily dismissed. 'There is no place to change into it, even if you had it.' He gave her an encouraging smile. 'In any case, there will not be room enough to take much luggage. You will have to make do with a single bag; the rest will travel north to meet you when you reach your destination.'

'I do not have more than that now,' she said, glaring at him again. 'I left in rather a hurry and am not such a great ninny that I wasted what time I had in packing band boxes.'

Damn. 'Of course, my lady.'

Then she whispered more urgently, 'But, Mr Hendricks, there is a problem. This saddle is…wrong.'

'You are referring to the lack of a side saddle?' he asked. 'Coach horses are not generally equipped for a lady's Sunday ride. These are accustomed to having a postillion, so at least we will not have to worry about being thrown into the dirt. But I cannot promise more than that.'

Such an enormous beast would frighten a normal woman to tears, but his employer was staring at the horse with a raised chin and a dark look. Then she stared back at the saddle with apprehension. 'But what am I to do?'

There, at last, he saw the frightened girl under the iron façade. Perhaps this trip was not as easy as she made it out to be. He tried to hide his smile at the well-bred delicacy that thought spreading her legs was more risky than breaking her neck on a coach horse. 'You must weigh your desire for further rapid progress against the need to retain your modesty in the wilds of the country, where no one will see you.' He hoped she would take the more sensible choice, but knew that she would not.

'I cannot ride astride,' she said, finally, 'but I must continue north.'

'Then you can balance on your hip as best you can with no pommel to hold on to. Or we can use one horse for the luggage and you may ride with me.' It would be faster than walking the horses so that she did not slip from the saddle, but it would mean that he would have to hold her close as they travelled, which would be awkward in ways she could not possibly imagine.

She stared back at him, brow smooth, eyes cool, chin raised and lips narrowed. 'It cannot be helped, I suppose.' The expression put him firmly in his place, assuring him that the ride would not be a pleasant one for either of them.

And yet… He thought for a moment that he saw a fluttering in the pulse of her neck and a nervous swallow. And the faintest of pink flushes to her cheek. Then it was gone.

He cursed his wayward imagination and mounted the larger of the two horses, then offered her a hand up. To assure her, he said, 'Let us go a short way and see how we manage. You need have no concern for your safety, for I am an excellent horseman.'

'I know you will not let me fall,' she said. Her confidence in his abilities would have pleased him had it not been delivered in a testy voice, as though she'd just as soon be dropped upon her head than share his saddle. But she sat before him comfortably enough, posture good, and an arm about his waist with a grip that was firm and not the least bit missish.

It took only a few miles for him to begin wishing she'd taken the other choice. It was nice to ride with her—far too nice. She fit easily into the space before him, her soft hip pressed into his thigh as though it belonged there. As he spurred the horse, wisps of her fine black hair escaped from her bonnet and whipped in the breeze, teasing the skin of his cheeks. It was a tickling sweetness, bringing with it a whiff of cologne that made him want to lean forwards and bury his face in the side of her throat. He had to work to stifle the urge to loosen the bonnet and free the rest of it to let it stream in the wind.

He wished he was in a position to make conversation with her, for it might have helped to pass the time and occupy his mind in anything other than the scent of her hair.

'Who are you?' The words came from her suddenly, with no preamble. And then she stopped herself, probably shocked at sounding ridiculous, nonsensical and, worst of all, rude.

But she was unaware of what a blessed relief it was to him.

'I am John Hendricks, as I have already told you. I worked for the Earl of Folbroke as a personal secretary.'

She relaxed a little as though she'd been bracing for some sort of harsh retort. It made him wonder at the sort of conversation she was accustomed to, if a simple question was not met with a polite answer.

'But I think that is not what you are asking me,' he said. 'I would be happy to answer you in detail, if you would clarify your meaning.'

'How did you come to be who you are? Who are your people? Where did you come from?' And again he felt her tense, as though she were expecting ridicule. It made him want to reach out and offer physical comfort of some kind—a touch on the shoulder, a word in her ear urging her to relax in his company. Or, worse yet, to ask similar questions of her. He must remember that conversation between them, given his position and hers, was a one-sided affair at best. A desire to know his personal history did not demonstrate a desire to share hers.

He answered carefully, giving just the information required.

'I was born in London, though I spent very little time there. My mother died when I was quite young; there is not much I can tell you of her, other than that she was beautiful. But that is what all children say of their mothers and so it hardly signifies.'

And that had been enough to loosen her tongue and relax her rigid posture. 'I suppose you are right, Mr Hendricks. I would say the same of my departed mother. Beautiful and happy.'

'Mine was sad.' He reflected for a moment, surprised that her questions had raised a fresh feeling of loss for something that had happened so long ago. 'I was sent away to school when she died. To Eton and then to Cambridge. There was never any question of how it would be paid for. But around the time of the death of Duke of Summersly, I received a nice settlement. I think that tells us both all we need to know about the identity of my father.'

'A bastard son of a duke?' Again she had blurted the words in a way that was the height of bad manners. He could almost hear her mouth snap shut.

'Of him, or some member of that family. While he did not acknowledge me in life, I cannot really complain about the way I was treated.' At least, he had no right to. 'I was a natural student and quite happy at all the schools I attended. I cannot say the same of my fellows. I took great pleasure in besting them when I could, at lessons or at games. It proved...' and then he remembered his audience and shut his own mouth.

'That it is not always one's parentage that proves one's abilities,' she finished for him, unbothered by the idea. Of course, she had no reason to feel threatened by it. She was a symbol of the rank he'd been denied; nothing he could say would change her status in society. 'And when you were finished with your education?' she prompted.

'I used the money I was given to buy a commission and did quite handsomely for myself as a soldier. I was aide-de-camp to the Earl of Folbroke. We were friends as well as comrades. When he returned home, I followed and took a position in his household.'

'And you might have been equals…'

'Or perhaps his superior,' he added calmly, 'had I been born on the right side of the blanket.' He waited for her chilly response and the inevitable withdrawal. Their circumstances were unusual and some curiosity was natural. But a well-bred young lady would not stoop to befriend a by-blow.

Instead, she continued as though she found nothing particularly unusual about his past. 'I enjoyed my schooling as well. There is a great comfort to be found in books.'

And why did you need comforting, I wonder? The woman was a curiosity.

'But in such places as I was sent, most of the time is spent ensuring that young ladies are properly prepared to take their roles as wives and mothers, and are assets to the households of their intended husbands.'

Which made them sound little better than servants. Perhaps they had more in common then he'd thought.

She sighed. 'When Mother died, it was agreed, amongst us, that it would be for the best that I come home from school and see to things.'

Liar. Her father had commanded it, he was sure. He risked a question. 'And what sorts of things needed seeing to?'

'Once we were out of mourning, my younger sister, Priscilla, was ready to make her come out. And it has been decided that I must be her guard, until she finds a husband. The stronger must protect the weaker, after all.'

'And you are the stronger,' he said, softly.

Her eyes narrowed. 'I am. In mind and in body. I am older and wiser, as well. And with no mother to advise or protect her, someone must care for Priscilla.' There had been the faintest, most fleeting hint of a something on her face as she had said it, as though she remembered a time not so long ago when she had not thought that way at all. But her father had called her home. And like an obedient daughter, she had come and done exactly as she was told, putting all of her own dreams aside for the good of her sister. More than her mother had died on that day, John was sure of it, but Lady Dru had convinced herself otherwise.

Out of the blue, she added, 'Priscilla is the prettier of the two of us, and with the extra attention she receives from so many gentlemen, there is an increased risk.'

'Prettier than you?'

For a moment, her frown faded into a look of surprise, softening her features into a dark attractiveness that quickened his pulse. 'Of course. She is of a more appropriate height, delicate of frame, fair of hair, pale of skin.'

And that explained why she would run to Scotland after a man who no longer wanted her. If she thought this Mr Gervaise was her only opportunity, if their understanding was that he would wait until she felt free to marry, she would be loathe to let him go.

It pained him to see such hesitance in one who was normally so sure of herself. Would it do any harm to give her some assurance on her looks? For it was clear that no one else, not even the errant Gervaise, had done so. 'There is nothing inappropriate about your height,' he said. 'It suits you. And your frame suits your height. In my experience, delicacy is as likely to go hand in hand with sickness as it is with beauty. A lack of frailty on your part is hardly an imperfection.'

She was blinking at him again, as though she could not quite understand what it was that he meant. But it had brought a faint flush to her pale cheeks that made her all the more attractive, so he dared and went on, 'Your colouring might not be the same as your sister's, but it is most fetching. I am sure the two of you, when side by side, are an attractive counterpoint to each other.' Now he was wishing he had a hand free to adjust his spectacles so that he might get a better look at her face before continuing. 'That is only my opinion, of course. But there is nothing unusual about my tastes and assessment of feminine beauty. There are men who prefer the fair sex to be fair. And there are an equal number that enjoy raven hair and large dark eyes.' At the moment, he fell too much in the latter category to say more.

In fact, he had said too much already. He checked his watch. They were making good time, now that they could leave the roads as needed. He gave his passenger a brief warning and took the horses up a steep embankment, in an effort to find higher ground for them.

And since he'd put his hand on her waist to steady her, it had seemed only natural to leave it there and enjoy the warmth of her ribs. It was a shame that she did not see beauty when she looked into the mirror, for he found nothing wrong with her. Perhaps she was tall for a woman, but there was nothing in the least masculine about the rest of her. He spread his fingers to span as much of her as he could, easing her body back against him.

She responded by nestling closer. She relaxed against him,

almost as if it required conscious effort to depend on the strength of another.

And he wanted to be her strength. In the years he had worked for Folbroke and doted on the man's wife, she had never once shown an interest in his past. They had been friends, of course, but not particularly close.

But in less than a day together, Lady Drusilla Rudney had ferreted out the truth of his birth and forged a connection between them. This trip was not the only time she'd felt alone. He could see it in her guarded eyes, in the way she held herself, carefully self-contained at all times, and the way she was leaning into him, unguarded and fragile.

Because of that fragility, he was a danger to her. Though his mind might want to reach out and comfort, his body felt the flesh-and-blood woman beside him and wanted a much more earthy connection. The movement of the horse shifted her against him and he had idle thoughts of stretching his fingers upwards to graze the bottoms of her breasts. And each change in gait raised a fresh fantasy as she rocked against him. Walking brought to mind a languid afternoon of love making. A canter made him think of a quick coupling and fear of discovery. And as he nudged them to a full gallop, he thought of a night of wild, uncontrolled, vigorous…

'Mr Hendricks!'

Chapter Six

He pulled on the reins, bringing the horse up short, suddenly afraid that she had guessed the contents of his mind or felt his obvious physical response. 'My lady?'

He glanced around him, checking his surroundings, his watch and his compass, and comparing the results to the last mile marker he had seen to pretend that their progress had been the only thing on his mind.

'Could we stop to rest? I think—'

'An excellent idea.' He practically leapt from the horse, helping her down and stepping quickly away from her. 'The stand of trees over there looks quite inviting.' He waited for the rebuke that must be coming. There should be shock and outrage, or at least some sign that she feared to be near him.

Instead, she was biting her lip as though unsure what to say or do next. Then she gave a hesitant nod and half-muttered, 'Perhaps that is it. I need to rest.'

He let out a sigh of relief. She did not seem to be worrying about him at all. 'Was the ride tiring for you?' He offered her an arm to help her over the uneven ground as they walked the horses towards a stream by the grove.

She gave an uneasy laugh. 'I fear I do not make the best passenger. I could not seem to sit still.' There was a gruffness about her words, as though they were more denial than total innocence. But the look in her eyes was confusion, and perhaps embarrassment. It seemed he was not the only one affected by their nearness.

'It did not bother me overly,' he said, for it hardly seemed fair to call such pleasant sensations an annoyance.

'All the same, I do not think I wish to ride that way any longer. Is there no other way?' She was looking at him, vulnerable and desperate, trusting that he would understand and help her. And though he wanted nothing more than to tumble her in the grass, or sweep her into his arms and back into the saddle, he knew that he would not.

He stared at her, wondering if he dared suggest what he was thinking. 'There is a way that we can make better progress, if you are willing to take certain risks.'

'Anything,' she said eagerly, then looked at him, trying to appraise his plan and regain some of her old composure. 'Well, nearly anything. What do you suggest, Mr Hendricks?'

He went to the other horse and pulled down his bag, removing the clothing he had stashed there. He held them out to her. 'Leather riding breeches, Lady Drusilla. And I have a spare shirt as well. If you were dressed in a less feminine way, you could ride astride with more comfort.'

'Men's clothing?' she said, clearly appalled. 'You expect me to wear breeches?'

'From a distance, you would be mistaken for a boy. It would

lessen the risk of someone recognising you as the Duke of Benbridge's daughter.'

'But it is very improper. I do not think I could...'

'They will fit,' he assured her. 'While you appear to be...' He cleared his throat, trying not to comment on the shape of her, which was as far from a man's as he could imagine. 'Well, at least we are of a similar height and, in most ways, I am larger than you. If we can cobble together a disguise out of spare clothing from my pack, it would do quite well for you.'

She touched the clothes gently and he noticed how fine her hand looked, lying against the leather. 'Would it add so much to the speed of our progress?'

'You will find that men's clothing is much less restrictive for trips like this. We will be able to move more quickly and will stop before returning to populated areas, to allow you to change into something more appropriate to your gender.'

'And no one would ever know?' she asked hopefully.

'I will certainly tell no one,' he said. 'It is much better, is it not, that Lady Drusilla not be seen travelling alone with a strange man?'

She gave a little shiver at the thought. He did not know whether to be angry or flattered by it, for at least it proved that she recognised him as a threat and not some neutered tool. 'That is probably true. If the story of this trip gets out, I have already done great harm to my reputation. Can the addition of breeches make it worse?'

He smiled encouragingly. 'Very well, then. Take these and step behind the trees to change. If you run into difficulties...' He thought of her half-dressed body and realised that there was not a damned thing he dared to do for her. 'Make a brave attempt.'

He waited where he was as she took the proffered clothing and concealed herself. To prevent temptation, he turned his back on the scene as well, so that he would not catch even a glimpse of bare skin through the sparse leaves.

Or, worse yet, he might catch himself straining to see something. Though he had managed to keep his eyes respectfully averted for most of last night, after the ride they'd just shared, his will was not so strong.

He heard her return a short time later and turned to find her standing with hands spread before her, in a gesture that sought approval. 'Is this all right?'

'Yes,' he responded, trying to modulate his own voice and looking hurriedly away. 'Yes. That will be quite satisfactory.'

Dear God.

When he'd made the suggestion, he had not given two thoughts to it. They were his own clothes, after all. He had seen them before.

But never like this. The shirt was full, and covered her to the throat, obscuring the curves underneath it with billows of fabric. But it was far too thin. The dark peaks of her breasts were displayed plain for anyone who wished to look. The tender budding tips jutted against the cloth. And his eyes strained to see, like dogs at the end of a lead. He forced them back to her face, and stripped off his topcoat and handed it to her. 'Perhaps this will help.'

It did not. Not really. Her legs still protruded from the tails of the coat and the shapeliness of her calves was not obscured through the heavy stockings. The leather of the breeches pulled tight against her thighs and her nicely rounded bottom. The buff colour looked almost like bare skin. And it all seemed to settle into that final crease at the top of her legs, drawing his gaze to a place that he should never look, but that he very much wanted to admire. They were alone, far from interruption, and only a few buttons separated him from paradise.

He turned away from her, busying himself with the harnessing of the horses, trying not to notice the increasing tightness in his own trousers, then pulled his glasses off, folded them and tucked them into the pocket of his coat.

'Mr Hendricks,' she said, 'will you not need those to see what you are doing?'

'Resting my eyes for a moment,' he assured her. 'It has been a long day, has it not?' He turned back to the horse and raised the stirrups as though this were the only thing on his mind. 'You must manage in your own boots, I'm afraid. Even if I had spares to offer, mine would fall off your feet.'

Such dainty little feet.

He rummaged in his pack for a soft hat. 'Here. Put this over your hair.'

She smiled at him in approval and pulled it into place. 'It is a relief to know that you do not expect me to cut it. There are some things I would not do in the name of disguise.'

'No. Never.' He hoped that his sigh had not been too obvious to her. But he'd have as soon asked her to cut off her arm as lose that glorious dark hair. He imagined it, down, smooth and thick in his hands. Then he did his best to imagine anything else. For a moment, he tried to think of Emily, who had occupied so much of his thoughts only two days ago. Her hair had been shorter and blond. It was strange how quickly a thing that had seemed so important to him, had faded so quickly from memory.

The same would likely be true of Lady Drusilla, once he was

out of her sphere of influence. It must be, or it would drive him mad. When he glanced back at her, looking into her eyes this time, he could see that she would not. Or almost see, at any rate. For the blurring of his vision without the spectacles made her face soft, more childlike, her eyes large and bewildered, and her mouth rounded into a soft red bow. This was how she would look when he made love to her.

Which he would never do, he reminded himself. He had no right to even think such things about her. The list of reasons against it was almost too long to count.

'It is time we were going again,' he said, staring up at the sun. 'I do not mean to stop until dark. Then we will return to the main road, find an inn and enquire about your friend.'

He went to her and offered her a leg up into the saddle of the big horse. For a moment, her foot rested in the cradle of his hands, and his face was far too near to her leg. He felt light headed with the desire to press his lips against the place he could reach. Then it was over and she was mounted, the horse dancing until she took control of the reins.

He looked up critically. 'You are sure that you will be all right with this?'

She straightened, stiffened and seemed to grow braver with each passing moment, though her eyes widened at the feel of the horse between her legs. 'It will be fine, because it must be so. And you are right. I can tell already that it is easier to ride when one can control the beast under one and not perch on it like a decoration.' She glared down at him, eyebrows and chin raised. 'And if you ever tell anyone I said that, I shall sack you immediately.'

'Yes, my lady,' he responded, with a small bow, dropping with difficulty back into the role of servant.

He rearranged the luggage and mounted his own horse. Then he pointed her in the right direction and allowed her to set the pace, for he did not wish to push her beyond her capacities.

He watched her ride. For someone with little experience, she had a good seat and showed no signs of fearing the animal he had given her. That was fortunate; he had no wish to end the day tearing across the open country after a runaway stallion, trying to save her from a fall. She chose a gait that was not too arduous on horse or rider, but still gained them time over the unreliable coach. It was hard not to admire her almost masculine single-mindedness in pursuit of a goal.

From his position behind her, he could admire her body as well. Now that the coat hid her form, there was really nothing to see. But his imagination was good, as was his memory. At some point, they would have to stop. And he would sleep in the stable before sharing another bed with her, lest he forget himself again.

Chapter Seven

Mr Hendricks pulled up beside her, and signalled her to slow her horse to a walk. 'We shall be stopping soon,' he said, checking his watch against the position of the sun. 'While it might be possible to travel farther, we must change horses to keep this pace. We could take a room—' He corrected himself '—rooms. And get some dinner.'

'Or we can hire fresh mounts and continue for a few more hours,' she said.

'You are not tired?'

'Not if there is a chance that we are gaining on them.' They'd had no information since the stop this morning. And she must hope that the speed they were moving had closed the distance.

'And you are comfortable as you are attired?' He looked doubtfully at her borrowed costume.

'I am accustomed to it,' she said, not wishing to commit herself. It was strangely freeing to go without skirts, as long as she did not think of how it must look. She could bend low over the horse's neck and gallop if she wished, unencumbered by petticoats, not worrying about the set of her hat or the attractive arrangement of the garments. And while she felt the stretching of unused muscles, it was not so much painful as troubling. There was a guilty pleasure in it that would not be repeated. And she wished to prolong that a few more hours, if she could.

'Very well, then. We will stop at the next inn, and I will check for your wayward carriage and hire us some new steeds. You…' He looked her up and down before speaking again. 'You had best remain in the courtyard. Keep your coat buttoned and your hat pulled low. Speak to no one and do not wander off.' He looked at her again as though he expected to see something he had not noticed before. 'I am sorry to say it, my lady, but you do not make a very convincing man.'

And then he laughed, a kind of choking snort as though his proper demeanour had failed him.

'Is there something amusing that I am not aware of?' she said in a voice that should have frozen him to silence.

He was still chuckling slightly. 'You seemed most unhappy with a statement that, in any other context, would have been good news. Just now, you were glaring into the air as though you had wished to hear you wore it better. I found the juxtaposition funny.'

'I do not like to be reminded that I am unable to perform a role to the satisfaction of others.' She'd had enough of that at home to last a lifetime.

'It is no fault of yours, I assure you,' he said. 'Perhaps a less attractive woman might have managed it.' He laughed again.

'Please do not joke with me about my appearance,' she snapped. 'If you thought that I was angling for a compliment, I assure you, that was not the case.'

'I am not laughing at your appearance,' he said in the same

mild patient tone he'd used to coax her into wearing his clothes, but stifling a smile. 'Only at the way you frowned again upon being told that you were attractive.'

'Because it is nonsense,' she said. 'Fine words meant to flatter me into a better humour.'

'Give me more credit than that, Lady Drusilla. I have not been in your employ for long, but I am smart enough to realise that it would take more than flattery to put you in a good humour.' Before she could reprimand him, he shot her another sidelong glance, then turned his attention to the road. 'This is what comes from reading sermons,' he muttered. 'You think too much. If I wished to flatter you, I would have mentioned your pleasant features and your beautiful dark hair. Both comments would have been true. But they would have nothing to do with your inability to disguise such an obviously female body in masculine clothing with any degree of success. And now, if you tell me that the Lord has given it to you, and you deserve no credit for it, then I will take that little book of sermons from your pocket and throw it into the next stream.'

To put an end to the conversation, he gave his beast a gentle kick in the sides and was off at such a pace that she had to struggle to follow him.

He needn't have bothered. Any retorts she had for him had flown quite out of her head. Left in their place was a swirl of words: attractive, pleasant, beautiful and, best of all, obviously female. Somewhere in the midst of it, he had commented on her bad humour. But she was hardly bothered by a comment on something which was seen as a universal truth by those close to her.

And he had laughed, not exactly at her, but in her direction, as though her temper amused more than it upset him. The negatives he'd thrown into the last interchange were like salt in a pudding, serving to emphasise the sweetness and bring out the subtle flavours of the rest.

And he had threatened to throw her sermon book into the river. Taken as a whole, she could not decide if she wanted to stammer a blushing thank you, or ring a peal over him. But the last statement could not be allowed to stand.

She spurred her horse to draw even with him. 'I would not care if you did throw the sermons in a stream,' she said, a little breathless from the ride. 'It is not as if they are my exclusive reading.'

'You brought other books with you?'

'Not on this journey, no.'

His features had returned to mild-mannered passivity, as though he had collected enough evidence for a decision, but saw no reason to comment on it.

'Perhaps it was because I thought that the couple I was searching for needed a reminder of their duty.'

'So you sought to give a sermon and not to read one?' It was an innocent observation. But it made her feel horribly priggish, not at all like the beautiful hoyden of a moment ago.

'We cannot always have what we want,' she said firmly. 'Where would the world be if everyone went haring off after their desires, eloping to Scotland on the least provocation?'

'Where indeed?'

'It would be chaos,' she said, sounding depressingly like the voice of her father.

'And you are sure you wish to stop this particular elopement,' he said carefully. 'If we are lucky, we might catch up with your friends tonight. Or perhaps tomorrow. But sometimes, when people are in love and intent upon their goal, they cannot be turned from it. If you stop them now, they will find another way.'

'If they run again, I will chase them again,' she said, feeling as stiff and flat as her sermon book. 'I do not mean to give them any choice in the matter. This marriage cannot take place. It simply cannot.' She was already near to on the shelf. With a scandal in the family, her own reputation would be in tatters. Her father would be livid at Priscilla and in no mood to launch the other daughter: the one who had failed to protect his favourite.

The man beside her sighed. 'Very well, then. If you are resolute, I load my pistols and prepare myself for the inevitable.'

'The inevitable?'

'To haul the loving couple back across the border by force, if necessary.'

'You would do that?'

'If you wished me to.'

And now she was the one smiling at incongruity. He had replaced his spectacles since their last stop and the sun glinted off his lenses, causing him to squint slightly. He hardly looked the type to resort to physical violence. 'If you will remember our conversation last evening, I requested discretion.'

'The sound of a single shot will not carry all the way to London,' he replied. 'And from what I understand of females, a wound in a non-vital spot is often deemed quite romantic.'

'It is not my goal to make Mr Gervaise even more attractive to the opposite gender.'

'Perhaps not, then.' He thought again. 'Maybe I should punch him. A broken nose will solve the problem of his good looks quite nicely, I am sure.'

The idea did have appeal. As did dragging Priscilla back to London by the hair. But it would only make her run away again. And the last thing she needed to risk was engendering sympathy for the villain who had taken her away. 'No, as I said, discretion is the watchword.' She glanced at him again. 'But thank you for the offer.'

He ducked his head. 'At your service, Lady Drusilla.'

Of course. That was all it had been. She had employed him to solve the problem and he had offered suggestions. The protectiveness that she was sure she'd heard were imaginings on her part. Nothing more than that.

She sighed. For a moment, it had felt quite nice to think that there was a man on the planet who could be moved to brutal overreaction in defence of her.

They kept the pace until they arrived at the next inn, and Mr Hendricks left her standing by a wall in the courtyard, out of the way of departing coaches, as he went to see about the horses and make enquiries about recent guests. While she waited, she did as he'd suggested and buttoned the coat, pulling his hat low over her eyes and thrusting her hands into her pockets in a way that she hoped looked insolent and unwelcoming.

But she could tell from the looks she got from the stable hands that they saw easily through her disguise. She shrank back into Mr Hendricks's overcoat, vowing that whatever might happen between here and Scotland, she would not be out of his sight for another moment. He had been right. There was no way that she would be taken for a male. She did not want to think about what the clothes might be exposing to view. Even hidden in the coat, she was exposing so much of her legs that she might as well be standing naked in the courtyard.

But despite her fears, the boys' attitudes were not so much menacing as amused. She could hear the muttered conversation between them, as they came for the horses and brought out the fresh pair. One was guessing it was an elopement. The other disagreed. The gentleman seemed more interested in who had gone before than who might come from behind. It must be some sort of bet or a strange prank.

The first insisted that the man was too old to be just down from Oxford. And the woman was too fine to be the sort of woman who would don breeches for the amusement of the lads. Only love made people act as cork-brained as this. It was an elopement for sure. He'd bet a penny on it.

Drusilla tried not to smile. There was some comfort in knowing that though she did not look like a boy, neither did everyone mistake her for a whore. But the idea that she might be thought the one eloping?

What a wonderful thought that was. For a moment, she imagined herself as being that sort of girl. Just once, she wished to be the one racing for the border with a laughing lover as the hue and cry was raised after her. And chaperons all over London would shake their heads and murmur to their charges about the bad end one was likely to come to, if one behaved like the notorious Silly Rudney.

Mr Hendricks was in the doorway, haggling back and forth with the innkeeper, struggling to pull coins from his pockets and muttering to himself. Then he walked back to her through the busy coach yard, dipping his head low to speak in confidence to her. 'Are you still carrying your reticule?'

She nodded.

'Please give it to me.'

She produced the blue silk bag from the pocket of her man's coat and was certain she heard laughter from the boys who had been watching her. It became even louder as they saw Mr Hendricks rooting through the contents for the sad collection of coins remaining there, swearing at the little money in his hand. Then he thrust the purse back to her and stalked away.

One stable boy passed a penny to the other, agreeing that only a man in love could be brought so low, and Dru cringed in embarrassment for her companion. And the boys glanced in the direction of the doorway to the inn, then looked hurriedly away.

There was a young lady, standing alone beside a stack of bandboxes, waving a handkerchief in the hopes of receiving aid. The burden was light and would have been no trouble for boys strong enough to handle cart horses. But when Dru got a better look at the identity of the girl, she disappeared into Mr Hendricks's coat, sympathising with the sudden deafness of the stable hands.

Priss's friend, Charlotte Deveral, was not someone she might wish to meet under the best circumstances. The girl was too young and pretty to be a harridan, but it was only a matter of time. If her disposition was as Dru remembered, she was most likely in a temper over nothing. And she would take it out on a tardy servant, or any lad who left a smudge on a package while trying to earn a penny or two.

'Boy!' Char's voice was sharp and ugly. 'Boy!' And then she muttered an aside to her paid companion. But it was a theatrical *sotto voce*, meant to embarrass the targets of her wrath. 'These country clods are all either deaf or stupid. One must shout to make them understand. I say! Boy!'

For a moment, Dru was reminded of her own tone as she ordered Mr Hendricks about. Did it sound like that to him? she wondered. She felt suddenly ashamed of herself and more than a little embarrassed for Char, who was making a spectacle of herself with all the shouting and flapping of linen.

'Boy, I am talking to you.'

And it was then that it occurred to Dru that there was no one else near and that Char was addressing her. 'Eh?' She managed a deep masculine grunt, and thrust her hands even deeper into her pockets, as though she did not care a bit for what some London piece might think of her.

'Help me with these packages. My coachman is nowhere to be found.' And another aside, loud enough so the stable boys might hear, 'And the rest of the staff here are useless.'

Dru touched the brim of her hat in what she hoped was a respectfully masculine way, managing to pull it even lower over her face as she did so. Then she sauntered towards Charlotte.

She heard one of the stable boys snicker.

But Charlotte noticed nothing unusual about the 'boy' she'd called to aid her, looking right through Dru and refusing to recognise someone she had seen dozens of times before. Of course, a lad in an inn yard was so far beneath her that he might as well have been an ant upon the ground. What reason would she have to assume he was no lad at all? And he was not nearly as important as the bandboxes, to which Char gave her full attention. 'Help me place my packages in the carriage.'

'Miss,' Dru said with false respect, bowing low to take them from the ground at Char's feet.

'The correct form of address is my lady.'

The devil it was. The Deveral family was gentle enough, but there was not a title in it. And though Charlotte had her hopes, she would be settling for a plain Mister at the end of the season. But Dru could not exactly announce a fact that she should be in total ignorance of. 'My lady,' she corrected herself and bowed deeper.

And heard another snicker from the boys behind her.

She went around to the back of the carriage and clambered into the basket, securing the packages with the rest of the luggage and, quite by accident, placing Char's bonnet where it might be crushed at the next stretch of rough road. Then she helped Char and her chaperon into their seats as the groom who should be doing the job appeared from the taproom, too late to be of help to anyone.

As Drusilla closed the door and withdrew, Char gave an insolent toss of her head and said, 'For your trouble.' And then she pulled a coin from her purse and made as if to hand it out of the window. But she realised at the last moment that she had no wish to touch a filthy stranger and dropped it in the direction of Dru's hand.

Before she could snatch it from the air, the shilling hit the cobbles and rolled into the muck.

Dru stared down at it in disgust. Under normal circumstances, she would not have noticed the loss of it. But things were far from normal and she was still far from Scotland. She stooped and grabbed, trying to ignore the dirt clinging to her fingers. To add insult to injury, the Deveral carriage had started on its way.

Before she could step clear, the wheels and hooves sent up a fine spray of mud that struck her cheek.

To make her humiliation complete, Mr Hendricks appeared with two fresh horses, just in time for a view of the tableau: Lady Drusilla Rudney, muck spattered and scrambling for coins, to the great amusement of ladies and stable boys alike. She could expect no more fine words about her obvious feminine beauty now that he'd seen her debased, dismissed as something less than human by a woman of her own kind. Even worse, she had disobeyed him by talking to Char at all. She waited for a stern lecture on speaking to strangers and the need for secrecy. Or, worse yet, laughter.

Instead, he said nothing, offering her his handkerchief to wipe off the mud. Then he spoke as though he had seen nothing un-usual. 'The news is both good and bad, I'm afraid. The couple you seek were here just this morning.'

She hurriedly wiped her face, clinging to this one small suc-cess. 'How many hours ago?'

'Four, perhaps. Maybe less. They stayed for luncheon, before starting out again. They seemed in no hurry, wherever it was they were going.'

'So we are gaining on them.' Dru smiled in satisfaction. 'They were a day ahead when I started off. If they continue to dawdle, then we are likely to catch them before they reach the border.'

'If that is still what you wish,' Hendricks replied. 'We are at the end of our funds, I am afraid.'

'I thought you had ample money to help me,' she said, feeling even worse than before. If she'd taken the man's last groat to catch her sister, she could hardly fault him if they failed.

'I thought I had sufficient funds as well,' he said. 'But now that I have brought us to the middle of nowhere, I find that my purse is still in my pocket, but its contents are gone.' His brows knit and the darkness of his expression was truly fearsome. She braced herself, ready to bear the brunt of the inevitable tirade.

Instead, he turned it inwards upon himself. 'I have only myself to blame for our circumstances. Like a fool, I left my coat behind in the mail coach, as I helped to push. And that grudge-bearing, bacon-fed cit went through my pockets and helped himself to it. Now I am reduced to picking through a lady's reticule and letting you grovel for pennies in a coach yard.' He looked to her again, obviously pained by the confession. 'I am sorry, Lady Drusilla. I have failed you.'

She felt a rush of sympathy. After all he had done to get her this far, she was amazed that he would think so harshly of himself. 'You most certainly have not failed me,' she said. 'We have simply hit another difficulty and must take the time to examine our options. What do you suggest?'

'As I see it, we have two alternatives. We return to the place we left and find the man responsible.'

'And what good would that do us? He would likely deny that he had taken anything.'

'At first, perhaps. But all the same, I would give him a thrashing that would shake the coins from his pockets.' His cold smile and the glint in his eye said that the experience would be the most emotionally satisfying option and the one he favoured.

'Mr Hendricks!' Drusilla said sharply. 'Attend, please. To return to find the thief would put my goal quite out of reach. If I have come this far, I do not wish to turn back without some satisfaction. Is there no other way to get to Scotland?'

Now, he was staring at her in silence, as though she were a piece in the puzzle that he could not quite seem to make fit. He did not immediately answer and she repeated, 'Mr Hendricks?'

'I am thinking,' he said, a little too sharply for a servant, and then corrected his tone before responding. 'There is another way, if you are dead set on continuing. We will press northwards as we have been doing and ride this change of horses to the end. We will be forced to sleep rough. We will take the shilling in your hand to buy some bread and cheese for our supper. But after that, we will have to beg or steal what we need for sustenance.' He looked heartily sorry that he could not do better. 'I fear it is not what you are accustomed to. But the only other alternative I can offer is to admit defeat and appeal to your father for help.'

'And that is precisely what I will not do.' She stood straight again, remembering that she was the daughter of a duke and not some slouching farm boy. Then she wiped the muddy coin and handed it back to Hendricks along with his handkerchief. 'Take this and buy us some dinner, so that we might set off again.' She glanced up the road at the dust of the retreating carriage, focusing all her anger and frustration on it, longing for revenge. And then an idea occurred to her. 'And if you hurry I think there is a way that we might solve all our problems, given a little darkness and a little luck.'

Chapter Eight

'This is mad, you know.' Mr Hendricks spoke in the same soft voice he used on those times when he managed to remember that she employed him.

'You have told me that on several occasions already.'

'I did not think one more would make a difference,' he said, with a sigh. 'But if there was even the smallest chance, then I had to try. When I suggested we steal to survive, this was not at all what I was intending. I meant that we would take only what was necessary. A loaf from a farmer's window sill, perhaps.'

'Which would leave the poor family there with nothing to eat,' she said. 'Does it not diminish the hurt to all concerned if we steal from someone who lives a life of excess?'

'Perhaps that is true, in theory. But you are not discussing some distant and romantic utopia. You are asking me to rob a coach on a modern highway. I believe, my lady, that you have confused me with some idealised combination of Robin Hood and Dick Turpin.'

'Just as you have confused me with a character in a Drury Lane comedy,' she snapped back, 'and persuaded me to traipse halfway across England in your cast-off clothing.' His tone annoyed her, for it was no longer mild subservience. There was a distinct air of derision. And it was just another example of the way those around her had no trouble leading her into jeopardy with their outrageous plans, then resisting when she offered an equally outrageous plan of her own.

'If you mean to rob every farm between here and Scotland, we will never reach our destination. Rather than stealing one loaf at a time, we could take a single purse from someone who can afford a closed carriage and have more than enough gold to finish the trip. In the eyes of the Lord, the latter is far worse.'

'It is to be my misfortune that you were reading the story of the widow's mite,' he said. 'I should have taken that book from you when I had a chance.'

'If you had, my opinion now would be the same,' she snapped back. 'I have no desire to spend a week sleeping in barns and munching on stolen bread and green apples.' Although, were she honest, the prospect of being forced to sleep in the wilderness, huddled against Mr Hendricks for warmth, had a certain appeal to her.

'I am sorry, my lady, if all that I can offer you is not to your liking.' There was a surprising bitterness in the way he said her title, as though it were caught in his teeth.

'And I am sorry if you do not like the position you have been engaged to perform.' She gave him her cruellest smile and let the words be an equally bitter reminder for him, as well as herself, that her present condition was nothing more than a colossal inconvenience.

'Begging your pardon, my lady.' He offered a false bow and tugged his forelock. 'I will not forget my place again.'

The soft blond hair falling in his eye gave her the sudden and inappropriate impulse to smooth it back with her fingers. She ignored it and said, 'Your apology is accepted. Now, about the matter of the coach robbery...'

'Which I cannot in any way condone.'

She huffed in disgust. 'Your weak resolve had been duly noted. And I dismiss it. The occupants of the vehicle we will be stopping are unworthy of your sympathy. Char Deveral is a pampered, foolish girl of carefully cultivated prettiness, who would leave a full purse on the ground rather than soil her hands picking it out of the mud.'

Or a coin from a coach yard. The incident still stung, even now that her hands were clean. She had made Mr Hendricks ride the next miles hard and well off the road, until her anger had abated. But at least she was sure they had passed the carriage and could lie in wait for it.

And now, even if she did not get to Priscilla in time, she would have her revenge for that muddy coin and for a host of other small tricks and social slights delivered over the years by Char and her friends. She smiled at the prospect. 'I know her type well. They are always talking behind their hands at those not of their set, laughing at their own empty jokes, and despite all the warnings of those who know better, running off with men who are little better than servants, heedless of what it might to their reputations, leaving the more rational members of their family to rescue them from their own foolishness, causing no end of misery...'

Now she had gone totally off her track and could tell by the look in his eye that he thought her even madder than before. He broke into her tirade. 'It is not the character of your potential victims that concerns me, Lady Drusilla. Or their tendency to fraternise with men who are beneath them. It is the result of our likely capture.'

She waved away his objections. 'If we are caught, then I shall tell everyone who I am and that you are my servant, forced into the actions by my misguided desire for adventure.'

He held his hand heavenwards as though to summon the angels to witness what he was forced to endure. 'And I suppose, when they ignore you, and I am hanged for highway robbery, it will be a consolation to know that it was not really my fault.'

'Nonsense,' she insisted. 'My father has bought justice to a halt for my sister more often than you can imagine. If this time the felonious prank perpetrated was the fault of Silly Rudney instead of his darling Priss, he will be annoyed with me, but will not hesitate. While the world has heard of no such actions on my part, a single mistake of mine can hardly compare to the sum total of the rest of my family.'

Mr Hendricks swore aloud, not caring that she heard the words, and said, in a more moderate tone, 'The upper classes are all quite mad. For a time I had hoped that you were proving to be otherwise. But you are blessed with a stubbornness that is well outside the bounds of sanity and a single-mindedness that could wear reason down to a nub.'

So, she had lost the good opinion of the man who sat beside her. 'At least I am consistent, Mr Hendricks.'

'You are that, my lady.'

Then she tried something that had not occurred to her before and dipped her head slightly, doing her best at a shy smile, as her sister would have done when trying to charm a man. She looked up at him through her long dark lashes. 'I am sorry to have been such a bother. You have done your best to keep me safe and I have much to be grateful for. If you can help me in this one last thing, I will see to it that you are properly rewarded for the inconvenience of it.'

He laughed. 'So it has come to this, has it? You mean to use your wiles on me, now that all else has failed?' There was a strange pause before his response, as he stared boldly back at her in challenge. 'And how might you reward me, if I risk my neck for you?' His voice was not mild at all, but hoarse, deep and strangely thick. She could feel the answering thickness in her blood as her pulse slowed.

She swallowed, wondering what she had meant to tell him. Some part of her mind was sure that her sister would have offered a single kiss as though it had some material value, but she doubted the currency of her inexperienced lips was of comparable worth. Nor could she inform him that, should they manage to find Priscilla, she could procure that kiss for him from her sister.

Then a thought occurred to her. She could tell him to take what he liked for a reward. Then *he* would kiss *her*. And though it would seem like a forfeit, only she would know that she had been rewarded twice.

But now that she needed it most, her nerve failed her. 'My father will pay you double whatever you intended to receive from this escapade. What else could I possibly mean?'

He shook his head in amazement. 'I cannot imagine. Double the pay it is, then. And enough money to replace what was stolen from me?'

'Of course.'

'Then for you, I shall turn highwayman, my Lady Dru.'

His anger with her must have dissipated, for the way he'd shortened her name had none of the frustrated affection that she felt when someone called her Silly. This made her feel odd. She tingled, almost as though he had reached out and touched her cheek to show her that they were friends again, and she needn't worry.

He stared down the road. The sun was near to dipping behind the horizon; with each moment, it became more difficult to make out details of their surroundings. But from just behind the last hill she could hear the sound of horses, and the jingling of harnesses growing louder as they drew near.

Mr Hendricks removed his spectacles and tucked them into the pocket of his coat.

'Do you not need them to see what you are about to do?' she asked.

He shook his head. 'Sometimes it is better not to see. It will be easier to do something as foolish as we are doing tonight without a clear view of it.' Then he reached behind him to the bag that was strapped to the back of his saddle and removed a pair of pistols and two black neckcloths. He tossed a cloth to her, and then carefully handed her one of the guns. 'Pull the cravat up and over your face,' he cautioned. 'Stay well out of the way, up on this hill with the setting sun to your back. You will seem much more intimidating if they do not have a clear view of you. And keep the pistol pointed up and over the heads of the drivers.'

'It is not loaded.' She said, trying not to sound relieved, for he had not troubled with ball and powder for her gun as he had with his own.

'But they do not need to know that and I do not mean you to shoot. Just hold it as if it is properly ready. They will have no idea, unless you do something that might cause them to fire at you and do not respond.' Then he looked at her seriously. 'And if they do, if there is any trouble at all, then you will turn and ride away, do you understand?'

'But that will leave you here alone.' At last, she saw the truth of the risk she had forced him to take. The empty gun trembled in her hand.

His face was dark, as threatening as one would expect from someone desperate enough to rob a coach. But it was with concern for her, not anger. 'If there is gunplay, it is no place for a lady to be, much less a lady disguised that might be treated with as little care as one might treat another man. If there is a problem, you will leave me to my fate.'

'I am your employer and I ordered you to this.' If he was hurt, it would be her fault. The thought almost choked her with anxiety.

'You have not answered me,' he said firmly. 'I brook no discussion of this, nor will I waste time listening to any suggestions you might give me. Swear that you will do as I say, or I will not proceed. And hurry, for there is not much time.' Without his glasses, there was no mildness in him at all. And the way he was staring at her made her feel small, easily managed.

It made her wish that there would be cause for him to look at her like that again. Perhaps in a situation where she had not put his life in jeopardy. For if he did, she would respond to any command he might give. She stifled a sigh and said, 'As you wish.'

'Very good. The coach is almost here and we have no more time to argue.' He pointed to a spot well up the hill from the road. 'Wait for me there. The height will appear to give you a good shooting position and will make retaliation difficult. You will be perfectly safe, as long as you do what I say.'

He pulled his own dark scarf over his face, and she masked

herself as well. There was nothing attractive about highway robbery. Or, at least, there should not have been. But the way he sat atop his horse, and the sight of him with nothing but those strange amber eyes visible above the scarf, was quite dashing.

It was incongruous with the look of quiet competence that she had come to expect when seeing Mr Hendricks. The man before her now was the very devil on horseback. His thighs were muscular, the dark coat stretched over broad shoulders and a shock of blond hair crept out from beneath the low brim of his hat. And, once again, her body tingled in the unexpected way it had when she had first sat upon the horse with him. He had been so strong, when he'd helped her easily in and out of the saddle. Now she wondered how those strong hands would feel if they lingered on her body.

They waited in silence, as the carriage approached. Suddenly, it was too late to lay a hand on his arm, or call out a warning to stay him. He was thundering down the road into the path of it, causing the driver to pull up and the horses to shy.

'Stand and deliver!' Mr Hendricks's voice echoed off the surrounding hills, and his horse reared as he fired a single shot into the air. But he kept his seat as though there were nothing in it, waving the driver and groom to the ground with his pistol.

And she would do everything she could to help him, even if it meant doing nothing at all. She kept her horse still and the pistol steady, held high so that the coachmen below her could see it.

They got down from their seats and made no effort to defend the family they served. Having met the inhabitants of the carriage, Dru could guess why. There was little to recommend Char that would give one the desire to risk life and limb.

Mr Hendricks was down from his horse in a trice, waving the

coachmen to the side of the road and directing them to lie upon their bellies and out of the way, gesturing up at her to show them it would go harsh with them should they try anything. When he was sure that they would do as directed, he strode up to the carriage and opened the door.

Charlotte gave a ladylike shriek from inside. 'My jewels!'

Hendricks gave a slight bow and a tip of his hat, then said in a plummy voice, 'I would not, for all the world, threaten your lovely person, nor steal the baubles from your beautiful throat.' Under his mask, she was sure he was smiling. 'I seek the money in your purse and mean to take only as much as I need.' He held open the door, then held out his hand for her reticule.

And the foolish girl leaned so far forwards, trying to get a good look at the man in the road, that she tumbled out into his arms.

From Dru's position, it was the most contrived thing she had ever seen in her life. Char's shameless behaviour very nearly made her forget the two men she was supposed to be watching. But when she looked back at them, they showed no signs of rising and seemed more interested in a flask they were passing back and forth between them, than in regaining the pistols resting on the seat of the carriage.

Mr Hendricks caught Charlotte easily before she hit the ground. Then he said, in a voice deeper than usual, 'You needn't fear, my lady. Your person and your jewels are perfectly safe. Though indeed, now that I see you, they are hardly necessary to enhance your beauty.'

Dru's eyes narrowed. For while she had no wish to see Mr Hendricks shoot Char, Priss's friend was doing it much too brown. The girl reached to open the reticule, pretended to fumble, dropping her purse in the dust of the road. Then she began to sag.

Hendricks rescued the money and tightened his grip on the girl fainting in his arms. Dru could remember how nice those arms felt when they had been around her body. But he'd never had cause to hold her as tightly as this. And he never would, if the only way to accomplish it was to fake a swoon.

Charlotte gave a weak laugh. 'I fear I am close to overcome.' She put her hands upon his bicep, so she could feel the muscle there. 'You are very strong.' She tipped her head back in an obvious invitation. 'And I am quite defenceless.'

'Are you, now?' She could tell, even from this distance, that Hendricks was responding favourably to the shameless playacting. And it irked her to see the trick she'd tried on him played better by one who had no responsibilities to prevent her from feigning helplessness when it suited her.

In the carriage, Char's chaperon gave a warning tutting noise, but did little more than fan herself and watch eagerly. In Dru's opinion, the woman did far too little to put a stop to her charge's behaviour, even when there was not a pistol drawn.

Hendricks had pulled the coin purse from inside the bag and was feeling the weight of it in his hand. 'This will do nicely, I think. I will not take from your companion. If she has any money, she will need it more than you.' He glanced over his shoulder, gauged the distance and tossed the purse expertly up to Dru, who loosed the strings and counted the substantial curl of notes inside.

'If there is anything else you want sir, you are welcome to it. As long as you spare my life and my necklace.'

She'd said nothing of her innocence, Dru noted. And now Char was batting her eyelashes as though she had cinders in her eyes.

Mr Hendricks gave a little laugh and reached to undo the

bottom of his mask. 'Then you shall sacrifice a kiss, my dear, and I will go on my way.' And then he put his lips upon hers. It was hard for Dru to see past the edge of the mask and the red haze forming in her own eyes. But it appeared that he had opened her mouth. His mouth was open as well. There was much movement and what looked like mutual chewing.

The coachmen were nudging each other and chuckling where they lay on the ground. The rate of the chaperon's fan increased, as though she was about to overheat in the closed carriage.

Now Char was making little noises in the back of her throat that sounded suspiciously like moans of pleasure. Her body trembled and her hands clutched urgently at Mr Hendricks's coat, as though she wished to crawl inside it with him.

And Dru felt sick, wishing that she could call the last few moments back and beg bread from farm wives as he'd first suggested. Her petty desire to take revenge on Charlotte might have gained them the money needed to finish the trip, but it had earned Charlotte a conquest.

And Char had got *her* kiss. If she had only chosen the right words a few moments ago, she would be the one bent over Mr Hendricks's arm. It would be her mouth he'd opened. And she would be the one shuddering in ecstasy and hanging from his lapels.

Instead, she had offered him money.

Dru stared down at the purse. Then she pocketed the bills, which were more than enough to get them to Scotland and back, and let the little bag drop again to the ground. She gave her horse a little kick that caused him to shift uneasily and stamp the thing into the mud at his feet.

When she looked back to the road again, Mr Hendricks was

setting Char back upon her feet to more ineffectual noises from the companion. Dru could see the look of dazed happiness on the face of her sister's friend.

She felt the strange, hot feeling again, in her cheeks and lower. Her throat felt flushed; the fabric of her shirt seemed to chafe at her breasts. And in the tight confining cases of leather there was a spot between her legs that seemed to pulse and burn and make her want to leap from the horse and rip the breeches from her body.

Now Mr Hendricks had secured his mask again and was helping Charlotte back into the coach. Then he ran to his horse, springing easily into the seat as though invigorated by the robbery. He tipped his hat again. 'Thank you, my lady.' And then, another tip of the hat for the chaperon. 'Apologies, ma'am.'

The casual courtesy annoyed her almost as much as the kiss had. How many times had she experienced that polite, dismissive attention from an attractive man, only to have him turn back to Priss?

'And now, I must be going.' Mr Hendricks looked back to the coachmen. 'See to your mistress, gentlemen. And if you are smart, you'll take your time about it.' Then he spurred his horse up the hill towards her, and they were off, into the open country, far away from the road.

They rode for some time without stopping; she ripped off her mask when he did and followed him without question. But her mind was seething and her body still in turmoil. If there was such a thing as a chaperon's corner for highwaymen, she had been left there tonight, holding an empty gun instead of her knitting. As usual, the real excitement was occurring close enough to be seen. And, as usual, no one had wanted her participation.

Mr Hendricks pulled up suddenly in the shelter of a copse of trees. Then he reached into his pocket and retrieved his glasses, looking through them and polishing the lenses. Without her having to ask, he supplied, 'I stayed not far from here, while growing up. There is no reason to ride blind. But it was pleasant to learn that I still know the roads well enough for pranks such as this.' He adjusted the spectacles and gave her a dark look. 'Not that I mean to pull any more of them.' Then he held out his hand for the money and counted it.

'And no more robberies should be necessary. This is enough that we might hire a carriage for the remainder of the journey. Once we reach Lancaster you may put on skirts again and travel properly, as a lady.'

As though that would matter to him, for she doubted he thought any more of her than he had of the unfortunate young lady fanning herself in Char's carriage. 'I do not have to put on skirts again, if it is more convenient to proceed as we have been.'

'I should think you'd be happy for the chance to ride in comfort. We can resume a normal rate of travel, rather than tearing across country, higgledy-piggledy.' He looked off in the direction of the northern horizon. 'Although we will keep it up for some time yet. There is a short cut I know that will bring us out on the road far away from the carriage we have just visited and closer to the one you seek.' He glanced back at her, taking in her unusual costume. 'The night is clear and I do not expect pursuit. We shall stay as we are and sleep under the stars. But tomorrow, it would be better that you were a woman again and I take back my hat and coat.'

'If I were a woman?' This was even worse than being ignored.

It seemed she had lost her gender altogether, with a simple change of clothes.

'If you were dressed as one,' he corrected. 'Of course, I know you are a woman.' He laughed in a funny, awkward way that did not match his earlier self-assurance.

'Do you really?' Suddenly it was very important that he say it aloud.

'And my employer as well,' he added quickly. And this was worse than neutering her. She might as well have been another species. But to choose now, of all times, to remind her of the distance between them was particularly cruel. 'If I am so far above you,' she snapped, 'then I am surprised that you think yourself entitled to choose my attire.'

A difference in their stations had not mattered a bit when he had been kissing Char. And the fact that she employed him did not mean that she was without feeling. She had a good mind to show him…to prove to him…to make him see…

Something. It was as if there was a word on the tip of her tongue that she could not quite remember. But she was sure that, whatever she meant to say, it was a uniquely female thing that everyone had learned but she. And if she'd asked Char or Priss what it was, they'd have looked knowingly one to another and then laughed at her.

She was tired of sitting in the corner while others danced, and even more tired of watching others being kissed in the moonlight. And beyond everything else, she was tired of Mr John Hendricks looking through her and holding another woman in his arms.

He was looking at her, aghast, and she wondered if some portion of her thoughts could be read on her face. Then he said in a mild, servile voice, 'I only meant that if any are searching for two daring highwaymen, they will not recognise them in us, should you choose to don a dress.'

It was so perfectly rational, and had so little to do with her femininity or his awareness of it, that she felt a complete fool. So she pulled herself together, gathered what little respect she had left, and answered just as reasonably, 'You are probably right. It is time to put this foolishness aside and behave properly.'

But her heart said something far different. Before the night was over, she would teach the man beside her that she would not be overlooked.

Chapter Nine

For their evening resting place, John chose a field that was at least a mile from the highway and every bit as remote as he could have hoped. There were trees for shelter, a nearby stream and not even a house in the distance. And there was a hay-stack with a single, rather uninterested cow munching upon it. He jumped down from his horse, feeling well satisfied with the night's doings.

Although it had been the height of foolishness to take to high-way robbery, it had been strangely exhilarating. Rather like being back in the army where every moment might mean one's death. He had acquitted himself well and survived the incident with an intact skin and a purse in his pocket.

And Lady Drusilla was safe as well. And a living example of why men should not take foolish risks for the glory of it. There were far better ways to expend energy waiting at home in England for those lucky men who could win them.

Not that he was the man for the lovely Drusilla. But the little fool in the carriage would have tumbled for him, easy enough, had he coaxed her. Kissing her had done nothing to ease his desire for dark eyes and luscious red lips. But it was an assurance that he was not the eunuch that his position required him to be. 'We will stop here,' he said.

'And sleep in a haystack?'

'You will find it a more comfortable bed than the ground is likely to be,' he assured her. His employer was out of sorts with him again and had been behaving more curiously than usual since the robbery. He had assumed that she would have some reaction to her participation in the robbery. But he had assumed that it would be fear, or perhaps excitement. He had not been prepared for annoyance.

Although it took some experience to gather what behaviour was unusual for the Lady Drusilla. The girl was a genuine eccentric. She rode like a man when the situation required it, miles at a time and without complaint. Where another woman might have held even an unloaded pistol with shaking hand, she'd played her part like a veteran of the road. And she'd snatched the booty from the air as he'd tossed it to her as though they were true partners and the action was old hand.

But now her silence had a prickly quality to it. And it seemed to stem not from the hay in front of them, but his earlier suggestion that she would be able to hire a post-chaise and travel in skirts like a normal lady of the *ton*, sleeping in inns and ordering him about in front of the coachman. After the day's easy camaraderie, the change in her grated on his nerves. 'Well?' he asked.

She frowned at him in the moonlight, the pucker of her mouth deeper than usual. He tried not to be flustered by it. But he could hardly look elsewhere because of what he had come to term in his mind 'the issue of the breeches'. While it was difficult to look at her face and not think of kissing her, it was even more difficult to deal with the thoughts that arose when he looked anywhere else.

'What do you mean by that?' she demanded.

'You are cross with me, though I have done just as you asked. I wish to know the reason for it. I can hardly remedy the problem if you do not state clearly what it is.'

'There is nothing,' she said, removing her hat and giving an imperious toss of her head meant to put him in his place.

'There damn well is,' he snapped back, looking at the cascade of shining black hair and forgetting his place yet again. After what they had just been through together, it irked him that she felt the need to play high and mighty.

'It is nothing important,' she corrected.

'If it is important to you, then it is important to me as well. Now tell me what is bothering you.'

She bit her lip in the way that she had when she feared she was revealing a weakness, as though she were accustomed to having any such used against her. 'I am tired, is all. And my muscles are sore from too much riding.'

'You have not been eating or sleeping properly and you are stiff from exertion. And not accustomed to riding astride.' She did look tired, swaying a little as she dropped to the ground beside her horse. It made him want to take her in his arms to soothe her, stroking her hair as one might a sleepy child.

Then she squirmed. 'I think I am not accustomed to these breeches.'

Nor was he accustomed to seeing her in them. And his thoughts changed instantly from innocence to hunger. 'I trust that they are not too uncomfortable.'

'It is not that.' She shifted again, but made no effort to explain.

'All the more reason you should return to your own clothing tomorrow,' he prodded. 'If mine is so disturbing, I should think you'd be happy to be rid of it.'

And that was badly phrased. It made him imagine her without any clothes at all. He stepped closer until she was so close that he had no choice but to look into her eyes. If she released his gaze, he'd not have been able to take his eyes from the place where her legs met, imagining the hot wetness of it, wanting to touch, to smell, to taste.

It was absolutely the last thing he should be thinking. And nothing like the chaste devotion he'd felt for Emily Folbroke. This was an all-consuming lust.

And Dru was looking back at him with eyes fixed and yet unfocused, the pupils large in the thin dark irises. But the firm set of her lips had a slight curve to it, as though she was daring him to reveal his feelings.

And he wondered—could it be that the tight clothing was arousing her? Perhaps she had learned more from her wayward lover than she'd let on. While it was flattering to imagine that she wanted him, it was far more likely that what she was experiencing was little more than a passing urge.

If so, there was no real harm in indulging it. A slight bruising of his pride, perhaps, when she cast him off in the morning. But it was better than feeling unmanned and invisible as he rode at her side.

As an experiment, he smiled at her in a way intended to charm.

In response, she bit her lip again, as though plumping it before a kiss.

And so he gave her permission to reveal herself. 'We have not really been speaking of doffing a disguise, have we?'

'We have not.' The words were half-statement, half-question, as though she was aware of what they did not mean, but was unsure of what they did.

He took a step closer. 'Or whether my clothing is an ill fit. Which it is not, if you were wondering.'

'It is not uncomfortable. But it is very improper.' She'd said it with a half-smile, as though telling him a secret.

'The impropriety is probably what makes it so damned fetching.' He waited for the firm snap of her disapproval at his impertinence and a return to the cold and aloof woman who had been ordering him around Britain.

Instead, there was only a slight gasp and the whispered words, 'You have been admiring me?'

'Any sane man would. And I could recommend something that might ease your distress, if you are feeling unsettled. Do you wish me to be of assistance?'

'In what way?' Perhaps she was not as experienced as he suspected. There was no trace of guile in the question, or any sense that she was trying to shift the responsibility for what was about to happen.

Which was why he ought to turn away, and do nothing at all. If she was unaware of the truth, it was not his job to change that fact.

But he could not help himself. After the adventures they'd had together, he was as restless as she was. There might never be a night when she was less of a lady, and he more of a rogue.

The distance between them had shrunk until it hardly seemed to matter. For better or worse, he would take advantage of the opportunity and touch the woman who had been driving him mad, almost from the first. He put a hand on her shoulder.

And she did not pull away.

So he said in a voice that was low and full of seduction, 'Sometimes, after a long ride, it helps to massage the stiff muscles, to return the natural ebb and flow of the blood.'

'I see,' she said, though clearly she did not, for she added, 'Like currying the horses.'

'Yes. Rather.' He was thrown momentarily off his stride.

'And you would do that for me.'

He regained his balance and lowered his voice again. 'If you wished.' Again, he waited for the outraged dismissal.

And again it did not come. Instead, she said, very softly, 'Perhaps you could demonstrate.'

So he stepped behind her, letting his fingers caress her shoulders as he moved, and eased the heavy coat from her body. He began, very innocently, by rubbing her neck and shoulders, stroking his hands down her back. She wore nothing beneath the shirt, having discarded her stays with her dress. It allowed him to enjoy the delicious feel of firm, smooth flesh under the linen, and the way the knots in her muscles seemed to melt at his touch.

It would be wrong of him to do more than this. And it was not as if he could pretend there was mutual seduction in play. Despite her forward nature, Lady Drusilla was considerably more innocent than the girl in the carriage had been. But he told himself that he was performing a service. She was tense and tired, and would sleep better after his ministrations.

She swayed against him; he heard her sigh and imagined her lips parted for a kiss.

So he put his arms around her waist and laid his cheek against her hair. No point in pretending that he was soothing her aching back. He was holding her for his own enjoyment, his lips resting an inch from the skin of her throat.

She did not move or tense, but stayed comfortably in his grip. And then, suddenly, she spoke, blunt and alert. 'Why did you kiss Charlotte?'

He started, but did not release her. It had not occurred to him that she had seen the kiss. But she could not have missed it. He just had not thought it would bother her.

And this sounded almost like jealousy. It was really quite flattering and a very good sign that further action on his part would be welcomed. So he pretended for a moment that he had room in his head for thoughts about the silly chit in the carriage they'd robbed. 'I knew she would be much less likely to send the law after us if I left her in a good humour. And she seemed to wish me to kiss her, did she not? When a woman makes such an effort to fall all over a man, it is cruel not to oblige her with a kiss.'

'So you knew she was shamming her faint?'

'Of course.' *But what are you are fishing for, in asking me these questions?* Dru was naïve, of course. But surprisingly savvy, when she had a need to be. There must be a purpose to this. And her movements against his body seemed almost an invitation. If she wanted to be aroused by a detailed description of the event, he was happy to oblige her.

'The kiss was pleasant for me as well,' he admitted. Then he could not resist goading her. 'Your friend is a very pretty girl, is she not?'

'I suppose.' He could feel Dru's shoulders tighten, as though he had struck her. 'And she is not my friend,' she added. Then she lifted her head again, rubbing her hair against his cheek as a cat might rub against its owner. 'I expect she will tell everyone who will listen that she was forced into submission by a wicked stranger, while revelling in the details of the experience.'

He felt his body tighten in response to her words and wondered how much of the discomfort she was feeling had to do with the sight of that kiss, and the hunger it had raised in her. 'Well, I expect that a well-bred young girl would find it an unusual and exciting thing to be kissed by a highwayman.'

Dru made a sound of displeasure and he imagined the bow of her lips, moist and waiting for him. 'She is not so young, come to that. She has been out for two years, already. Nor do I find her particularly well-bred. She really is the most appalling gossip.'

'And not too innocent,' he supplied, slipping his hands around her waist. 'It was quite clear to me, as I kissed her, that she knew exactly what to do with herself, from previous experience.'

'What do you mean?' she asked.

So she wanted the details, did she? He smiled and obliged her, shifting his lips so they touched her ear. 'She pressed close against me as I held her, to make sure that I could feel her breasts against my own body. She opened her mouth at the first touch of my lips, and took my tongue into it as though she could not get enough of me.'

Under his hands, he could feel the slight hitch in her breath as she listened. It had nothing to do with hisses of disapproval, and everything to do with salacious curiosity.

'But she is a blonde. And fair-haired women are not to my

taste.' And he stroked up over her ribs and took her breasts in his hands.

She started. 'That is not the area which was affected by riding.'

He stilled, but did not remove them. 'One cannot treat one area of the body without seeing to the others, any more than one grooms just one leg of a horse.' It was a most unromantic analogy, but she was not a particularly romantic female.

Her shoulders pressed into his chest and then relaxed. 'I suppose that makes sense.'

'You will find it quite satisfying, I promise.'

'Well, then,' she said again, 'carry on with your story.'

'Of course, Lady Drusilla.' He stopped to wet his lips, allowing the tip of his tongue to accidentally stroke the shell of her ear and felt her hips settle against his in reward. She could feel him now, he was sure, for she was pressing herself against the growing desire he had for her. But she did not pull away from him, so he continued their game. 'I meant to be gentle with her. Just a light touch of the lips and then I would be gone. But when a woman is willing, it is hard to resist.'

And the woman in his arms was giving her evidence of that, right enough. Her hands reached behind her to steady herself and gripped his thighs, sending another surge of desire through him.

'So I held her firmly and thrust my tongue deep into her mouth over and over, until she was quite weak with it.'

And it had felt nothing like this. Drusilla was heavy in his hands, warm and round, and he thanked God to his very soul for the wonder of her, massaging gently, and then more vigorously until the nipples stood out hard against his palms. He pinched them easily between his fingers and felt her gasp in pleasure at his touch.

'Oh.' The word was little better than a moan, as she writhed against his body, and a cue that he must stop before things got out of hand.

'Are you feeling better?' he asked.

'Somewhat.' Her head was lolling back, now, against his shoulder. 'But I do not wish you to stop, just yet.' She turned enough so he could see her eyes half-closed in the moonlight and her lips relaxed and parted. 'It was very wrong of Char to behave in that way,' she said, pursing her lips and wetting them with her tongue.

He threw caution to the winds. 'Perhaps you had best show me how a proper girl ought to react,' he offered.

'I do not know—if that is wise...' she said, slowly and deliberately, as though she had over-imbibed and were trying to remember why it was that she should not agree. But even as she said it, she turned in his arms and lifted her face for a kiss.

'For the purposes of edification, if nothing else,' he whispered, and gathered her close to him, one hand around her waist, the other sinking his fingers into her hair. It was heavy, as he'd imagined it to be, still smelling faintly of soap, even after three days on the road. Her lips, when he touched them, were perfect. As soft and full as her breasts and with that same pucker to them.

If he stopped to look at them, they might seem to be set in disapproval. But on closer inspection, they were open slightly, ready and waiting, as the other girl's had been. More hopeful than demanding, his Drusilla wanted a kiss as much as he longed to give her one.

And so he did, brushing her lips with his, and then licking

deep into her mouth, settling there, as though he had a right to possess her. In response, her hands came up to touch his shoulders and she brought her body close to his, brushing her breasts against his chest as though she was not sure that she was doing it correctly.

He struggled to hold himself still, to allow her to grow used to the feeling of his mouth on hers. And to enjoy the feel of her kissing him back: the gentle touch of her tongue on his and the soft movements of her lips as they parted with his, to touch the line of his jaw.

When they reached his ear, she whispered, 'You make me feel most unusual, Mr Hendricks.'

He could feel, in her sweet and uneven breaths against his hair, that she desired him, just as he did her. 'The way you feel is the most natural thing in the world and nothing to be concerned about.'

'The fact that something is natural does not mean there is no cause for concern,' she said.

'Very logical of you, Lady Drusilla,' he answered and laughed to himself that she would even try to think at a moment like this. But it was very her, and very appealing, and it only made him want to touch her all the more. 'Does it frighten you?'

He had found his question aright if he wanted to urge more passion from her—he ought to know by now that there was nothing that frightened this woman. At least nothing that she might admit to. 'Certainly not. I only wonder if it is a wise course of action.'

'Probably not,' he admitted.

'But it is…' she wet her lips and touched them to his earlobe

'...quite pleasant. And I suppose, as long as we are still standing and not lying down together...'

'Which we will not,' he assured her.

'And we are both fully dressed...'

'Which we will remain,' he added, swearing to himself that it was true and realising that she must understand very little of what he could accomplish without breaking either of her restrictions.

'Then it cannot be so very bad.' She then smiled against his skin.

'That is good. For I am not ready to let you go.' He kissed her again, dragging his lips along the curve of her jaw, to her throat and shoulder, and back up again, until his lips were resting beside her ear and he could whisper back to her, 'May I touch you again?'

'Please do.'

Then he let his hands go where they wished, exploring every inch of her that he could reach. Firm breasts. Tiny waist. Flat belly. He let his thumb sink into the dent that was her navel and imagined joining with her. Round bottom. Soft lush thighs. He pushed his hand between them and imagined those thighs wrapped around his waist. Then he cupped her womanhood, pressing his palm upwards, squeezing it possessively, feeling the heat of her in his hand and envisioning how she would look if he undid the drop of his breeches. 'Does this do anything to ease your suffering?' For it was increasing his, sure enough.

He waited for her to struggle free of his grasp, but instead her hands reached out to grasp his biceps to steady herself and she pushed back against his palm, groaning at the increased sensation. 'That is the spot, exactly,' she said, clearly amazed that he had guessed. And then added, 'Perhaps, a little less gently.'

'Very well, Lady Drusilla.' He looked into her eyes and smiled, then allowed himself the freedom to stroke more vigorously, imagining the flesh heating and growing damp at his touch. She closed her eyes. But her lashes still fluttered, as though she could not control them, and her neck arched ever so slightly as she caught her lower lip in her teeth. 'More?' he asked, leaning close and letting his breath caress her skin.

But she was quite beyond speech at this point, lost in the beginnings of a wordless response to his touch. She gave the barest nod of encouragement. In a few more strokes of his hand, her lips were trembling, open, moist and perfect. And so he kissed her roughly, pulling her body to meet his, safely separated by their clothing as he thrust himself against her and imagined being inside her, surrounded by her, consumed.

Her tongue came to life, darting against his in frenzy as her hands tightened on his arms. He was desperately hard and more than half-wishing that he had not started a game that could not end in his own satisfaction, but equally happy to have his supposed employer gasping into his mouth and pressing her sex eagerly against his as though she could not get enough of him. And he felt the moment that she lost the last of her control and came for him, breaking the kiss in a desperate bid for air as her back arched and her body went limp, swooning in his arms.

He held her like that for a moment, almost lifeless. And he brushed the hair from her eyes and thought, *I did this to you. And it was the first time.* 'Dru,' he said softly, loving the sound of the word.

She took a great, smiling, shuddering breath.

Then she realised how she had behaved and was shaking off the near-swoon and pushing away from him, brushing hands down to straighten the skirts that she was not wearing, trying to pull together the injured dignity of Lady Drusilla Rudney and pretend that she was still in charge. 'What was that?' The words were said with a stern frown as though her own physical response to his touch was somehow a trick that had been played upon her.

He gave her a benign smile. 'That was a perfectly normal, physical reaction.'

'To your kiss?'

'I suspect it had more to do with the way the breeches were fitting, and my—' he glanced down and then quickly back up at her outraged face '—ministrations in that area. You will find you feel much more relaxed, now that the moment has passed. And you can just as easily perform the actions yourself, should you feel the need again.'

'Certainly not.'

'Or I will continue to help you, if you wish.' He smiled, thinking that it was unlikely anyone would give him a reference should they find out what had happened and deciding that he did not care one whit who her father was, or what it might do to his career. He would not take back a moment of what had gone on between them.

'You know that is not what I meant at all,' she snapped. 'I would prefer not to feel this way. Certainly not ever again.'

The thought that she would not want to experience unbridled response was disheartening. But by the look in her angry eyes, Lady Drusilla had no real complaints with the way he performed his duties. There was a softness in them that she was trying very hard to hide from him.

'I feel unsettled. Even, after…the improper thing you just did to me.' Then she added in a whisper, 'It is as if I have forgotten to finish a task. And I do not know, for the life of me, what it is.'

If he was not careful, he would have those breeches off her and lay her down in the grass right now to help her remember. He was a careless fool and this had been a mistake. A horrible lapse of judgement. It was the first step on a journey that he would never be allowed to take.

He caught her warm brown eyes with his gaze and held them. 'I am afraid you are quite as finished as I can allow you to be, Lady Dru. Pleasurable though it would be, I do not dare show you the rest. I apologise for my behaviour,' he said, taking the burden of the indiscretion upon himself. 'It will not happen again and we need never speak of it. We will treat it as if it never occurred, if you wish.'

He was backing away from her now and it felt as if he were backing away from the act itself. *Do not make me go.*

'Thank you,' she said, her voice brittle.

'I had best see to the horses. And you…can take this to prepare a bed.' He tossed her a blanket from his pack. 'You will find the hay is quite comfortable. And I will just… The horses…' And he turned from her, stumbling towards the horses and wading into the icy cold stream.

Chapter Ten

It will not happen again.

That was rather a shame, she thought, as Dru gathered the blanket to her body and went to shoo the cow from the hay. The less sensible part of her wanted to demand an immediate repeat of the experience.

All she had wanted was a kiss. And she had assumed that, if she allowed him, that was all he would take, as he had with Char. But she had underestimated Mr Hendricks, just as she had from the first. Things had got quite out of hand. And while he had claimed that what he was doing was meant for edification and was merely meant to assist her in being comfortable, she suspected that there was much more to it than he had let on.

But she was not likely to know what had occurred without further experimentation and questioning of the man. What had happened was so pleasant that she was quite sure it must be unusual, unhealthy or improper. She sighed. Many things that were pleasant seemed to fall into those categories.

But, if this was what came of wearing trousers, then it explained much of what she had heard of men and their insatiable desires. There had been nothing in Mr Hendricks's other behaviour that had made her think of a man crazed by lust. But her governesses had assured her that all men became so on the least provocation.

Of course, they had been quite sketchy on the details of what such a mania might entail. But she was sure that there would be some obvious sign of it. In any case, she doubted that she was the sort of female that would engender such emotions. Especially not attired in muddied breeches and smelling slightly of horse.

Still, it would be nice to know. And to imagine what it would be like to drive Mr Hendricks mad. Because, if there was an answering madness, she suspected that she might be experiencing some of the symptoms. It was probably all the fault of the breeches.

The idea that they would be sleeping side by side again tonight made her... She shook her head in disgust. It made her want to giggle. To simper, just as girls did in the retiring room after having had a waltz with a particularly handsome gentleman. There was nothing about the current situation that should be so amusing. Or even give rise to the sort of nervous tittering that other girls engaged in.

Sleeping beside him was a necessary evil of the trip, a way to share warmth without laying a fire. Or at least it had been, until he had touched her. Her body resonated like rung crystal. And it proved that, no matter what she had feared, he did not think of her as genderless. He knew she was a woman and had apparently given the matter some thought. The look in his eyes had been confident, knowing and faintly amused. It had been there in the kiss as well, as though he had known what to expect from her mouth and her body. He had seen potential in her and had sought to develop it.

After, he had looked as she had felt: utterly confused. As he had promised, she was relaxed, more sure of herself and her surroundings. But he looked tense. Nervous. Unable to meet her eyes. And she had ruined everything by being harsh with him, scolding and pretending that she had not wanted exactly what he'd given her.

And then he had hurried away from her with muttered excuses about seeing to the horses. If she did not change her tone with him, it was unlikely that he would share the blanket with her at all tonight. He would go to sleep beside his horse and she would sleep alone.

Tomorrow, they would ride on, she would find Priss and they would take her back to London. She would explain to her father what had occurred and Mr Hendricks's part in it. Omitting certain details, of course. He would be paid and she would see to it that he received a polite but vague letter of thanks and recommendation for his help in handling a delicate matter with utmost discretion.

Then he would go. And she would never see him again. All the anxiety of the previous days came flooding back to her at once. What was she to do without him?

The same things she had always done, of course. She would manage herself and those around her. She would raise her chin, standing firm in the face of all the nonsense her family was capable of, and put up with her father's endless disapproval. She would put her needs to one side in the vain hope that, some day, things would be settled and she would have time for herself.

For the first time since childhood, she wanted to stamp her foot and cry. Sometimes, she worried that there would never be more to her life than what she already had, an endless string of duties and loneliness. In the moment she had kicked the strange man seated across the carriage from her, the burden of responsibility had been lifted. Now she did not want to take it back. It would be even more difficult to return home, knowing that there was a wonderful world of experience that she had sampled just one small corner of.

She wanted him to come back, so she could put her arms around his neck and pull him down into the haystack. Then she would demand that he tell her everything. He must teach her to touch him in the way he had touched her, right to the very soul, until he was lying beside her, as happy and sated as she felt.

She wanted him to assure her that there was more between them as well, that it didn't have to end in a week, with a discreet thank you and a return to their normal stations.

She bundled the blanket in her arms and set off towards the trees to find him. 'Mr Hendricks!'

He was leaning against a tree, eyes closed and at peace, almost as if he meant to sleep standing up. But when he realised she was near, he started in panic, glancing around himself as though he thought to run. 'Lady Drusilla.'

'Mr Hendricks,' she said, more gently. 'I wish to retire. Will you be joining me on the haystack this evening?' It sounded ridiculously formal. But what else did one say, at a moment like this?

But it must have been right. When she caught his eyes, he smiled. No. Not a smile. He grinned. It was insolent and inappropriate.

Without even thinking, she grinned back at him, then they

both looked hurriedly away. She straightened her clothing; he polished his spectacles.

And then he said, 'I do not think it wise that I join you, after what just occurred. That is, if you do not wish...'

'I do not wish to be cold or alone, either,' she said firmly. 'And in the hay, there are likely to be...other residents. Vermin, perhaps, or adders.'

'And that frightens you?'

Of course it didn't. It would be unpleasant, of course, but it was foolish to worry about things that were so small. But for once, she managed to answer correctly. 'Yes, the very idea terrifies me.'

He let out a bark of laughter to show that he did not believe her in the least, then he stood up and took the blanket from her. 'Of course I shall share a haystack with you, Lady Drusilla. I would not dream of leaving you, a frail female, alone and afraid.' They walked back to the hay and he took the blanket from her, spreading it out to make a kind of nest for them. Then he climbed up and helped her up beside him. And added, more quietly, 'At the very least, I will come to see what you look like when frightened. In my experience, it must be a rare thing.'

'Not really,' she admitted. 'But I have found there is little point in displaying such emotions. Fear is invariably used against one by those who sense it. In the end, one is worse off than before.'

He made a noise, low in his throat, like a beast growling at an intruder, then he pulled her to him, so that she could form herself around the bumps and hollows of his body. They were as close as pieces of a puzzle. 'You need have no fear of showing your true colours to me, Dru. You are safe, as are your secrets.'

She felt something deep inside of her relax, as though she'd kept a spring coiled tight and just now released it. Had she really been frightened, all this time? 'Mr Hendricks,' she said, testing her newfound bravery.

'Yes, my lady?' If he was trying to go back to the way it had been before, when he was nothing more than a solicitous servant, he was not quite succeeding. Though his words seemed innocent enough, there was an added depth to them, as though he meant something quite different.

'If I had not hired you...' she wet her lips '...would you still have helped me? I know I trapped you into accompanying me, at least a little way. But there was no real need. Even from the first, you could have exposed the lie.'

'Of course I would have helped you. While the offer of remuneration was certainly welcome, I could not have left a woman in need.' He smiled. 'And while you might not like to admit it, you had need of me.'

'Oh.' As always, her voice sounded gruffer than she wished. And the tone, which Priss would have called her schoolmistress voice, hid the little stab of joy she felt.

Then she stifled it. Of course he would have helped her. He was a gentleman, after all—not rich or titled like her father. But in the sense that he had proper manners, and respect for the fairer sex.

As though he had guessed her next question, he said, 'If you are now thinking that I would have treated any woman I found just the same, then the answer is, no, I would not. I would never have abandoned a lady in distress. And once my services were engaged, I was bound to do as you wished. But there are some things that cannot be commanded, by manners or money. Robbing a coach, for instance. It would take an exceptionally persuasive woman to achieve that.'

She took a deep breath and said, 'And what happened after?'

'That was something I did by choice, not out of a sense of obligation to anyone.' He tipped his head to the side and looked at her. 'While I might kiss some women on a whim, it is unusual to be so moved by the presence of another that I lose all common sense. Nor do I usually take to…grooming horses…to keep the incident from getting totally out of control.'

She stifled another sudden smile, glad that it was dark and he was close by. He seemed to understand her, and she would not be required to explain herself. For she hardly knew where to begin.

His arm draped easily over her side now, holding her with more tenderness than passion. 'What happened was not about money, or duty. It was something very special; I doubt it would have happened had you been here with another, or had I. Do you understand?'

She gave a slight nod; they were so close that he must feel the motion of it against his shoulder.

'And you do not have to be worry that it will go any further. You are safe with me, just as you were before.'

Safe. Then clearly he knew less about the situation than she did. For there had been nothing safe between them from the first moment they had been alone together. But the lack of safety bothered her less than her reaction to it. She had never felt so alive and so strangely happy.

From now on, when she looked at Mr Hendricks with one eye she could still find the quiet, responsible man in spectacles that would follow her instructions to a T. But with the other, she saw a highway robber, a devil-may-care rogue, up for any challenge, who might help a lady politely down from a coach only as an excuse to urge her to impropriety. And instead of giving him the disapproving sermon he deserved, her heart fluttered with excitement.

'I wish to ask you a question as well.'

She knew the sort of questions that a gentleman should ask, once they had behaved as Mr Hendricks had with her. He meant to offer. She was sure of it. And if he did, she would say yes to him. It would be quite impossible, for her father would never permit them to be together. But no matter what happened when they returned to London, tonight she would tell him the truth of her feelings. 'After the last few days, I think you are entitled to any answers you wish,' she said, trying to sound soft and approachable.

'After all that has happened, are you still intent on going to Scotland to find and retrieve your friend?'

She tried to hide her disappointment. Though her goal was the most important thing, she did not really wish to speak of it now. 'Yes. I am not bothered in the least by the difficulties we have had. And we do seem to be gaining on them, do we not? This stop is not putting us too far behind?' If dallying in the arms of Mr Hendricks had lost her a sister, it would be difficult to forgive herself. But was it so wrong to wish for just a small share of what Priss took for granted?

'I suspect we shall be quite close behind them, once we take to the main road again,' he assured her. 'But you understand that this means they have not been hurrying towards their goal. They have not hesitated to take meals together where people can see them. And they spend their nights at an inn and not on the road.'

She had known, of course. But she had not wished to think about it.

'The lady involved is hopelessly compromised. A gentleman would have only one honourable course of action towards her. And was I not pledged to aid you in stopping the marriage, I would feel honour-bound to make him go through with it for the sake of the girl.'

'I understand.' She put her hands between them, flat on his chest to feel the beat of his heart. It was steady and true and a great comfort. 'But you will help me, just as you promised? Because they cannot marry. I will not allow it.'

His body stiffened under her hands and he let out his breath in a slow exhalation, as though he had kept it in check to hear her words. When he spoke, his voice was placid. 'Of course, my lady. If you truly wish it, it will be so.'

He sounded like her servant again. She had done something wrong, or failed some test. But she had no idea what the mistake might have been.

'Tell me about this Mr Gervaise that we are seeking.' And he had changed again. This time, it was his voice that was gruff, like the growling of a dog when meeting a rival. The sheer masculinity of it made the hair on the back of her neck prickle.

She thought for a moment, searching for a way to answer the question without revealing too many of the details of Priss's embarrassing flight from home. 'Mr Gervaise is a most pleasant gentleman,' she said. And then added, 'I believe he is a French viscount.' That was most likely a complete invention. For all she knew Gerard Gervaise had been born plain Gerry Jarvis.

Mr Hendricks grunted in disgust.

'He ran from France when Boney came to power,' she assured him, fearing that he thought that her family was consorting with the enemy.

'How very tragic for him,' Hendricks allowed in a flat voice. 'And yet it is romantic in just the way that ladies appreciate. They think a French title is better than none at all. He is wealthy as well, I suppose?'

'A man of independent means,' she hedged. For wasn't his temporary employment a form of independence? Mr Hendricks was similarly self-reliant, now that she thought of it.

The independent man next to her grunted again. 'And I'll wager he is handsome as well.'

'Very.' That at least she could answer with sincerity. 'He is a little taller than you, well formed and with clear dark eyes and features that manage to be both strong and fine. He is quite charming as well. And an excellent dancer.' Of course, his profession required that of him. But his looks and manners were an asset. Taking it all into account, she could not blame her impressionable sister for running away with him.

'And the woman he is with?'

'Of no consequence,' she said hurriedly. The last person she wished to discuss, when a man was holding her in his arms, was her prettier and more charming sister. He would see her soon enough and note the differences between them. If her luck continued as it had so far, his attention to her would evaporate like a morning mist in the face of the sunny blonde delicacy that was Priss.

'I would find it difficult to live with myself if our actions in parting them caused her hardship or disgrace.'

'Do not worry about her,' Dru added hurriedly. 'I will see to it that she is back in the fold of her family by the end of the week.' With the doors and windows locked to prevent any more nonsense. 'If we manage to keep the trip a secret, her honour will be untouched.' Because appearance was all. 'And after?'

'After?' Mr Hendricks said dully, as though he had not thought that there would be an end to the trip.

'Your plans, as I remember them, were somewhat vague when we met.' Perhaps a nudge would be all it took to remind him that there was a woman in his arms.

'That is a kind way to describe my situation,' he replied. 'I was drunk and broken hearted. And ready to throw myself into the North Sea.'

'And how are you now?' she asked, hopefully.

'Sober. But otherwise unchanged.'

She had forgotten the story he'd told her the first night, dismissing his past as unimportant, since it did not concern the trip. 'When we met, you said that you were avoiding the company of a lady…'

'I had the misfortune to fall in love with her,' he finished. 'But I did not tell you that she was the wife of my employer.'

'Lady Folbroke?' Though she could not remember meeting the Earl, she had met Emily Longesley at a rout, during one of the countess's rare appearances in London. She had been as beautiful as Priss, and with a lively wit that held the attention of every man in the room. She had been friendly and welcoming, even to a spinster elder sister, urging her away from the chaperons' corner to sit with one of Priss's beaus. The prospect that her Mr Hendricks might, even now, be comparing her with such a nonpareil made her want to sink beneath the hay in embarrassment.

'She and her husband were estranged for much of the last three years. I spent most of my time relaying information between the two. I grew to be quite smitten with her.'

'And I suppose she is very unhappy in her marriage,' she said, wanting to think the best of the situation.

'Not particularly. If you are spinning wild fancies about an evil husband and a beautiful countess in need of rescue, do not bother yourself.' His arm tightened about her for a moment, as though drawing strength before remembering something painful. 'While Emily was certainly beautiful enough to be such a heroine, her husband was equally handsome and vastly superior to me in wealth and position. He was also a man I counted as a friend.'

'Then she was unfaithful to him,' Drusilla supplied. 'And led you astray.'

'On the contrary. Even when they were apart, she doted on him. She had no interest in me whatsoever, and made the fact quite plain.'

'How very cruel.'

'Cruelty is a kindness, when the object is being as obtuse as I was. It had reached the point where the parties involved could no longer ignore my feelings. I revealed myself not in some sort of dramatic and romantic declaration, but in a few and fumbling words that were unwelcome and ill received.'

Dru wound her arms around him and pressed her face into his shirt front. She felt his embarrassment as if it were her own: a replay of a dozen days, where some chance word revealed her feelings to those around her, only to find them unwelcome.

In return, he gave her an awkward pat on the back. 'Adrian was very understanding about the whole thing. Emily would have looked the other way as well. But I was too embarrassed to remain in the house. I quit my position that same day. Then I packed my bag, drank myself into oblivion and took a seat in the wrong coach.'

'How awful for you,' she managed. And for her as well, if his actions tonight were an attempt to forget another.

'Not so very bad, I think.' He gave her a kind smile. 'Travelling with you has taken my mind off my troubles.'

So that was all she had been to him: a temporary diversion. 'I am glad to be of help,' she said, closing her eyes tight and burrowing into his coat.

'Emily was delightful company and we worked well together. I have many fond memories of time spent with her and the dreams I had when I thought there might be hope for me.'

'I can see where you would be tempted, if you worked in close proximity with her. She is quite lovely.' *Please, do not tell me about her and all the ways she is unlike me.* 'But in the end, I think you made a sensible choice in leaving,' she said, wanting the conversation to end.

There was a pause and he brought a hand up to stroke her hair. 'I just wanted you to know that the revelation of my infatuation with Lady Folbroke, and my behaviour when you met me, were out of character for me. I can always be counted on to do the sensible thing in the end, Lady Drusilla. Some of us are cursed with a natural stability.'

'Lucky for the rest of the world that we are,' she said.

'But even the most sensible of us are not immune to love.'

'You make it sound rather like influenza.'

He laughed again. 'It is like a sickness, in a way.'

And you have given it to me. How could he lie beside her and have no idea what she felt for him, or what his philosophical musing was doing to her?

He went on as though it were nothing. 'I pined over Emily for several years in silence. But recently, being forced to see the hopelessness of it...' His hands on her stilled again. 'In telling you this, I meant to dissuade you from your cause and show you the hopelessness of reasoning with people who love. But it seems, Lady Drusilla, that you have persuaded me. It is not that I do not believe in constancy of affection. While I was caught up in them, I would have sworn that my feelings for Emily were everlasting. They are fading, after only a few days. If the union you seek to dissolve is of such a transient nature, then perhaps you will have more success than I first thought.'

'I am glad you think so. It is good to have hope.' *In something, at least.*

'I think so as well. If I land on my feet after this, I mean to take my recent behaviour as a sign and find a wife, if only to clear the nonsense from my head.' He did not sound terribly enthused about it. But she understood the need to have some plan to anchor his future to. Marriage was certainly better than throwing himself into the sea.

He laughed. 'Of course, the girls that I have the right to court would bore me to tears.'

'And what sort of women might they be?' she pressed, almost afraid of the answer.

'Women with parents who are not bothered that my own father will not claim me,' he said. 'And I should learn to accept that fact as well. When I was enamoured of the countess, it was not just her husband that was the problem. I tend to overreach myself. It is the height of foolishness on my part. I will not allow myself to make that mistake again, I assure you.' He pulled away from her and looked into her eyes with his serious amber ones. 'It is time I learned my place and to be content in it.'

He traced the curve of his bottom lip as though the touch were a farewell kiss. Then he pulled his coat up to cover them both and pulled her close, offering his arm for a pillow. 'And now we should rest. If we get an early start, we will steal a march on your escaping lovers and have them before luncheon.'

Chapter Eleven

*D*amn it. *Damn it. Damn it.*

The curses in John's mind rung in time to the strike of the horse's hooves. Dru had lain in his arms all night and he had slept not a wink. And the sweet torment of loving Emily was nothing, compared to what he was experiencing now.

He'd lulled her, and touched her, and brought her to climax. Then she'd spurned him. And five minutes later, she'd lured him back to bed, so she could tell him that she had no intention of giving up the trumped-up French noble she was chasing after.

He gave a snort of disgust. It was just as likely that, if he gave the man a firm shaking, he'd turn out to be an English nobody putting on a fine accent and a tight coat to get on the right side of the ladies. When they caught up to the beggar today, he'd have to put up with his Dru fawning all over the man and holding the handkerchief while some other poor chit wept her eyes out.

And she was not *his Dru* at all, he reminded himself firmly. She was Lady Drusilla Rudney. He should call her by her title as often as he could, to re-establish the distance between them. Seeing a woman's legs did not entitle him to an intimate acquaintance.

Although grabbing her between those legs should have. Apparently, the peerage, when one got them alone in the dark, was a different sort of animal entirely. She had awoken the next morning showing no sign that the previous day had affected her at all. She'd combed the straw from her hair, splashed a bit of water in her face and declared herself ready to travel. And it had all been done without so much as a 'Good morning, John'.

It had been Mr Hendricks this and Mr Hendricks that since the first night. And 'a little farther before we stop, Mr Hendricks' all this morning. Of course, now that he thought of it, she had never used his first name at all. That should have been a warning to him.

He had learned nothing at all by his experience. He had given a fine speech to her last night about knowing his place, and not repeating past mistakes. But it was all lies. In less than a week, he had transferred the affection he had felt for Emily to the next inappropriate female.

Of course, Dru was as unlike Emily as it was possible to be. Dark where Emily was pale. Cool where she had been warm, awkward where she had been graceful. And interested in him in a very personal way. She had shown more than a passionate response to his touches. She had been curious about him, sympathetic, and desired to be reassured that he would be well, even after they'd parted.

She cared.

Or she had last night. This morning, she seemed to have forgotten what had gone on between them and to be utterly indifferent to his presence. She was back to stalking the unfortunate Gervaise like she had ice in her veins.

And it was likely his own fault. If he had wanted more from

her, then he should have declared his interest and not made a dramatic show of setting her free. He could have spared them both the pretty words about not overreaching and his plans to stick to his own class in the future. If she'd felt any lasting affection for him, he had crushed it with his reminders of the unbreachable distance between and his decisions to set up housekeeping on the other side of it.

This morning he should not be encouraging her to pursue a man who did not deserve her. When they'd come to an inn, he'd hopped off his horse and raced inside to hear that the elegant black carriage they were seeking was just ahead of them. After that, he'd persuaded her it was time to cast off his clothes and dress like a lady again before they came to another inn, reminding her that she did not want to catch up with the man looking like she'd spent two days in a haystack with him.

She had taken her bag down from her horse, stepped behind a hedge beside the road and he had stood guard, back politely turned so that he would not catch a glimpse of his employer's delectable flesh. She'd reappeared a short time later in a travelling gown of deep green, braiding her long black hair so that she could pin it up under her bonnet.

He reached out and plucked another bit of hay from it, then stepped a respectful distance away.

She gave him a curt thank you, then said, without much confidence, 'Is the rest of me all right? It has been so long since I've seen a mirror.'

'Very fetching, Lady Drusilla. But straighten the bow on your bonnet. To the left. Just so.' And when he was sure she was occupied with her ribbon, he tucked the hay into his pocket as a keepsake.

He'd helped her up on his horse to ride the last few miles to the inn where they would hire a carriage; he had tried not to think of the extremely sensible drop-front gowns she favoured. He'd enough experience with women to know that they were a boon to mankind. Without even undoing a button, he could slip a hand inside her bodice and bid her a proper goodbye.

Then he had reminded himself that the fact they were alone did not give him the right to take liberties. She was young, although she pretended that she was not. And a virgin, even though she was not as innocent as when he'd found her. She was not married, but she might as well have been. She had given her heart elsewhere.

Take it back. He could rein in the horse and tell her how he felt, pull her to the ground and prove to her that there was no need to chase an unwilling man all the way to Scotland, when there was one right beside her who would stick like a burr if she gave him a chance. *Take her heart back and keep it for yourself.*

And do what with her? Shout, 'I love you. It has only been three days. And I am not worthy. But I am falling in love with you.'

Marry me.

He wished he could think of a way to make it all more palatable. They were well suited in temperament, used to being the ones pushed to the side and left to clean up the messes of others. That alone should have gained some sympathy from her. He understood her in a way that no other man could. He would make her happy, as she would him.

If he'd had savings, or family, or even a position…but no. Employment was likely to make it worse. 'Come away with me, my darling, to my tiny room in Cheapside and live as a clerk's wife.' He winced at the banality of it. Perhaps he could beg his way back to Folbroke. They would probably allow him to bring a wife into the household, relieved that he would no longer be sniffing after the countess.

But what kind of future might that be for Dru? Not at all what she'd been raised to expect from marriage. She was trained to navigate flawlessly in society and control a large household staff while her husband made laws and collected rents gained from the labour of others. She would be equal in birth to his employers. Yet, because of him, she would always be set aside. There was no hope for them at all. No place for him in her life, other than as a lackey. And no place in his world that she could possibly want.

So he did nothing. She sat primly in front of him on the saddle and he touched her no more than was necessary, riding as quickly as he could for the next inn.

When they arrived, John dropped to the ground and steeled nerves that had been worn to tissue since he'd received that fateful kick on the ankle. Then he held out his arms and Dru slid from the horse and down his body to the ground. It would have been better to let her stumble than to ever touch her again. But touching her was far too nice and he was running out of reasons to do it.

And he'd sworn as her breasts grazed his chest that the nipples tightened to demonstrate their awareness of him, even though their owner did not. There was nothing in those huge dark eyes to indicate any arousal at all. Only a deeper furrowing of her brow, and a slight tightening of her lush lips. She probably thought it was a grimace of disapproval, but it only made them seem more kissable.

'What are we to do now?'

'You may wait in the parlour, my lady. Take refreshment. Relax and let me see to all. I will ask about the ones you seek and hire a post-chaise and driver.'

As he escorted her into a room already crowded with waiting travellers, he could see the wistful gratitude in her eyes at the thought of a soft chair and a cool drink. It made him wish that he'd had a right to put that small smile upon her face by offering something other than such a mundane service. Then he pushed the thought away, led her to her seat and went about his business, as he was paid to do it.

The hostler informed him that Mr Gervaise and his 'sister' had indeed stayed the previous night in his best room. The innkeeper gave a disapproving shake of his head that said that the girl was clearly no one's sister, but that it was no business of his. The couple had argued endlessly, much to the annoyance of the other guests. The gentleman had ended the night shut out from his bed and asleep in a chair by the parlour fire. The girl had been slow in rising, and there had been much more fighting and slamming of doors to get her out of her bed and back into the carriage. But at last, they had gone, travelling northwards little more than an hour before.

If the couple was the sort to dally, which it was obvious they were, then they might be found at the next stop, or perhaps the one after. John could feel the eagerness to be done, like an itch that must be scratched. They would catch up before they reached Scotland. Lady Drusilla would have her Frenchman back and they would tack a plaster on the wounded honour of the other girl. There would be much weeping all around; John would be left to nod sympathetically, get the coach turned around and get everyone back to London before their absences were noted.

It would be over. And he could pocket his earnings, open his flask and return to his original plan to drown his broken heart. But as God was his witness, he would ride on top with the driver before getting back in a closed carriage to sit opposite Dru and her lover. There was a limit to the extent his gentlemanly manners would carry him and he expected to reach it well before nightfall.

A short time later, after a visit to the stables, he was back before his lady to explain why everything could not be accomplished as promised.

'If there is no chaise to let us, then get the innkeeper to give us more horses,' she said. 'I will don trousers again, and we can bump along as we have been.'

John shook his head. 'I have seen the poor nags in the stable, and I doubt they will take us one mile, much less ten. All the beasts with any spirit are saved for harness, and the best of them are hitched to the Reliant, the coach that runs regularly on this stretch of road. It is waiting in the courtyard now.'

'Then buy us two tickets for the stage.' She gave him a stubborn smile as though wondering why he had not suggested the obvious solution.

'It is full up,' he said with equal mulishness. 'And delayed to boot. The passengers surround you now. It seems the driver imbibed too deeply last night and has his head stuck in a slop bucket. He is in no condition to drive anyone anywhere, and unlikely to be so for several hours.'

Dru's eyes narrowed, clearly looking for someone to blame. 'You are telling me they are nearly in our grasp, we have money in our pocket and yet they will escape us?'

He gritted his teeth. All he had to say was 'yes', and offer an apology. The man she loved would slip through her fingers and over the border with another girl, leaving Drusilla angry, but free.

But free for what? There was no chance that he would have her. None at all. He would only be leaving her free for some other man. And if he was unfortunate, she would compliment his efforts to her father and he could stay on in the household to watch her marry another.

'No,' he said. 'This is not the end, unless you wish it to be. How strong are your nerves?'

She smiled at him; there was the playful spark in her eyes that made his heart tighten. 'You ought to know the answer to that by now.'

'Then keep the innkeeper occupied, while I ready the horses. We will steal the coach.'

For a moment, he had surprised her. 'You cannot mean it.'

'You did not baulk at highway robbery when I begged you to reconsider. Do not tell me you are having second thoughts about a life of crime, just as I develop a taste for it.'

'But who shall drive?'

He smiled at her and was pleased to see a flush on her cheeks and a slight dip of her head, as though she did not want to show him the excitement that was written plain on her face. 'Just do as I say.'

Chapter Twelve

Dru kept one eye on the innkeeper, and circulated amongst the passengers, whispering that if they were up for an adventure and could get to their seats, the coach would be leaving directly. One by one they escaped into the courtyard; she watched Mr Hendricks slipping pound notes to the stable hands to keep them quiet, carefully checking harnesses and blinders, examining wheels and making sure that all was at the ready. Then he hopped up into the driver's seat without letting go of the ribbons. He took up the whip and waited.

She ran for the carriage and he whistled to her, offering a hand to swing her up into the seat beside him. He gave a quick snap of the reins—they were on their way.

They were gaining speed, heading for the end of the stones and the beginning of the open road. Behind them, the coachman came roaring out of the taproom, and she turned to see the man shaking a fist and swearing.

'May I suggest you cover your ears, Lady Drusilla? I fear the man behind us does not realise there is a lady present. And head down, please.' He reached over and forced her to duck as they went under the stone arch that marked the edge of the coach yard, then released her, letting her spring erect again like a bent reed.

She looked behind her at the rapidly disappearing inn, then in front of her, then at him again. 'You drive four in hand?' she said, unable to contain a gasp of feminine admiration that would have done Priss proud.

'When I was a wag at Cambridge, I was considered the best of my lot at foolish stunts like this,' he answered calmly, keeping an eye on the horses. 'It will be more work for you than riding, but far more comfortable. And if you do as I say, we shall make quite good time. I expect we will find your friend within the hour. Then we shall see if Mr Gervaise is quite the man you remember him to be.'

That was an odd remark. She remembered Gervaise to be pretty, but soft and useless. She doubted he had changed a bit in three days. She glanced again at the man next to her, as he gave a smart crack of the whip to speed the horses. She sighed happily. Gervaise certainly would not have been able to drive himself to Scotland. She dared not tell her sister how they'd made the last leg of the journey. A man that could handle the ribbons as her Mr Hendricks was doing could likely dance as well. And manage an elopement without getting caught. When Priss learned of that, poor Gervaise would be out on the street and Hendricks would be left fighting to save his honour.

He cracked the whip over the horses' heads again, and said, 'Keep your reticule handy, my lady, for there are likely to be tollgates. It is up to you to pay, and to keep a watch on the passengers, while I manage the team. And if you can learn to blow the horn to warn oncoming traffic, as well? I think you will make an admirable guard.'

The wind was buffeting her bonnet, so she removed it and placed it behind her feet, letting the breeze blow the pins from her hair. The sun was touching her cheeks and there was a strong and handsome man at her side. It was bittersweet to think it was almost at an end. But the moment was glorious. So she smiled, and persuaded herself that it was a lark he'd arranged, just to amuse her. 'Mr Hendricks, is there anything that you cannot do?'

'It is a wonder what can be accomplished, if one only tries,' he said, as modestly as possible. 'And being born with fewer opportunities gives one reason to dare.'

As he stared down the road, his spectacles slipped down the bridge of his nose. And without another thought, she reached out a finger and adjusted them for him. Then she blurted the truth.

'I beg your pardon?' he said, tipping his head to the side to better catch the words.

'It was nothing important,' she said hurriedly. 'I was wondering how fast we were going.'

As they took the next turn in the road, the carriage rocked dramatically to the side, and he slipped his arm around her waist for a moment to keep her from sliding off the seat. Behind him, she could hear the angry mutters of the passengers, and offered a silent prayer that they would arrive in one piece and hear no complaints about the inexperience of the driver.

'We are going as fast as we are able and somewhat faster than the coachman would have gone. At least eleven miles an hour, I think. But do not worry, I will have us there safely.'

Dru gave him a satisfied nod, and turned her attention to

learning the coach horn, afraid that she would speak again, where the road was quiet and he might hear the truth.

I love you.

She might have managed to turn the words into a statement of respect for his abilities, which were prodigious. But more likely she'd have clung to him like a foolish girl, and said it again with the sort of sheep-eyed expression that made her near to nauseous when she saw it on others. Now, at least, she could understand the reason for it and the idea that it really was possible to fall in a swoon of rapture, as she nearly had in the hayfield. She was in love with Mr Hendricks. And when he left her, she would weep as loudly as any girl in London.

They took another turn and she grabbed for his coat tails with one hand and raised the carriage horn to her lips with the other. The best she could manage was a gooselike squawk and not the sprightly tunes that some guards could play. But if there were obstructions in the way, it was better to give them some sort of warning and she must do her best.

Of course, puckering her lips on the mouthpiece made her think of kissing. And kissing would, now and for ever, make her think of Mr Hendricks.

In response to her grab for him, he caught her waist again and held her until danger was past. It was so like him that it made her want to cry in frustration. If he had not been there, every step of the way, smoothing her path, seeing to her comfort and making her happy, she would not be thinking such foolish thoughts now.

And none of it had meant anything to him. He was an employee. A servant. He had been doing his job. Her father would pay him, he would leave and that would be the end of it. Unless, of course, she went to her father and insisted that he be kept on in some permanent way, so that she could have his company whenever she liked.

Although what he would do, she had no idea. Father already had clerks and secretaries and stewards enough. And she could not exactly ask for a manservant of her own.

But he had assured her that what had happened last night had not been part of the position. It was instead the thing which they were both trying very hard not to speak of.

She was trying, at least. There was no indication in Mr Hendricks's usually tranquil demeanour that it required any effort on his part at all. Even if she could convince Father to hire him, she could not keep him like a pet. He would have duties to perform. She would wander about the house, mooning after the man, hoping to catch sight of him, just as she would have cautioned Priss not to have done. And Mr Hendricks would continue to politely ignore it.

And when he found the wife he claimed to be seeking, a girl of modest expectations with a father who valued good sense over parentage, it would break her heart.

Hendricks nudged her; she let go with another feeble blast on the horn and dropped the required coins to the toll keeper. Then he gave a nod in the direction of a building on the horizon. 'There is your inn. And still twenty miles to Scotland.' He was pulling up on the reins and the carriage was slowing marginally.

'Well done, Mr Hendricks.' She put a hand on his arm and felt the muscles. They did not seem to strain to control the horses, but they were taut with the effort. Such strong arms, but gentle as they held her. She took a breath and let her hand drop away, pointing towards the courtyard, as though she still cared. 'There is the carriage, plain and black, with a crest on the door. And there is our livery.'

'Your livery?' He'd tensed on the reins in a way that made the horses start and the carriage jolted at the sudden slowing of the pace.

'Yes,' she said, lifting her chin as though the truth was a small omission that should have been obvious to him. 'It is my family's carriage that we have been seeking.'

'And you could not have mentioned this before?' he said. 'For when I asked about it, in all the inns between here and London, another detail would have been a welcome aid.'

'I did not want to run the risk of someone identifying the crest,' she replied. 'The fewer people that realise the identity of the couple, the better.'

'But, apparently, I could not be trusted with the information.' There was definitely reproof in his voice.

'A few days' acquaintance is hardly a reason to take someone totally into confidence,' she said.

'Of course not. What reason would I have to expect such intimacy? My lady.' Her title was added as an ice-cold afterthought, to make it plain that she had been badly mistaken if she thought him unmoved by recent events.

He cracked the whip for emphasis. 'Now do you mean to tell me, before we arrive, how Mr Gervaise came to be riding in your father's carriage? Or is it to be a surprise? Speak quickly, for we are almost in the courtyard.'

He was right. There was no reason to keep the secret any longer, for he would know the answer the moment they saw Priss. 'Mr Gervaise is riding in my father's carriage, because he has eloped with my sister, Priscilla.'

The horses broke their gait and a cry of complaint went up from the passengers. And then, all was right again, and they were slowing to an orderly stop in front of the inn. 'Speak to your coachman, to make sure he does not leave. He is your servant and will do your bidding, just as I have. And then, tend to your sister. I will speak to your precious Mr Gervaise.' And before she could say another word to him, he was out of the seat, handing the ribbons to the stable boy and stalking towards the door of the inn.

Chapter Thirteen

John pushed through the doors and into the taproom, in no mood to explain the stolen carriage to the stable hands, or to share one more word with the woman in the driver's seat. She had dragged him all this way, never mentioning the coat of arms on the carriage, or the fact that this meeting was nothing more than a sibling squabble over the same man. If she'd kept those secrets, then what else did he not know?

Although, knowing Dru as he did, he could not see that a battle between the sisters would be a fair fight. Young Priscilla had been wise to run, for her elder sister had to be the stronger-willed of the two. If she had wanted Mr Gervaise, the other girl would have no chance at him, had she stayed in London.

He scanned the occupants of the room quickly. Seeing no one, he asked the innkeeper about the couple attached to the carriage in the yard. He was directed to a private sitting room. He pushed through the door without a second word.

On a banquette near the windows sat the young couple, the plates on the table before them pushed to one side and their heads close together in some sort of heated conversation. The man looked up suddenly at his arrival, guilty, and quite aware of how this must look.

The girl looked strangely triumphant. As John watched, her arms twined about the elbow of the man at her side as though she wished to make clear their relationship.

Of course, it might just have been to hold her escort in his seat. The infamous Mr Gervaise was half out of his chair and leaning towards the door before the girl could pull him down again.

'Mr Gervaise, I presume? And Lady Priscilla?' He offered a bow to Dru's sister, and turned his attention to the man involved, watching the fellow's Adam's apple bobbing in his throat as his hand reached for the ale in front of him. There was none of the outrage at an interruption that he'd have expected from a peer, or the bluster of a soldier. Only a man who was thin but well built, hands neatly manicured and soft, with a coat cut tight to his body, of good quality but perhaps a little too flash to be tasteful.

A dancing master?

John looked at the pathetic excuse for a Lothario before him, sure of the truth. Then he turned to the girl clinging to him like a damp handkerchief. She was nothing at all like his Dru. Priscilla was petite and insubstantial, with an excess of strawberry blonde hair and bright blue-green eyes. But those eyes had a mutinous light in them that put him in mind of his own lover's iron will as it might look if disguised with candy floss and ribbons. It was the sort of combination that could turn a man inside out, if he was not prepared for it.

But then he remembered that recent events were proving that Dru's character was not as he'd expected either. John had imagined a young lord for her, being forced into a marriage by her father. His breeding would be excellent, but his character weak.

He'd have bolted with Dru's rival for the border, rather than wed the formidable lady he'd won. Or perhaps Gervaise was a rake whose house and title would more than make up for his disgraceful behaviour.

But of all the men he'd pictured, there had never been a doubt that the gentleman would be worthy. When Dru went to him, John would know that blood had bested him again. He could step quietly to the side, because it was best for her.

But a dancing master? Was the girl mad? Or as foolish as the rest of her kind, and willing to throw aside her honour for an elopement with a dandified nothing?

'Well, man? Are you going to stand there all day or explain yourself? What is the meaning of this intrusion?' Gervaise's French accent was as atrocious as he knew it would be.

'It is not I who must explain myself, Gervaise. I am not trying to steal over the border with the Duke of Benbridge's daughter.' The whole thing would drive the duke to fury, once he heard of it. He would have stopped it long before now, had he known a tenth of what was going on.

Priscilla gave her fiancé a slap on the arm. 'Do not be an idiot, Gerard. He is from Father, aren't you, sir?' She looked up at John with eyes as blue and liquid as a mountain lake. 'Is Papa here? Has he come for me?'

Gervaise turned in a panic to the window behind him, searching the courtyard.

'My name is John Hendricks,' he said with a polite bow to Lady Priscilla. 'I am in the employ of your sister, Lady Drusilla.'

Though Priscilla drooped in disappointment, the man beside her looked even more frightened at the mention of the sister. 'Silly sent you here?'

'Lady Drusilla did not send me,' he said, eyeing the man with contempt. 'She engaged me to accompany her.'

'She is here, as well?' Lady Priscilla slumped in her chair and put a hand to her temple. 'That will not do at all. Take her away immediately. Send for my father. I wish to go home.'

'Now, sweetness,' Gervaise said, petting her arm, 'we are very nearly to Gretna Green.'

'You are yet in England, Gervaise. And no marriage has yet taken place.'

'But it will once we cross the border,' he said with an arched brow. 'Just as Priss wished it to.'

'I wished no such thing, you great oaf,' the girl said, slapping at Gervaise again.

John held a hand out to the girl. 'If I might suggest that you go to your sister, my lady, I will take care of everything.' He shot Gervaise a warning look.

Gervaise ignored him, turning to the girl. 'It was not as if I forced you into the carriage. You arranged for the transport yourself. It was your idea from start to finish, and I will tell your shrew of a sister the whole truth, when next I see her.'

'I never wished to marry you, Gerard. Only to elope.' Having spent his life dealing with her kind, it was just the sort of non-sensical statement that John expected to hear from a young lady of quality. He took a breath before another wave of foolishness grabbed him and sucked him under the impending tide.

'The one leads to the other, Priss,' Gervaise explained. 'As I told you before, when a girl runs off with a man and behaves in a certain way, it gives that man certain expectations—'

'You worthless bounder!' John slammed his fist down upon the table, trying not to imagine what liberties the cad had taken with either of the daughters to get them into such a state over him. 'Lady Priscilla, I must insist that you come away so that I might deal with this...thing.' He gestured to Gervaise.

'I have no idea who you are, sir. But I am not moving an inch until Father arrives.'

'He is not coming, Priss, though you sit here 'til doomsday.' Dru stood in the doorway, arms folded.

Priss looked at her desperately. 'But if I go home now, you will ruin everything for me.'

'And if I allow you to stay, you will ruin everything for me. Now come to the carriage. We are leaving immediately.'

'You may do as you please. But I am not going anywhere.' The younger girl rushed past her, towards the hall. 'I am going to my room and I do not wish to be disturbed.'

'We do not have rooms here, Priss,' Gervaise called after her.

'Then I will take one,' Priss announced.

'And I am putting you in it and locking the door,' Dru muttered. Then she turned to the dancing master. 'But first, I shall deal with you, Gerard.'

'You most certainly will not,' John said. God help him, he would not see one sister dislodged from the clutches of this parasite, only to have the other take her place.

'This is none of your concern, Mr Hendricks,' she snapped.

'I beg to differ.'

She turned her anger from Gervaise to him, furious that he had disobeyed. 'While I employ you, it is not your decision to make. If you will excuse us, I wish to speak to Mr Gervaise alone.'

'Then I resign,' he barked back. 'Now that I have seen the whole of it, the chances of my winning your father's favour are all but moot should I continue to follow the mad orders that you have been giving me. You will not spend a moment unchaperoned in the company of this louse. In fact, you will spend no time with him at all. You will go immediately to tend to your weeping sister and give me no further trouble. And once you are gone, I will deal with Mr Gervaise. Now, go!'

He waited for the angry outburst, the shower of tears, or even the worthless Gervaise rising to her defence. But all he received was a muttered, 'Discretion, Mr Hendricks…' as though it were the only thing that mattered.

'Oh, I shall be discreet, my lady. Have no fear of that.' But what he would not be was the poor fool who watched the woman he loved clinging to a primping caper merchant all the way back to London. Or, worse yet, a witness as she dragged him to the anvil. He removed his glasses so that they would not be damaged.

'Now, sir,' Gervaise said with a nervous laugh, staring at the retreating back of Drusilla. 'You seem to be suffering under a misapprehension.' Then he looked back to Hendricks. 'Lady Priscilla was quite insistent that we make this trip. I meant no disrespect to her, for I hold the girl in high esteem.'

'Do not think you can shift the blame to an innocent girl, you muckworm!' Hendricks spat.

'There can be no sin in love, Mr Hendricks. No sense of blame in following one's heart.' Gervaise said it with such convincing piety that it was no wonder the girls had been swayed. 'And I would do anything to get the lovely Priscilla out from under the thumb of the Lady Drusilla. She has the eyes of a hawk and the tongue of a viper. And she would not let me alone.'

After three days in her company, John might have felt some small bit of sympathy for his rival, had he not just then imagined the pair on the dance floor, Gervaise's oily good looks a good match for the pale skin of his travelling companion.

'Now she has caught up to you. And she has brought me as well.' John flexed his arms. 'And I will make you wish you'd never met either of them.'

'I can wish that without your help, Hendricks,' Gervaise said, shaking his head. 'You must have sussed out the truth of it by now. Both the hot and eager Priscilla and her silly spinster of a sister are totally mad, and in need of a hearty prigging to set their wits to right.'

For a moment, John saw nothing but red. When he came back to himself, his hands were on the man's throat, dragging him towards the door.

'What…what…what…?' Gervaise was flopping in his hands like a fish on a boat dock.

'For talking in such a way about a lady, I would meet you on the field of honour. But it is clear that you have none. And so I think a good thrashing is in order.'

The man under his hands gave out a small sound that was rather like 'Akkk'. Hendricks loosened his grip, pushing Gervaise ahead of him through the taproom and out into the courtyard of the inn.

'This will do, I think. Unless you have a better choice. Boy,' he called to a stable hand, 'hold my coat.' He released Gervaise, so that he could remove it.

His rival rubbed his windpipe and uprighted himself, brushing at his garments as though it were possible to gather his dignity. 'I have no intention of fighting you.'

'Then I fear you shall be soundly beaten,' Hendricks said reasonably and raised his fists.

'Very well, then. But be warned. Mr Jackson says I am quite handy with my fives,' Gervaise announced, raising his bony fists and giving them a threatening rattle.

'It is a pity that he is not here to see how you acquit yourself,' said Hendricks, and punched him in the nose.

Gervaise let out a yowl of pain and cupped his face in his hands. 'You hit me.'

'Perhaps you do not understand the principles behind the art you practise,' Hendricks responded. 'Now come back here, for I mean to hit you again.'

'Help!' cried Gervaise, his eyes watering in outrage and pain and peeping between the spread fingers of the hands that guarded his nose.

'Oh, for God's sake,' Hendricks muttered, almost embarrassed to be harassing the man.

And then he thought of Dru, and decided that perhaps he was not embarrassed after all. 'Stop squalling, Gervaise, and take your medicine.'

'I will not.' The man rubbed his nose. 'If I do, you will only hit me again.'

'You dishonoured the ladies.' Hendricks said, as reasonably as possible. 'You did not think your behaviour would have no repercussions. And I called you a louse. A muckworm. A prancing dunghill,' he added for good measure, trying to reason the man into defending his honour.

Gervaise picked himself up, shook the dust from his coat and shrugged. *'Cherchez la femme.'*

Hendricks knocked him down again and glared at the coward lying at his feet. 'Did I not tell you not to blame what has happened on the ladies involved?'

Gervaise shrugged again, from his place on the ground. 'Miss Priscilla wished to escape the restrictive confines that her father and sister had set for her. Since I was tired of wooing her in secret, I was happy to aid her.' He gave John a significant glance. 'One would think, after all this time without a chaperon, that it might be better for a gentleman to wish us well, and escort us to Scotland. There he could witness that the job is done properly.

Hendricks debated the honour of kicking a man when he was down, decided against it and hauled Gervaise to his feet. 'I have heard from the lady's own lips that she does not wish to go. Her sister is equally insistent that no marriage take place.'

Gervaise produced a handkerchief and tended to the blood leaking from his nose. 'Then it seems that I should be owed something for my silence. And the damage to my person and my coat, as well.' He looked sadly at his tailoring, then in accusation at John.

'I suppose you expect it from me.'

'You are here as Lord Benbridge's agent, aren't you?'

'Actually, I am not,' Hendricks admitted. 'At the moment, I am without employment of any kind and acting according to my own desires. And I have decided, Mr Gervaise, that I do not like you.'

He caught the man by the lapels and gave a twist and a lift that put Gervaise up his toes and flailing his arms, complete with torn sleeve and bloody handkerchief.

Then he continued in a voice, low and full of menace. 'I do not care what happened between you and either of the ladies. Nor do I mean to buy your silence. I have found, Mr Gervaise, that when dealing with a certain type of person there are more effective and inexpensive ways to ensure a permanent and total silence.'

'You would not...'

'You would be surprised, sir, just what I am capable of, if it concerns the welfare of Lady Drusilla. Or her sister,' he added, trying to be less transparent. 'But I can assure you, if you ever return to London, and if I ever hear so much as a word of scandal about either of the Rudney sisters, I will find you and make an end to you.' He glanced at the stable boy. 'Young man, get me the coach ticket from the breast pocket of my coat.'

The boy brought him the ticket and he released Gervaise and forced the thing into his hand. 'I suggest, Mr Gervaise, that you go north. For your health. I hear that Orkney is lovely this time of year.'

Gervaise looked puzzled. 'But the Orkneys are on the other coast. With this ticket it would make far more sense—'

'Never mind!' John spun away and snatched the coat from the hands of the shocked stable boy. Then he turned to the Benbridge servants, who had been observing the scene without comment. 'Take this refuse and his baggage away. Anywhere he likes as long as you drop him on a north-bound coach route. Return in the morning for the ladies. They shall be ready to depart after breakfast.'

Then he returned to the inn to deal with Dru.

Chapter Fourteen

Dru paced the confines of the little room she had taken to freshen herself and await the return of Mr Hendricks. There was no point in trying to talk to Priss, for the girl was as good as her word. She had shut herself up in the largest room that the innkeeper could offer and was deep in the throes of a tantrum that would last the better part of the day. It would go on even longer if Dru indulged it by giving it any attention.

That left her alone and with time enough to worry. Through the door, Priss had sobbed something about Gervaise having a pistol. Dru could not know if it was an attempt by her sister to make her departure look more coerced than simply willful. But if it was true, then surely Mr Hendricks deserved a warning that the man he faced might be armed.

When she had announced she was going down to ascertain the direction of things, Priss had roused sufficiently to open the door and offer to join her. She was eager to see the duel being fought in her honour. Dru had renewed hectoring the girl until she was sure that the tears were flowing properly again, then made them all the worse by pointing out that no man would fight for a woman with a red nose and streaming eyes. With that, she was sure she would see no more of her sister until morning.

It would have been much worse had they not rescued Priss before she got to the border. But the idea that Mr Hendricks might come to harm through any of it was quite the worst thing she could imagine. She would never forgive herself if Gervaise managed to do him an injury.

She had told him as they travelled that a physical altercation was hardly necessary. Silence and discretion were key. If he had allowed her to deal with Gervaise as she had wanted, she could have arranged a settlement and sent him on his way without a scene. She had never intended that, when the moment came, Mr Hendricks would have to fight her battles for her, with fist or weapon.

That was foolishness, when all it would take to dislodge Gervaise was money. If it even took that. After a few days alone with Priss, it was quite possible that he'd grown bloated with the contact like a tick and was ready to drop off on his own.

But judging by how angry he had looked in the dining room, the non-violent solution did not seem to be enough to satisfy Mr Hendricks. Perhaps a few days in her company had driven him mad. He had been as inflammatory as possible until enough insults had been exchanged to make a duel inevitable. And before the end of it, he had quit her service, giving her no authority to stop him.

Mr Hendricks was strong and resourceful in his own way, of course. He hardly seemed the sort that would resort to such extremes when he had sufficient brains to find another solution. But it seemed when a girl like Priss was involved, men did not use their brains to lead their actions. Now he was likely to come to a bad end, brawling with a stranger.

She thought of the Countess of Folbroke, who, had she been more charitably disposed to poor John, might have saved him from this fate. Although the woman could hardly cuckold her husband as a matter of gratitude, surely there must have been some way to release him gently, instead of discarding him as though he were nothing.

As Dru had. She wished she could call back the last three days, and start again, to be kinder to him. And to give him some small clue how she felt. Or at least to be sure that he would not go to his grave angry with her.

The door burst suddenly open and Hendricks strode through, alone, slamming it behind him.

'You are safe?' Without another thought she threw herself at him, clinging to his arm, weak with relief. She patted his body and stroked his arms and chest, but could find no wounds or marks upon it, no evidence of the duel that Priss had envisioned.

He glared down at her, but did not shake her off. 'Of course I am. Not that you have any reason to thank yourself for it. After two years in Portugal, I have more than enough battle seasoning to take on a dancing master.' The words came out of him in a sneer, as though it were something he did not want to think, much less speak aloud.

'And Gervaise?'

John gave her a grim smile. 'Is gone, with his pretty nose broken, just as I promised you.'

'But the scandal…'

'There will be none. Wherever the coach takes him, it will not be London.' He shook her from his arm and grabbed his cravat, tearing it from his throat and dashing it to the ground. 'And why young ladies are fascinated with the likes of him, I have really no idea. I should think, if you had any sense at all, you would not bother to cross the street to see to his safety. But to come all the way to Scotland...'

'It would be very distressing, should he come to harm,' she assured him. 'Priss is already distraught. And I did not give you leave to fight the man.'

'Give me leave?' He tossed the coat he was holding over the chair nearest the bed. 'As you remember, Lady Drusilla, I left your employ before putting up my fists.'

'And if the altercation had led to his demise...?'

His eyes narrowed. 'Then it would have served the three of you right. If I had had any idea that such a man was to be the reason for your journey, I would have denied you on the first night.'

'Well, I am thankful that you did not know,' she said, lifting her chin a fraction. 'If you felt so strongly about this, but thought so little of me, then you needn't have risked yourself in confronting him.'

'Oh, ho, ho!' John reached to undo the buttons of his vest. 'Now we have the truth of it. You chose me as your aide in this because you did not think me man enough to stand against him. Did you expect me to stand by, polishing my spectacles as he insulted you, awaiting my dismissal?' The vest was open now and he removed it and tossed it uncaring after his coat, only to miss the chair and send it slithering to the floor.

'That is terribly unfair of you,' she said, retrieving his vest and placing it properly on the chair so that it would not wrinkle. And then she stopped to look at it, puzzled. It was barely supper time, and there was no reason for them to be changing for bed.

Nor was this his room. It was hers and there was no reason to share it. They had money enough to stay properly separated and she had reserved a place for him just down the hall. He must leave this room immediately. At least, after he had put his coat on again. She had her honour to think of, although why she had not thought of it before, she was not sure.

She turned back to him to demand an explanation. And he stood before her, shirt open and showing more bare male skin than she had ever seen in her life.

He went on, heedless of her stare. 'You were the one who was unfair, my Lady Drusilla. You expected me to sleep by your side like some kind of damned monk, so that you could stop this foolish marriage. You sneered at your friend for throwing herself at men beneath her class—'

'Actually she was Priss's friend, and it was not her...' she interjected, trying to tear her eyes away from his body.

But there was no indication that Mr Hendricks had heard her. 'Then you expect me to clear the field for you, so you can throw yourself on that primped-up popinjay.'

'Clear the field for me? Now just a minute, Mr Hendricks.'

'Not another minute longer.' He took a menacing step towards her, looming in the confines of the little room, making her feel small and helpless. 'If you think I will stand idly by while you make the same mistake as your foolish sister, you are sorely mistaken. I have thwarted one elopement and can just as easily thwart another.'

'My sister is not foolish,' she insisted. Priss was exceptionally so, but that did not give Hendricks the right to comment on it.

Then she realised that he was removing his glasses, folding

them with a snap and setting them upon the table, staring at her with those angry amber eyes.

She looked back into them and what she saw frightened her; she could not seem to look away from it, it was terrifying, yet intriguing, wild and unstoppable. She took another step back and felt herself bumping into the edge of the bed.

Then he smiled and it was hard and predatory. And if she was to be totally honest, quite exciting. 'I mean, my dear Dru, that you have dragged me half the length of Britain on a fool's errand, treating me like nothing more than a sexless lackey. And now it is time for you to pay the piper. Run to tend the wounds of your dancing master, if you must. But you will do it when I am through with you, and not a moment before.'

'Me?'

And he was on her, like a wolf in a sheep's fold.

There was a moment, before his lips touched hers, where she had time to suspect that he had misunderstood her motives. She had no intention of going after Gervaise, and owed Hendricks a 'thank you' for his swift handling of the situation. But it did seem that he had got confused about her reasons for the trip.

Then his tongue was in her mouth and she could hardly breathe, let alone think. When she could manage to gather her thoughts, she suspected that the last thing she wanted was to mention Priss and run the risk of receiving a polite apology and the sight of the door closing behind a retreating John Hendricks.

What had she done to imply he was sexless? she wondered. Did he not remember how she had swooned under his hand, that day in the hayfield? And now he was likely to do the same thing to her with a kiss. But there was nothing educational about it. This was to be a final test that assumed she had a complete knowledge of the subject. He was demanding that she prove competence, before moving on to the next lesson. His hand was on her jaw, opening her to him, stroking her throat as his tongue took hers, rhythmically, deeply, over and over.

He was here. He had not left her. She had been so afraid that she would never see him again. With relief, she let him master her.

But it seemed that the kiss was not enough. His hand went lower, reaching between them to undo the drop front of her gown, and he thrust his hand inside of it. When his fingers brushed against her nipples where they peeked out from the lacings that held them, she let out a little squeak of shock, and he pulled away from her to look into her eyes.

'Now you mean to be the prim-and-proper miss again? As though you have no idea what you do to a man, with those big brown eyes and that delicious body? Your tricks will not work with me any longer.'

'What I do?' She was doing nothing. It was he who was driving her to madness. His fingers that were raking lightly along her skin, tormenting her, and outlining her nipples through the fabric of her shift. And now they were untying the ribbon at the neck until it gaped low to expose them. She felt cold and hot at the same time; her knees went weak as he pushed her backward to sit on the mattress. Then he stripped his shirt over his head and bent over her, cupping the back of her neck to push her face into his bare skin until she could feel one of the tiny buds on his chest pressed tight against her closed lips.

It was insanity. She wanted to open her mouth and take him in. She knew she shouldn't, but she did, licking eagerly at what he offered.

Above her, and against her, she could hear the low rumbling of his voice. 'Perhaps you thought it a grand romantic adventure to dangle me on a string while running to meet your lover. But damn it, Dru, a man can only take so much. And I have taken all that I can, and then more.' Then he was pushing her away, on to her back, dragging her up onto the bed and lying on top of her, taking her mouth with slow deep penetrations of his tongue as his hands untied her stays and pushed her bodice and shift to her waist until he could cup her naked breasts in his palms.

It had been good in the hayfield, daring and dangerous. But that was nothing compared to this. She had not been able to see his eyes as he'd touched her then—the bottomless smoky gold of them that seemed to trap her look of pleasure and give it back to her. And she had not seen the smile on his face as he watched her.

Her breasts felt so swollen that they almost hurt. And yet he continued to touch them and lowered his face slowly as though he meant to kiss them. 'Please,' she begged.

And he laughed at her. He took them into his mouth, each in turn, sucking upon them to give her relief. She relaxed back into the pillows, letting him take what he wanted. But it seemed that this was but a calm before a storm. The tension was growing in her again, as it had in the hayfield.

He paused again and climbed up on the bed to straddle her, 'Now, I will take the one thing I truly want from you in payment for this trip. Unfasten my trousers, Lady Drusilla. You know well enough how they come undone.'

And she almost obeyed him without thinking, before sanity returned. 'I mustn't.'

He caught her hand, running his fingers lightly across the

knuckles of it, and said, 'I do not mean to give you a choice.' Then he pinned it to her side and stooped to kiss his way down her chest, and settled on her breast again.

She had no choice. She did not have to worry about her father's anger, or her sister's welfare, or what tomorrow might bring for any of them. For a little time at least, John Hendricks was in complete control and demanding that he be allowed to pleasure her. And if he did not stop what he was doing this instant, she would scream with delight.

Then someone might come and discover them. If nothing else, the beating of her heart would draw them, for it must be so loud that the whole inn could hear it. So she bit her lip to turn the cry of shock into a throaty moan and did her best to slow her pulse to something not quite so deafening.

The cries that she could not manage to stifle were little more than a series of gasps, as the strange rippling inside of her grew, crested and faded. She let out a final sigh of relief that it had passed and they were undisturbed. For a moment, until he was through with her, she was the centre of a man's universe, and she did not want to yield the stage to an outraged knock upon the door.

He released her hand and gave a final lick of her nipple before letting it slip from his mouth. And when he looked up at her, he smiled.

It was a wicked smile that hinted of things to come. Delicious punishments. Wonderful tortures that would leave her helpless with satisfaction. She felt as though some part of her was going to burst like a grape and imagined him licking away the juice of it, staring at her with those strange golden eyes, and running his tongue over his teeth as he smiled.

And before he had even touched her, the trembling was begin-ning inside of her again. One of his hands was on her skirt now, lifting the hem until she lay exposed to his gaze. He stared, eyes hooded, intent. And then he trailed a finger up her stocking and higher, settling near the place he had touched her when they had stopped to rest.

And just as it had been with her breast, it was different when he was touching her bare skin. She had not imagined those sen-sations to be muted, but clearly they were. Now his fingers had the freedom to slide along the most sensitive places of her body, which felt wet and swollen. And suddenly, they speared into her, and the shock of it made her almost rise off the bed.

She struggled for a moment, unsure what was happening. But he held her with his gaze and his fingers pushed harder, deeper, faster.

And as though to prove to her mind how well he knew her, her body crested quickly and then relaxed, legs falling open of their own volition, and her back arched to offer herself to him as his mouth returned to her breasts.

And the spiral began again. She could feel herself slipping away, just as the sensations were blending, fusing, growing and there was a final touch, which was somehow both hard and gentle, and then her soul seemed to leave her body, helpless and shaking on the bed.

Then he rose to straddle her again and removed his fingers, making her moan in disappointment. Again, he smiled his know-ing smile and said, 'Now do as I asked.' And he gathered her hands and gave them an encouraging squeeze before placing them on the waistband of his trousers.

With a shudder of suppressed excitement, she undid the buttons until the drop front fell away. Then he pressed his manhood against the palm of her hand and leaned forwards to ring her throat with short eager kisses, as though he meant to eat her. He was rubbing himself gently against her fingers and he seemed to grow larger and harder with each touch. It did not feel as she'd expected it to, warm and heavy and alive.

Nor did she feel as she'd expected, frightened and vulnerable. She felt as she had when he'd finished with her out in the field, strange, tingly and wet. She had not known what was happening then. But as she looked at him now, and thought of what his fingers had been doing, she began to imagine something they might try that would feel even better. In fact, she was convinced that if he did not attempt it on his own, she would have to shock him by suggesting it.

Then she remembered that he was giving her no choice, so she smiled, spread her legs and waited.

And he must have known she was ready, for he pulled away from her and rose so that he could remove his boots and push his trousers down, off, out of the way. He stood above her for a moment, naked and magnificent, staring down at her in her tangle of rumpled bed linens and half-removed clothing as though he owned her, body and soul.

And it occurred to her again, in a quiet, distant way, that this was just the sort of situation that she'd meant to rescue Priss from. And that it was quite possible, if she'd felt as Dru did now, that Priss had not wanted to be saved.

Then his hands were on her ankles, spreading them even wider. He lay down on top of her and his weight was on her, between her, and then in her. And there was a sudden thrust. And pain. And he whispered, 'And now, you are mine.'

I am yours. Whatever became of her, it did not matter any more. In this instant, she belonged to someone and felt safer than she ever had before.

He was lying very still on top of her and she wondered if this was all. She had lost her maidenhead. It had not hurt as much as she had expected. Nor did it feel as good as she'd hoped, compared to what had come before. But the pain was fading, and his lips were on her shoulder, brushing back and forth ever so gently as though to soothe her. 'Lady Drusilla,' he crooned. 'My Lady Drusilla. You feel wonderful.'

And then he was moving again, very slowly. It made her gasp, for it was new and strange, and he was right. It felt wonderful. And she could feel herself beginning to tingle again. 'Mr Hendricks,' she said, a little breathlessly.

He laughed. 'Please, darling. Call me John.'

'John,' she said, trying to sound more confident than she felt. And then, 'Oh. John.' For he was rubbing relentlessly against a most sensitive place in her body, and it was all beginning again.

She reached for him, putting her hands on his shoulders, trying to remain steady. They were warm and smooth; she could not seem to stop touching him once she had started, roaming over his back and his arms and settling upon his bottom to find the rock-hard muscles that drove his thrusts.

In response, he bit her shoulder, just hard enough so that she arched her back and gasped. And when her hips rose to meet him he thrust harder, holding her as she did him, squeezing her from behind and locking her against him.

She should beg him to stop. Hadn't she heard that, even when things had progressed to this point, there was a way to stop that would minimise the possibility of a child? But instead she held him tighter and moved with him. And in opposition, as though she was only playing at escape so that she could come rushing back to meet him with equal force.

But Mr Hendricks showed no sign of slowing. 'John,' she said. And then, again, 'John.' What he was doing felt achingly good, and even better when she tightened the muscles of her body and spoke his name. With each flash of desire, she felt a little more control slipping away, and the madness that she had felt before was beginning to take her again.

Only this time it was better. His groans answered hers, and when she began to move against him, he answered with even more force. Then they both were lost in a hot wet rush of feeling and she thought she called his name, one last time, but she was not sure. She could think of nothing but the helpless, blissful feeling of being with him, under him, and around him.

He went limp against her for a moment, as though there was no strength left in him. But when she tried to struggle out from beneath him, he came to life again and rolled with her farther on to the bed, wrapping his arms around her and stroking her skin until the trembling grew in her muscles again, and then slowly subsided.

And as sanity returned, she realised that she was making sport with a strange man on the way to Scotland. If they had crossed the border, would this have made them married? she wondered. Perhaps it was the act that made the union, not the other way around.

'Drusilla?' The man with her sounded quite dispassionate again. Which was strange for one whose body was still... She flexed the muscles where they were still joined and realised that there was no situation of etiquette that covered just what it was she was supposed to do in this situation.

'Mr Hendricks,' she said at last, 'I think that was probably very unwise of us. Of you,' she corrected, for now that she thought of it, she had not encouraged the beginning, much as she might have enjoyed the end. 'And I think you should probably—'

'What?' he asked. He began to move his thumb over a spot very near the place they were joined. 'What do you wish me to do?'

She had meant to say, 'Leave here immediately.' But perhaps his leavetaking could be postponed for a few moments at least, until he finished what he was doing to her, which was making her body tighten on his.

He smiled against her skin as he kissed her. 'Because I think, for a time, I will decide what it is that I should do. And I mean to make it so you will never think of another man, ever again.' He had begun to move in her again, and his other hand cupped her from behind, lifting her hips to his. 'And I think I shall make you call me John, again.'

She drew her knees up until she could cradle his body with them, wondering, as his hands stroked her legs, lifting them even higher to rest on his shoulders as the shudders began to rack her body again, whether it was possible to be ruined more than once.

Chapter Fifteen

When John woke in the morning, he rolled over and reached without thinking for the woman at his side. The empty space beside him came as a shock; he groped blindly in the pillows for a moment, as though there were a way for her to have got lost in the narrow and uncomfortable bed on which he had slept.

Consciousness returned. After a few moments of waking clarity, he remembered. This was his room, not hers. He had left her only a few hours ago, when the horizon was lightening with the dawn, sneaking back down the hall to the room she had got for him so that he was not seen leaving hers in the morning. He had fallen into his own bed exhausted, to catch a few hours' sleep so that he might pretend to rise refreshed.

But with waking had come the beginnings of dread. The activities of the previous night had been earthshakingly wonderful. And when he had left her, she had been smiling in her sleep. But he would be lying to call them consensual. She had known nothing of lovemaking when he'd met her, only three days ago. She had been a proper, sermon-reading young lady and well on the way to becoming a spinster. And he was sure the kisses he had given her, only yesterday, were the first she had ever received.

He had worked to break down her defences, weaken her resistance and destroy her virtue. Of course, the idea of such a woman remaining unmarried and untouched was so wrong as to be almost criminal. If there was nothing in her sermon book about the need for fruitful multiplication, then its lessons were incomplete and she was in need of other reading material.

But that had given him no right to push his way into her room and have his way with her. He was little better than Gervaise if he tricked the girl out of her maidenhead with no promise of a future. Today, he owed her an apology and an offer.

But until it was too late to take them back, he would have no real evidence to assure him that his words would be well received. She was a duke's daughter and he was someone's unclaimed natural son. In the cold light of morning, she could be screaming for her father, who would administer the horsewhipping he deserved for touching his precious daughter.

Although John had to wonder how precious she might be to Benbridge, if he allowed the family to call her Silly, gave her younger sister a come out and relegated Dru to the background. Dru did not seem to find it unusual. But John felt a growing outrage on her behalf, a need to rescue her, to take her away and prove to her that she was beautiful, cherished and desired.

And to be honest, he had his own reasons for offering. Although he had thought he understood love and the loss of it, the feelings he experienced when he thought of Drusilla Rudney were unfamiliar to him. There was the madness and rage that had taken him when he feared he might lose her, and the bliss of lying with her. And at all other times, there was... He searched his vocabulary and decided to call it a surety. It was as though they shared secrets that no one else had heard. When they looked at each other, there was knowledge. Trust. Communion. Quite simply, when she was beside him, things were right. And when she was not, they were wrong.

He had no idea if she felt something similar, for he had not spoken of it, or given her time to speak last night. What if it had left her frightened into silence by him and the possible consequences and the results that could be visited on her from his actions: disgrace, discomfort, pregnancy... She might be meaning to keep silent, as though it was something shameful and best forgotten.

His guts clenched at the thought of her, hiding her feelings behind a mask of stoicism, as she did everything else. Now that her sister travelled with them, it would be much more difficult to get her alone so that he might declare himself. And the fact that he had rushed into action, rather than wooing her properly, would make it harder for her to believe that what he did was not from obligation.

For a few blissful hours he had been only a man and she had been a beautiful and impossibly high-born woman. Even now, while alone, he could barely find the words to explain what he felt for her. But last night he had let his body talk to hers, knowing that if he did not do something sudden and irrevocable, common sense would win the day and he would do the right thing. He would stay silent, take her back to London and give her up. Lying with her had been selfish, irrational and unwise. But he had wanted to do it more than he'd ever wanted anything in his life.

And it had made her happy. Because of that, if nothing else, he had known that it was the right thing to do. Now it was simply a matter of finding the right thing to do next.

When he came down to the taproom to arrange for breakfast and ready the carriage, he saw no sign of his Dru. He smiled. Perhaps she was sleeping late, for they'd had an active night.

He did see Priscilla, sitting on the same bench in the parlour that she had shared with Gervaise, soaking in a patch of sunshine like a pampered kitten. He hoped the sun was doing her good. Her cheeks were wan and her eyes rimmed faintly with red. It had been a difficult night for her. But she had already been unhappy when he'd found her. He doubted that parting from Gervaise had done her any lasting harm.

Lady Priscilla was as pretty as Dru had said, in a fragile, flawless way that seemed to come naturally to the aristocracy. And while he had found the same sort of look quite attractive in his friend's wife, the eyes of the girl before him lacked the natural intelligence that he had found in Emily Folbroke.

Of late, John had decided that he much preferred a woman who could combine that intelligence with a sharp wit and a sharp tongue. And deep brown eyes. He tried to stifle his smile at the thought of Dru as he'd left her, lying in the tousled sheets, staring up at the ceiling as though she could not quite fathom how she'd come to be there.

But the younger Rudney sister had caught his mood and now, thinking it was for her, she smiled back at him. It was brilliant and captivating. It made him uneasy. 'Good morning, Mr Hendricks, it is a lovely day, is it not?'

He nodded in greeting to her, and said, 'Good morning, Lady Priscilla.' And then he fell silent, for he had nothing to say. Nor was it his place to make his feelings known about the day or anything else.

'Silly has told me so much about you,' she said, smiling even more.

For a moment, his mind stumbled over the nickname, wanting to rush to her defence and argue that there was nothing the least bit silly about his Dru. Then he caught himself and remained silent. There was something about the statement that sounded like a trap. When had Dru found the time to speak to her sister? He'd been with her most of last night. He suspected she would not have told Priss a single thing about the last few days, even had she had the chance. And now Lady Priss was angling for details.

'She spoke frequently of you as well,' he said.

'I am sure I gave her a fright, running off like that. But she needn't have worried.' She turned a little in her seat, to put herself in the best light, so that he might better admire her. 'As you can see, I am quite all right and well able to take care of myself.'

That was a patent untruth. He had never seen a woman more foolishly in need of rescuing. 'I am sure Lady Drusilla is gratified to find you so.'

Priss smiled all the brighter. 'But she would not have done so without your help, I am sure. The roads were most difficult on our way north, and we were delayed several times. It is a wonder that you were able to catch us so quickly.'

So that was it. She wished to know what her sister had been up to, perhaps wanting to hold an impropriety over her head to fend off the anger of their father.

'Lady Drusilla was most eager that you be found and scandal

averted,' he said, still not sure if it was the sister or the man she had been trying to find.

'And you helped her.' Priscilla gave a moue of sympathy, rather as though, in looking at her sister's ability to appeal to a man for help in anything, she were staring at the runt of the litter.

'She engaged me to do so,' John said firmly.

'And it was nothing more than that?' she asked, quite candidly. And for a moment, he saw the firm look that Dru used so frequently on him. It was as though the younger girl were daring him to admit any impropriety so that she could punish him, had he caused harm.

'What else could it have been?' he said, lying through his teeth. 'I met your sister on the road, just three days ago. It was most fortuitous that I was in need of a position just at the time she needed help.'

The girl seemed to relax in relief. 'Oh, Mr Hendricks, you are so gallant that I am sure it was more than that.' Dru's sister fluttered her eyelashes at him, but the eyes under them were as sharp and discerning as her sister's.

'Not at all, Lady Priscilla.' There was something about the calculated way that she did not stare at him that put him on his guard.

'No, really. In helping her, you have saved me from a disastrous mistake, and I have much reason to thank you. If anything about this trip got out, my reputation would not survive it.'

He gave her a reassuring smile. 'No word of it will pass my lips, my lady.'

'And you have seen to it that Mr Gervaise will have no cause to speak either.' There was a slight tightening of her brow as she said it, as though that had not been what she'd intended at all.

She stepped closer to him, until he could almost feel the warmth of her little body. 'How can I ever repay you?'

He gave a dismissive shake of his head and took a step back, bumping against the table, suddenly sure that the girl had meant to say, *How can I pay you back for this?* He had spoiled some plan or other, and it had nothing to do with thwarting her chances for true love.

'No thanks are necessary. Your sister engaged me to help in this matter. I was most eager to discharge the duty.' He moved clear of the furniture and took another half-step back. There. That should put things back on a professional standing.

'No, really. I was quite overcome by the excitement of it. Men, fighting. And over me.' She looked to be near swooning, until he stared into those very large, very blue, very cagey eyes.

'Well, it was, in a sense, a battle for you,' he admitted. 'But it was to defend your honour, my lady. And that is a cause that any gentleman would be happy to defend.'

'But surely the victor deserves a reward.'

'As I said before, Lady Drusilla will be amply compensate—'

The girl made a sudden lunge forwards, as quick and deft as a trained fencer. As she did so, she rose on to tiptoe and seemed to fall into his arms and, openmouthed, onto his lips.

There was an awkward moment of surprise on his part, then a tangling of tongues—and the horrible realisation that there was too much experience on her part, far too much eagerness and the subtle shifting of her body against his that hinted he was likely far too late to save her honour by scaring off the dancing master. The best that could be hoped for at this point was to get her safely back to her family, so that the doors could be double locked to prevent another escape.

And then he would get Dru away from the girl. For if she was the one tasked with keeping Priss on the straight and narrow, she must see that it was a losing battle.

He slid her feet back to the floor as gently as possible, hearing her moan at the friction between them, and untwined her vine-like arms from his neck. 'As I said, my lady—' he did his best to sound properly subservient '—what I have done for you was all in a day's work.' He looked her squarely in the eye. 'No further thanks are needed.'

'So you say, now,' she suggested. 'But if your mind should change on the subject...'

'I will bear your offer in mind,' he responded.

The girl stepped away from him, at least temporarily satisfied that she had made a conquest of him. He would need to steer clear of her until he could speak to Dru. Once he had her heart secure, he could counter any further attacks on his person with the assurance that he held only brotherly affection for Priss, tempered with the need to keep on her good side lest she run to her father with tales.

He straightened his glasses, which had been knocked askew by the force of her attack. And when he looked up again, Dru stood in the doorway, a stricken look upon her face.

How much of that had she seen? he wondered. More than enough, no doubt. It would do no good to deny the occurrence. He could hardly claim to be an innocent victim of an attack by her sister, no matter how true that might be. Blood would tell then, he was sure. If Dru had brought them all this far for the girl and not the gentleman, then she would never forgive him if he said anything less than flattering about the foolish little trollop they had rescued.

He turned to her, giving a short formal bow. 'Lady Drusilla, I apologise for my behaviour. Your sister was overwrought. I offered comfort and the situation got quite out of hand. It will not happen again.'

'See that it does not, Mr Hendricks.' Her demeanour was as cool as it had been on the first day, but when he looked into her eyes he saw hurt. Tears. Damn it to hell, he had made her cry, when nothing else had. 'Priscilla, come away from Mr Hendricks this instant.'

Her sister gave a saucy smile and a half-shrug of apology to him. And then she winked, as though to say the only thing she was sorry for was the fact that they had been caught. 'Coming, Silly. Do not raise such a fuss.'

Dru's eyes narrowed and she pulled her body in tight, proud and studiously unaffected by what she had just seen. It was as though, in a heartbeat, she could somehow draw the tears back up her cheeks and inside of her again, so that no one would know her feelings. She gave John a withering glare, then turned her disdain on to her sister. 'I can see, Priscilla, that we will need to have another talk about the sort of people it is proper to associate with. First you run away with a dancing master. And now?' She gave a dismissive wave of her hand. 'This.'

He tried to cast his eyes in the direction of the open door and held out a hand in supplication, hoping that Dru would understand the awkwardness of the situation and his need to speak to her alone, to explain.

But either her almost preternatural perception failed her, or she chose to ignore it. And him as well. She was looking at him as though he was something less than a man, less even than a piece of furniture. Worse than that, after all that had happened between them, it was as if he did not even exist as a part of her world.

'My Lady Drusilla,' he said hurriedly, not wanting her to leave. 'I spoke hastily last night, when I tendered my resignation. If you still require my services...'

Dru glanced from him, to her sister, and he saw the slight slump of resignation in her shoulders. Did she seriously think he could change his heart so quickly?

Of course she did. She seemed to think Priscilla was irresistible and her superior in all things related to the male sex. And what reason would she have to trust him after all he had told her of Emily, and his undying love that had not lasted out a week of separation? If she thought him faithless, it was because he had given her ample reason.

When she spoke, her voice was cold and superior, and she sounded as one might when speaking to a servant that one did not much like. 'You still deserve compensation for what has gone before, and will receive it if you return to London with us. But neither of us will need or accept the kind of personal attention that you have provided these last few days. Is that clear, Mr Hendricks?'

'Of course, my lady.'

She gave another sharp gesture to her sister, demanding that she follow. Then she turned from him, retreating at an unhurried pace. But as she went, he saw her reach for the handkerchief tucked into her sleeve.

Chapter Sixteen

The Benbridge carriage rambled on at a sedate pace towards London, with the windows open to fight the oppressive summer heat that had followed the rains. Dru fanned at herself with the open book in her hand. For all that had occurred since she'd left London, it was perhaps the best use for sermons. Priss seemed to be unaffected by the temperature. She looked just as fresh as she had when they'd found her and fully recovered from her bout of tears.

Apparently, it had done her good to casually take the only thing of value from her older sister's drab life. The image sprang fresh in her mind of Priss in the arms of John Hendricks. And with it came the heat of rage, and the desire to clout Priss repeatedly with the book in her hand. The girl was unlikely to gain any sense from the disaster she'd made of the trip. But if Dru could raise a drop of sympathy in her heart for the feelings of others, and maybe a small bump on that pretty blond head…

She fanned herself all the faster, trying to cool her blood. She should have been prepared for the inevitable, when it happened.

Men invariably turned from her, once they had met her sister. But it had never hurt so much as this.

Of course, no other man had held her in his arms, nor whispered of her beauty and his uncontrollable desire, nor acted upon those feelings so enthusiastically before. While she understood that what had happened did not always mean marriage was forthcoming, was it too much to expect a day would pass before she was betrayed by both lover and sister?

If Priss had been willing to think of anything other than her own feelings, then Dru could have requested that, of all the men in the world, with just this one she might make an effort to be less than her completely charming self. And to try to act as though she was a little shamed by the trouble she'd caused, and not on a week-long holiday.

Of course, there was little wonder that Priss looked happy and rested. She had not been forced to drag herself through the mud, skip meals and sleep in the hay. When Dru had managed to part her from the contents of her reticule, she had found more than enough money to take them home properly and in comfort, stopping wherever they liked and sleeping in proper beds.

Dru's eyes narrowed as she looked at her sister. It was just like Priss to create a disaster, yet suffer no discomfort from it. But she did not usually finish by reducing her older sister to brokenhearted tears in the public room of an inn.

'Do stop harumpfing at me, Silly; it is quite a waste of your time,' Priss said. 'It is not as if I mean to learn my lesson from the experience. Better you should learn not to follow me.'

'As if Papa would ever let me forget it, should I leave you get up to such foolishness,' Dru bit back, annoyed at her own shrewishness.

'Papa would not let you forget it, even if I had behaved,' Priss said in disgust. 'I swear, Silly, you think far too much of him, and what he approves or disapproves. His favour is hard to earn and seldom lasts.'

'That is no way to speak of our father,' Dru said, almost as a reflex.

'But it is the truth,' Priss said firmly. 'Read that book in your hand and I am sure you will find something favourable on the subject of speaking the truth. Especially when it is plain before your face.'

'It also demands that we honour our parents,' Dru snapped.

'And so we have,' Priss replied. 'For we have little choice in the matter but to do so.' And then, wilting a little under her sister's critical gaze, she amended, 'And you do enough of that for the both of us, I think. And you get far too little of the credit for it.'

The compliment was surprisingly welcome. And though it did not make up for even half of what had occurred, Dru managed a weak but sincere, 'Thank you.'

Priss sighed. 'I have inherited Father's temperament, I am afraid. Being just as headstrong as he is makes it difficult to obey without question. And you are too often forced to play peacemaker.'

'Someone must,' Dru said, wishing she could stay angry with a girl who so heartily deserved a scolding.

'For the moment, you could try to enjoy your time away from that abominable house,' Priss encouraged, in a way that seemed like sincere concern. 'And I promise that I shall give you no trouble at all.'

Making trouble came as naturally to Priss as breathing did. There was no point in commenting on it.

And then her sister said, with a sly smile. 'I suspect that you would have no real complaints about travelling with Mr Hendricks, if you would allow yourself to relax. He really is the most fascinating man.' She was staring out the window, to where Mr Hendricks rode beside the coach. 'Although, behind those ridiculous glasses, it is hard to see the colour of his eyes.'

'Golden brown,' said Dru, absently, looking down at her hands. 'His eyes are amber.' In the moonlight, one might even call them gold.

Her sister continued, as though she had not heard. 'I wonder, can he see without them? For I expect he would be much more handsome, were he to forgo them.'

'It would be quite foolish of him to do so,' Dru snapped. 'He is very sensible, not the sort of man at all who would sacrifice clear vision in the name of vanity.' Surprised at her own outburst, Dru bit her lip to prevent herself from mentioning some of the occasions that had caused him to forgo the spectacles.

Priss smiled. 'But I am sure that he is not unaware of the effect he has on women when he takes them off. There is not a man alive who is as proper as you make him sound, Silly.'

Dru pulled her skirts more tightly around her legs. Last night should have proved to her that he was as prone to sins of the flesh as the worst of his kind, and willing to take advantage of a helpless female, without regard to her reputation or modesty. And to make no mention at all of it the next day, but instead, to begin a systematic wooing of the female's sister.

She could feel her knuckles going white as the nails cut little crescents in the palm of her hand. It was all the more foolish that she could not seem to manage the correct response to what had happened. She should have cried out last night, and to devil with the consequences. This morning, she should have been racked with guilt and shame and fearing for the safety of Priscilla while the villain stalked her under the guise of assisting them.

Instead? She felt…

Jealous. The sight of Priss in his arms had left her burning not with shame, but with anger. And not at him alone, but at her sister. It was Priss who had led them to this pass, and who now could not seem to understand the gravity of the situation for both their reputations, and the difficulties she faced in the future. After all the fuss over running off with Gervaise, she seemed not bothered in the least that the man was for ever gone from her life.

Instead, she had moved on to the next available man, using charms that had brought the males of the *ton* to their knees. Did she bother to think, even for a moment, that her quarry might have formed an attachment elsewhere? Or that someone might have formed an attachment to him?

Not that Dru had any real evidence that what had happened on the previous evening was any more than a biological reaction to stress. It was wishful thinking on her part that filled every corner of her head with fancies about John Hendricks on one knee before her, pleading for a chance to make things right. Or sweeping into her bedroom tonight, as he had on the previous one, overcome with desire and with no cares at all about right or wrong.

Instead, this morning she had found him, warm and soft with her sister, but stiff and formal to her, as though she no longer mattered to him, now that she had been bedded. It had given her the strangest feeling inside, cold and sharp and painful, as though she was full of broken glass. And so she had done what came naturally to her. She had focused her mind on them until the shards were on the outside, where they belonged. There, they would hurt others and not herself, and she would be protected, safe and untouched inside the barrier they created.

However, she was conscious of the emptiness at their absence and the way that John Hendricks had retreated to a safe distance. It was just as she had commanded him to do this morning. He was not bothering her, or her sister. He rode just outside the carriage, where she could catch only the occasional glimpse of him.

Now Priss was craning her head out the window, waving to catch his eye. She glanced back at her sister. 'It is a shame that he does not ride with us, is it not? I asked him to. But he told me that he does not enjoy being closed up in the body of the carriage.'

That was little more than a polite and unconvincing lie. He had not seemed to mind it much as he'd ridden with her. 'The way he was carrying on with you this morning, I think it is just as well that he remains outside, as I requested. It will save him from the stern lecture I would give, to remind him of his place. For the duration of this trip he will aid us in the task at hand. Just as Mr Gervaise was brought into the house to teach you to dance. Such men should know better than to get above themselves, and you should learn not to stoop.'

Perhaps if she could persuade Priss, she could learn the same thing herself. But after so long in his presence, just the sound of his voice as she scolded him would be a welcome thing. She missed the feel of his body close beside her, his leg pressed against her skirt and his arm at her waist to protect her.

Of course, the family carriage was exceptionally well sprung, and she hardly needed a sheltering body to guard her against the bumps and the jolts of the road. But luxury had never felt so empty and unwelcome.

Priss shook her from her reverie with a sharp tap upon the hand. 'Really, Silly, you mustn't brood so. One kiss is hardly a sign that I do not know a servant from a suitor.'

Nor, Dru supposed, did one night mean anything. No matter how much she might wish it did.

'The scenery is quite beautiful, and yet you are glaring out the window as though it were a dark day in December. Can we not stop for a time and enjoy the countryside?'

'It is only three miles to the next inn,' Dru cautioned, pulling herself away from the window to stare at her sister. 'If we are continually stopping, it will take ages to get home.'

'But now that you have your way and I am returning to there, must we rush the trip? There is no one fashionable in London in the summer.'

'Father is there,' Dru said, firmly. 'And that is where we will attend him.'

'And I know you well enough to be sure that you have notified Papa of our return. You can tell him just as easily that we are delayed. It is nearly noon. I am stifling, and hungry as well. It would be delightful to have a picnic. Please tell the driver to stop and get down the hamper so that we might refresh ourselves.'

Dru sighed; now that her sister had the idea in her head, there would be no peace until she had her way. So she signalled the driver to stop at a wide spot in the road.

Mr Hendricks reined his horse and displayed no emotion save one barely raised eyebrow when he realised the purpose of the delay. He was likely eager to meet her father, receive his payment and be totally out of their lives.

The thought made her jaw clench; she ordered him sharply to lay out the blanket and help with the opening of the wine and the slicing of meat and bread. If he wished to act like a servant towards her, as though there was nothing more between them, so she would treat him.

Once he had seen to the comfort of her and her sister, he moved a respectful distance away, taking a small portion of the food for himself and leaning his back against a nearby tree.

'This is much better, is it not?' Priss insisted, then glanced at their companion. 'Mr Hendricks, would you not be more comfortable sharing the blanket with us?'

'I am quite fine here, my lady.'

'Oh, but I insist.' She patted the ground at her side.

'Oh, yes, Mr Hendricks. Do come and join us.' The sarcasm in her own voice was so thick that even Priss recognised it and stuck out her tongue in response, before sending another hopeful look in the direction of Mr Hendricks.

There was the barest hesitation before he pulled himself smoothly to his feet and joined them, dropping into the space between the two of them and allowing exactly the same distance so as not to show any partiality. Then he went back to the piece of bread he had been eating, as though nothing had changed.

'There. That is much better, I think.' Priscilla favoured him with another brilliant smile. 'It is a lovely day, is it not?'

'As you remarked earlier,' he responded.

She considered for a moment. 'When we were at the inn, the air was not quite so fresh. Here, we have the scent of the dog roses growing along the road.'

He noted the position of the flowers and nodded politely.

'Are they not lovely as well?' Priss coloured up in a way that looked almost sincere. Dru wondered how she could manage to control what should have been an autonomic response.

He turned his gaze on them again and answered. 'Indeed, my lady, they are most pretty, if one likes such things.'

'I doubt there is anyone in England that does not like a rose,' Priss said with a definitive nod of her head.

'But those are rather common flowers,' Dru answered, in some annoyance. 'And I expect they have thorns.' The cloying scent of the things, combined with Priss's annoying prattle, was giving her the most abominable pain in her head.

'A wise man learns to look past the thorns, at the beauty,' Mr Hendricks said, after a small pause. 'There is much reward to be had if one is willing to get past the prickly bits.'

Dru looked down at her hands, worrying that, if she looked up at him, she would find him staring at her in a most improper manner. Or, worse yet, that she would see him staring at Priss, with no idea of how his last statement might have sounded to her. When she finally gained the nerve to check, he was staring at nothing in particular, eating the sandwich he had made of cold meat and cheese.

Dru's eyes wandered to their surroundings, which were as annoyingly beautiful as Priss had said. Sunshine and roses—a lover at her side whom she dared not speak to, not even in anger, and a sister who was both chaperon and rival. Priss might find it pleasant and long to dawdle. But to Dru it felt unnatural, as though she were play-acting at being Priscilla. Everything was unbalanced. Someone had to keep their head, even when the roses were in bloom. And Lord knew there was not room in any family for two of them to behave like Priscilla.

'If I might be so bold as to ask a question?' John Hendricks's voice was polite and proper, carrying the subtle undercurrent that had led her into trouble in the past.

Dru put up her guard, but Priss responded, 'Oh, do. Ask anything at all, Mr Hendricks.'

'Lady Drusilla has mentioned that you are out, Lady Priscilla.'

'Indeed, sir. I expect I shall be married by the end of the year. Of course, I am quite without suitors at the moment.'

'Really, Priss,' Dru hissed. 'You are barely clear of Gervaise.'

Hendricks ignored the tension, and went on. 'But Lady Drusilla has said nothing of the results of her Season. And she is the older of the two of you, is she not?'

'At twenty-three, I am hardly an ancient,' she snapped, feeling as faded and rough as a dog rose in a hot house.

'She is bitter about it, because she did not receive a Season.' Priss put the truth bluntly, and yet there was sympathy in her voice. 'Mama died and Papa and I were distraught. Dru was brought home from school to take charge of me. And after a year of mourning, we were both old enough for the marriage mart. But she put me in her place.'

'At the expense of herself?' Hendricks asked, as though she was not even there.

'To have both of us out at the same time would only have divided the attention of the *ton*,' Dru informed him, to remind him of her part in the decision.

'Other families have managed to launch two marriageable daughters, even when they are not as wealthy as yours. Did you not wish for your chance to shine?'

It was an impertinent question, made all the more painful by the presence of her sister. 'We cannot always have what we want,

Mr Hendricks. If there are two daughters in the family, one must needs be married first.'

'It is normally the elder daughter who experiences that honour.'

'But not always,' she said firmly. 'Sometimes, one child is more vivacious, more popular, more sought after. And when it is known that this is likely to be the case...' After four years, she could say it almost by rote.

'You sound almost as if the decision was made before you were brought home.'

'Priscilla was clearly the more eager of the two of us...'

'Because Mother filled my ears with talk of dancing and parties, Dru. You were sent off to school, to learn reason.' Priss looked directly at John, with none of her flirtatiousness and added, 'There is little mystery why we turned out as we have, sir. One of us was discouraged from being sensible. And the other was required to be.'

'Aptly put, Lady Priscilla. But you give yourself far less credit than you deserve. I suspect, in your own way, you are as astute as your sister.'

Now it felt as though the other two were passing messages between them that she was not privy to. Once again, she was on the outside, just as she had always been, looking hungrily at the green grass on the other side of the fence. But she was not hungry at all, really. She just wished that this horribly awkward conversation could be over. She nudged the food about on her plate and waited for Priss to declare herself ready to continue the journey.

Priss was still staring down the hill at the rosebush again. 'It is a rare man that pays me the honour of calling me astute, Mr

Hendricks. Probably because I would much rather be thought pretty. And now, I think I would very much like a flower,' she said, scuffing the toe of her slipper in the dirt at the edge of the blanket. 'But I could never get it for myself, for I should certainly prick my finger upon it.'

Mr Hendricks gave a little sigh of amusement and put aside his meal. 'Then let me be of service.' His voice was as bland as if he were performing any other task put to him by a member of the family that employed him.

But he no longer worked for them. What he did now was merely a courtesy. And it angered Dru to see him scraping and bowing, especially to her sister, who was trying to get a rise out of him, to see some kind of reaction that would prove his true feelings for her.

'Oh, do leave off, Priss,' she said, her patience nearing an end. 'Let the poor man finish his meal, so that we might get back to our journey.'

But Hendricks was going for the flower, and Priss gave her a sharp nudge with her shoe. 'Nonsense. He didn't mind at all, did you, Mr Hendricks?'

'Of course not, Lady Priscilla.' And, as she had a hundred times when chaperoning her sister, she watched his manner for the eagerness or amusement, or a sign of hesitation that would make the flower a token of affection.

Mr Hendricks reached into his pocket for a penknife and cut through a stem, wrapping it carefully in his handkerchief to protect Priss's fingers from the thorns and offering it to her.

'It is so lovely. Thank you, Mr Hendricks.' The smile practically blazed from her sister's face in a way guaranteed to melt the reserve of even the most proper gentleman. Then she pulled a small mirror from her reticule and used the thorns to their best advantage to fix the blossom in her hair.

His name is John. Dru held the words in her heart, wanting to blurt it out to prove that, even for a moment, she'd had him all to herself. She felt her cheeks burning with something other than the coy charm that her little sister could manage. How did Priss make it all look so easy, wrapping a man around her finger just as she wrapped her curls around the rose? And leaving her, with a blank look on her face and straight dark hair that would not hold flowers, any more than she could hold the attention of a man.

She stood up too quickly, muttering something about needing a moment's privacy, and turned to step behind a nearby bush, praying that they would think she needed to relieve herself of anything but a foul mood.

'Dru.' He had caught up to her in a step or two, saying her name so low that no one but she could hear. But there was no blandness about it. It was a low growl of command that touched her, making her head snap back to look at him. He had cut another blossom from the rosebush and was examining it carefully to make sure there were no cankers. He turned his back so that Priss would see nothing, skinned the thorns from the stem with his knife, and held the bloom to his own nose, as though admiring the scent, brushing it gently against his lips as he did so.

Then he presented it to her with a flourish, touching it lightly to her cheek as though he could transfer the kiss he had given the flower.

She gasped in surprise; when she took the flower from him she held it so tightly that she feared she might break its stem.

'We must talk.' His voice was rough and urgent.

And do so much more than that. For she was sure she could feel the touch of his lips still. And then she remembered the much more earthy kiss he had given Priscilla, just that morning, when her bed was hardly cold. 'Go back to my sister. For I am sure that she is most eager to speak with you.'

He stifled an oath that was delivered so quietly that even she could hardly hear it, though she stood close by. 'I come to pour my heart out to you, to offer apologies for my shameful behaviour. And I find you are jealous of your sister?'

Her cheeks were burning now. She gave her head a little shake, as though to deny the obvious.

He looked her in the eye, and his molten-gold eyes turned hard behind the lenses. 'It is unworthy of you. And unnecessary.' Then he spoke, even more quietly and more urgently, as though there were a great many things he wished to say, and no time or place to unburden himself. 'What you saw this morning was no fault of m—' As though he realised how it would sound to her, he stopped. 'It was of no importance; I will see that it does not happen again. But whatever your feelings towards me, we need to talk, and there is too little time for it. The things that must be said cannot be blurted in the open where anyone might hear them. When we have stopped for the night, if you can get away unobserved, come to my room.'

'I most certainly will not,' she whispered furiously. 'What must you think of me, that you believe I would even consider…?'

'Please.' He grabbed her hand, rose and all, and brought it up to touch his face, rubbing the back of it against his cheek, pressing his lips against it, breathing in as though her skin was some sort of rare perfume. 'Please. I will not risk coming to you again. Someone might see. But you will know when it is safe to get away.' He pushed her hand away and half-turned from her, as though he had been balancing precariously on the edge of a cliff, and had only just managed to step away. Then he looked up into her eyes. 'You must be the one to decide if I can be trusted. After what happened last night, I am not fit or able to make that decision. But if there is anything left to say between us, then come to me. I will wait.'

'Mr Hendricks?' Her sister's voice cut the thick air between them, and his head turned in the direction of the sound. Then he took a hurried step away from her, guilt plain on his face and searched the cover they stood behind for another exit. He went around the far side of a nearby tree, working his way through a small copse, to return to her as though to pretend that he had been nowhere near Dru.

She peered through the leaves of the hedge that hid her, to see Priss glancing over her shoulder in his direction, eyes alluring and the rose he had given her tucked into the curls at the side of her head.

'Yes, my lady.' He went to her. Attentive, obedient. Dru watched him closely. And nothing more than that. Though her sister tried with enthusiasm to evoke a stronger reaction, he stood politely to one side, well out of reach of her.

Dru's heart beat fast in her chest, and she put her hand against it, wishing that it would calm and let her think. What did he mean by that? What did he mean by any of it? Had he seriously kissed the rose in her hand or was it merely a wish on her part? And to ask her to his room was every bit as improper as coming to hers. How was she even to find it, without asking someone and revealing what she was searching for? And would she have the nerve? If he came to her, they both knew that she could pretend she had no part in the meeting. But if she went to him? Then it sent a clear meaning that she had gone where she had gone willingly and with intent.

Stuff and nonsense, she told herself. She had shared lodgings with the man for almost a week and had no such qualms. She had even slept in his arms.

And that experience had not been the least bit innocent, no matter what she might pretend. She could not speak of it, should not even think of it. Going to his room tonight was out of the question. It would be better that every moment of the last week be forgotten. Not that she could ever forget—but perhaps she could try.

She shuddered, for she could still feel his hands on her, his body in hers and his breath on her skin. Without thinking, she wrapped her arms around herself, trying to capture the feeling and still the trembling. Then she stepped out from behind the bush and back towards the place where the footman was gathering up the remains of the picnic.

From across the clearing, Mr Hendricks's head turned, as though he had sensed her response. His eyes were innocently blank. 'Lady Drusilla?'

'Nothing,' she assured him. 'A momentary chill.'

He nodded. 'They come on sometimes, even in the heat of the day. Do you wish me to get your shawl?' Ever the attentive servant, willing to see to her comfort and meet her every need.

The thought made her shudder even more. 'No. Thank you, Mr Hendricks. I think once we are on the road again, I shall be fine.'

And hardly thinking, she turned to catch his attention and slipped the rose down the front of her dress, letting the petals crush against the skin of her breast and release their scent, turning everything about the day from innocent sunshine to something hot and lush and exciting.

And she smiled as the man before her watched, stumbled and caught himself again, taking a moment to remove his spectacles and wipe at them, as though eager to focus on anything but the place the rose had gone.

Chapter Seventeen

John Hendricks waited patiently behind the partially open door of his room, as still as a man waiting at a springe to catch a hare. He had dropped a few rose petals on the threshold. Should Dru come to look for him she would guess their meaning and enter.

Anyone else who stuck their head in could be sent off with a curse and the slam of the door. But after last night, and the way she had looked at him today, there was little more he could do for her than to wait patiently for her to come to him.

He silently damned her sister for the trouble she had caused, hanging about his neck like an albatross and creating no end of trouble. But what could he say to Dru about it that would show him in a good light? *I am sorry, darling, but your sister is no better than a grasping whore.*

But a shrewd one at that. It was possible that Priss had taken Gervaise away from her older sister. And if she suspected even a modicum of affection between Dru and himself, she might try the same trick. But today, as they had eaten she'd been most candid in her assessment of Dru's place in the family and the unfairness of it. This evening, she had taken herself off to bed at an early hour and insisted that she have her own room, so that her sister would not bother her.

At first, he feared it was meant as an invitation to him. But Priss had given her sister a pointed look, as if issuing a last warning before turning a blind eye. It gave him some small hope that he had an ally in the winning of Dru's hand.

But now, there was a hesitant scuffling on the threshold, and a whispered, 'Mr Hendricks?'

John, he thought fervently. *By now, you are entitled.* 'Yes.' He rose quickly, opened the door and pulled her inside, closing it behind her.

In the candlelight, she was as lovely as he remembered. And all his plans for a rational conversation evaporated. She had a woman's body, ripe and curved, to match those full red lips. It was a body a man could sink into, hot and rich, heady and intoxicating like a good wine. He tried not to think about it. Instead, he touched her face, cupping the softly rounded cheeks in his hands, pulling the lips to his for a kiss. He had meant it as a chaste greeting, as gentle as the kiss he had given to the rose. But her lips parted to accept him and he could not resist.

She had been innocent, he reminded himself. Still was. To presume less was to insult her character. But still, it was amazing that such a gem had gone undiscovered. And that he had been the one to touch her. Now, she was willing and here in his room. And he wanted her, just as much as he had the previous evening.

The circumstances of that bit into his conscience. She had not fought him, but she had hardly given him leave to do what he had done to her. And now he was ready to do it again without a word of consent.

He pulled away from the kiss with a groan, feeling her lean after him as though she did not want to give him up. But when he tried to read her mood, her head dipped so that he would not see her expression. Her heavy black hair was unbraided and hung down past her shoulders, covering her breasts. He touched her chin, lifting her face to look into his eyes. Big, brown, liquid.

And fearful. She did not shrink from him, for her arms still clung to his waist as though she was afraid to lose him. But she was not smiling. And as he watched, her lower lip trembled and the first tear coursed down her cheek.

He wrapped an arm about her shoulders and damned himself for his hasty actions of the previous night. 'Sweet?' he said, brushing the drop away with the back of a knuckle, only to see another take its place. She closed her eyes then, and the heavy lashes grew wet. And then her lips moved, as though murmuring a prayer.

'Drusilla?' he asked again, more clearly. 'Speak to me.'

She gave a little shake of her head and he felt the pain of hurting her, sharp inside him, and a hunger to take back the last hour, to a time when she was not crying. 'I am sorry. I did not mean to hurt you.'

'Last night, you were upset,' she whispered.

'Not at you, love.'

'But you will be.'

He smoothed a hand over her hair. 'And why would I have any right to anger? It is you who must hate me, for I have been a brute, with no sympathy to your feelings, no consideration for your innocence. I should never have touched you. I had no right.'

'It is not that,' she whispered. 'It is that you did what you did with no understanding of who I am.'

And for a moment, the strange idea leapt in him that she was about to make some dark confession about being a governess or a serving girl, masquerading as Lady Dru. He almost crossed his fingers in hope of it, for it would make life so much easier if they were in any way equal. He would offer, she would accept and nothing would stand between them, ever again. 'If I do not know who you are, then you must tell me. I want to know, Dru. I want to know you.'

'No, you do not,' she was shaking her head again. 'My sister...'

'Priscilla?' he asked, hoping for a different answer. But she nodded.

'It is she who loved Mr Gervaise, however unwise that might be. And I came after her and her alone. She did not understand the damage she might do to her reputation.'

Damn fate. And damn Priscilla as well. Dru was as great a lady as he feared and had lost her own reputation in the flight to save her sister. 'You have rescued her. And there is an end to it.'

'Last night, you seemed to think that I held some feeling for Gervaise. That there was a penchant, perhaps.'

'And there is not?' That was some small scrap of good news. 'But when we first met, you said that you and he had an understanding.'

'It was not that sort of understanding. When he first came to the house, I saw the way he looked at her. But he was a very good dancer and only in the house for a few hours each week. So I paid him twice what he was worth and told him that the money would continue as long as he caused no trouble, but that he would get nothing but trouble if he tried anything more adventurous than a waltz.'

The plan was so very like his Dru that he smiled. 'I do not think you were successful.'

'I did not count on Priss,' she said with a sad shake of her head. 'But there was never anything between Gervaise and me. He did not care much for me. Nor did it matter to me how he felt, for I liked him no better.'

'And the reason for your tears...' He stared up at the ceiling, trying to fathom it. For her outpouring of emotion made no sense at all.

'You were angry with him when you came to me. If you did what you did—' she took a deep breath '...to punish him in some way, or to punish me for liking him...'

'No, love. No.' He put a finger to her lips to stop her nonsense.

'Then it would not have worked. Perhaps, if you had gone to Priss instead. This morning, you seemed to prefer her. But I did not want that. And so I said nothing.'

Now he felt near frantic with the truth of her feelings, and pushed himself away from her body. 'Lady Drusilla, you misunderstand me as well. I would not have gone to your sister, in any case. That is not how it was at all. I had no wish to hurt her, to spite Gervaise. Nor to hurt you. And if, in what happened between us, I forced you to endure and not to enjoy...' Now he felt sick, nauseous at the idea that he had forced himself on her, and that, to keep her sister safe from his clutches, she had said nothing.

She gave a deep, gulping sob, clutching her hands to her mouth, her arms shielding her body from his gaze. 'It is worse than that. I…I…enjoyed it. I wanted you to do what you did. Had wanted it for so long. But if you had known the truth, then I was afraid you might have stopped. So I waited until it was too late.'

She was saying something else, but he could hardly hear her, what with the rushing blood in his ears at the relief. And so he seized her again and kissed her, stopping her prattle with his tongue and kissing her until sanity came back to him. Her mouth was salty from the taste of her tears. But given the least reason, she was kissing him eagerly back, thrusting her tongue into his mouth in unsure little forays, as though still afraid that he would reject her. When he pulled away from her, he said firmly, 'Did you like that as well?'

She gave a hesitant nod.

'Then it is all settled between us. I had no intention of visiting your sister, either before or after. In fact, having met her, I am sorry, but there is nothing that could induce me to it.'

'But this morning?'

'Was a mistake.' He searched delicately for a way to phrase it. 'Your sister seems to have drawn the same conclusion as you did for my reasons to fight Mr Gervaise. But it was not in an effort to defend her honour so much as extreme frustration that such a worthless clod could have designs on you.' He smoothed a hand down her side, feeling the rich promise of her hip through the fabric, wondering if he dared to do what he was thinking. 'I will fight him again, if he comes back.'

'That will not be necessary,' she said absently. 'But this morning…you said nothing to me. You could hardly bear to look at me.'

'I did not dare, more like. Better for your sister to think she had ensnared me, than that I had dishonoured you. And I mean to give her no further encouragement. I just didn't want her guessing what had gone on between us. Even a hint of what has happened would hurt you—and destroy what little chance I have to offer honourably for you.'

'Offer,' she said, in a surprised whisper.

His pride stung along with his conscience now. They both knew that he was not a worthy suitor. But she could at least pretend otherwise. 'Of course I will offer. After last night, you must understand how I feel about you. When I found a beautiful woman rushing to stop an elopement, I incorrectly assumed that it was to retrieve your own wayward fiancé. And I damned the inequality of our births and my misfortune at not being the one to tempt you away from the life you deserve. But I doubt your virtue would have survived the first night, had I but known that your heart was unengaged.'

'You wanted me?' She had that curious little frown again that he found so appealing.

'Most certainly. Almost from the first moment.'

'But people do not—male people, that is, men—do not normally...once they have met Priss...' She was still trying to puzzle it out, so he kissed her again until he could feel the lines in her brow begin to relax, bringing his hands from her shoulders down to her waist and back up, over her ribs until the swell of her breasts filled his hands.

'Let us think no more of what other men want, Drusilla. My only care is for my own satisfaction. And my only desire is to find it in your bed. Not your sister's. Nor any other lady of my acquaintance, or of yours.

'Hmm.' He kissed her again, and felt her whole body relaxing against his, her arms creeping back around his waist. Her hips were locked against his, and after last night, she must have a much better idea of what was likely to happen, should she stay.

'Dru,' he murmured in a sigh against her hair, willing himself not to tighten his hands upon those delightful breasts. 'Must you return immediately to your room?'

'Priss is most adamant that I not disturb her until morning. And there is not another person for miles that would care what becomes of me.'

'There is one, darling.' He kissed the side of her throat and felt her laugh. 'I know it is a day too late to ask, but have you given any thought to your feelings towards me? If I were to offer, what might your answer be?'

She gave a frustrated sigh. 'Father would never permit it.' Then she bit his ear as though she did not want to bother her head with anything so unpleasant.

It was not the same as a no, he told himself. And she did seem to be kissing him eagerly, as though she wished him to forget any impediment. 'Your father is not the one I wish to marry. If it were only us, then what might your answer be?'

'If you wish to marry me, then it would be most foolish of me to refuse,' she said, rather primly for one separated from him by only a nightgown.

'That is a sensible "yes" and, therefore, little better than a "no".' It was certainly not the enthusiastic answer he required. 'How do you feel about me? While I would marry you for duty, should you wish me to, just to restore your reputation, I would much rather it be a union based on mutual affection.'

Then her expression turned strange. A cloudy, dreamy sort of smile was on her lips, and her eyes seemed to be gazing far away. 'I never expected to be asked that question. How do I feel?'

'Yes,' he said, more urgently. 'Could you love me, just a little?' For I swear, though I could love enough for both of us, it would be a burden happily shared.'

'I feel wonderful, Mr Hendricks,' she said, with a sigh. 'And while I do not know the emotion well, I think I might be in love with you.'

'John, darling. Please, call me John.' And then, he buried his face in her throat, wanting nothing more than to mark it with the force of his kisses. Instead, he inhaled her scent and licked gently along the cords of it.

'John,' she said resolutely, as though growing used to the name. And then, more softly, 'Oh, John.'

He laughed against her throat, drawing her back towards the bed with him, praying that it was not too great a liberty to want the woman he loved in any way he could get her, for the brief time they had to share. He whispered, 'This, darling, is where you are supposed to tell me that you will not countenance such behaviour from me until there is a ring on your finger.'

She sighed and pushed him back until he sat on the mattress. 'Then I fear I shall be no good at all. I have no intention of stopping you, and missing this opportunity. If I did, and some misfortune would befall us, if you were to change your mind...'

'I would never.' He laughed again, into the hollow between her breasts.

'Or if my father should forbid us...'

Now that was a distinct possibility, and one he did not wish to think about just now. So he leaned his head to the side and caught one of her nipples through the fabric of her nightgown.

She gave a gasp of shock, then put her hands to the back of his head to push his face into her breast, all thought of disaster fleeing from her mind.

And his as well. She was the sweetest thing, and her heart beat wildly against his cheek as he suckled her and reached to ease the hem of her gown up higher over her hip. With his other hand, he teased the place between her legs until her knees began to give way. 'Take off your nightgown for me. Let me see you.'

She hesitated, as though this act was the one that would prove her intentions to herself. But she did as he asked. And he fell to his knees before her, burying his face against her body. 'Do you know how long I have wanted to do this? Since the first moment I saw you in breeches.'

'You told me that it was only to make the riding easier...'

'And it was,' he assured her, kissing her thigh.

'But all the while you were looking at my legs.'

'They are very nice legs,' he admitted, kissing them again, and pushing his hand between them, slowly lifting the palm up until it could go no farther. He raised his head to look at her. 'I admired your breasts as well. Without a corset to hold them, they swayed whenever you moved.

'You are horrid.'

'Very much so. Let me show you.' And he followed his hand with his tongue and lapped at her sex.

'Mr Hendricks!' In her surprise, she had fallen back to her old ways of barking prim orders at him.

And so he responded in kind, and said, 'Lady Drusilla,' then covered her with his mouth. And for a while, all she could manage was a few stifled moans, then gasping as her hips bucked in his hands, and finally settled, soft and open as a dew-soaked flower.

He lifted his head to kiss her belly, regretting that he had not bothered to undress before her arrival. But her smooth white hands were tugging at his shirt, and he rose and let her fumble at the fastenings of his clothing, the timidity of her hands all the more erotic. When he could no longer stand to wait, he hurriedly undid the last of the buttons, stripped to his skin and then laid her down on the bed and himself down beside her. Then he placed his member on the palm of her outstretched hand, curling her fingers around it and teaching her to stroke.

Now it was his turn to moan, for she was a quick study, eager to please him, climbing on top of him and pleasuring herself by using his body to touch hers, rubbing him in the wetness between her legs until he was near to sliding inside her.

He cupped her bottom and pulled her forwards. 'Tonight I will remember to leave your body before I spill my seed.'

'You will not,' she said.

'But we dare not risk…'

'I do not care.'

There was much she did not understand about the risk of children and his inability to feed them should they arrive before he had secured another position.

And then the thought fled, for she was experimenting with movement, flexing the muscles inside her body to trap him, rising up and dropping back again in a slow rocking that felt incredibly good. He leaned away from her, wanting the feeling to last and watched her touching herself as she moved until she shuddered in the throes of orgasm, her hair damp with sweat, covering her beautiful face in a veil as she lost control.

She opened her eyes and looked down at him, smiling in wanton surprise as she realised that he was still hard, still in need.

And he felt the aching tightness growing inside him and tried to rein it in, remembering that one of them must keep their head. But she broke that control as easily as a twig, moving on him again, scratching his chest, pushing her ripe breasts into his palms and leaning forwards to bite and suck at his shoulders and throat, marking him as hers.

He could stand it no longer. He rolled with her until he was on top, driving into her over and over, his mouth on hers to stifle both their groans so that they came together in a rush of silent, shaking power. He collapsed on her body, skin to skin. 'A night is not enough,' he whispered. 'I need you. All of you. Naked beside me.'

'Me,' she whispered back, still surprised.

'Of course, you. My darling, my beautiful Dru.'

She nestled close to him, her smile growing soft and fond. 'Tell me again that you love me.'

'I love you,' he said simply, feeling the inadequacies of the words. 'I wish there was a way that I could prove it. I would shower you with diamonds, if I had them. Rubies and pearls. I'd dress you in silks—' and then he stopped. For the likelihood of any of that escaped him. If she came to his house and his bed, she would be leaving luxury behind.

'Just words, please. I like to hear you say it.' She thought for a moment. 'Words and actions.'

The night had passed quickly. And the dawn left John wondering how he would manage to sit a horse for another day's ride without falling asleep in the saddle. He stroked the hair of the woman in his arms, feeling thoroughly depleted by her and satisfied in all ways but one.

He prodded her arm. 'Dru, wake up and speak to me.'

She gave a groan and then ducked her head beneath the covers, kissing his chest.

'Enough.' He pulled her up his body, so that he might look her in the eyes again. 'Do not try to hide from me. For if you remember, when I invited you here, I said there were things to discuss.'

'And we have hardly talked at all,' she said, with a wicked smile, as though it were an achievement.

'We will be in London soon,' he said. 'A day or two at most.'

'I know,' she said with a sigh. 'And then it might all be over.'

'What the deuce? Of course it will not,' he said. 'You have not been thinking all this time that I meant to let you go, have you?'

'I fail to see any other way that this can end,' she responded.

There was a sudden and unexpected tightening in his throat at the fear that he had been mistaken in her feelings. 'I thought that, after what has happened, it would end in our marriage. You said you loved me. And that you would have me, if I wished.'

She looked at him with eyes full of both worry and pity. 'Do not feel that you have to do that, Mr Hendricks.'

And there was that 'Mister' again, as though she had not lain in his arms these past two nights, murmuring 'John'. 'You are still describing a possible union between us as though it were some sort of obligation.'

'Is it not?' she asked. 'You feel that, since you have dishonoured me, you must make the offer.'

'Of course I do,' he said, exasperated.

'And you have said you loved me,' she said, with a happy sigh. 'And I love you as well. And because of that, I do not wish you to feel bad for what shall happen.'

She was being puzzling again, as she was sometimes. 'You speak as though it would be a hardship to wed you.'

'It cannot be what you expected, when you set out from London,' she pointed out.

'Of course not. But just because a thing is unexpected does not make it unwelcome. And I know I am unworthy. But you must tell me plainly, right now—will you have me or no?'

'Of course I would have you. I would like nothing better. If...'

'There need be no ifs or buts, Drusilla.' He wrapped an arm around her body, hugging her close. 'I do not wish to hear them.'

She sat up, gathering the sheets around her body. 'But now you must. We cannot be for ever on the road, my love. We will be back in London, just as you have said. And while I will take you gladly, my father will most certainly refuse to let me go.' She hesitated. 'You do mean to ask him, don't you?'

It would be so much easier if he did not, for she was likely right. If they simply turned their backs on London and went back to where they had been, he could take her over the border, just as Gervaise had tried with her sister. And though there was nothing fragile about his Dru, their love was new and might not stand the shock of the duke's displeasure. 'Of course I will ask him.' He looked up at her, reassuring.

'And when he says no?'

John grinned at her. 'Do not be so sure of that. I mean to make a very persuasive case for myself.'

She smiled at him fondly. For a moment, he imagined seeing that smile, just as it was, each morning for the rest of his life. Then she said, 'It will not matter. He has plans of his own in regards to the marriage of his daughters. And for all we might want it to be otherwise, they do not include you.'

'Are you promised elsewhere?' Again, panic gripped him, low in his stomach. For though it had not been Gervaise, perhaps his assumptions had some small grain of truth in them.

She shook her head. 'I have been far too busy seeing to Priscilla to think of such a thing for myself. And my father has been satisfied to have it so. If I marry, then who shall watch over her?' It was clear that the obligation of her younger sister was such a solid and palpable thing that she could imagine life no other way.

'Your father has the means to hire a companion. He must have considered it at some time.'

And there, when he looked in her eyes, was a curious blankness and a growing puzzlement, as if it was hard for her to imagine a life where she was anything other than spinster companion to the vivacious Priss. 'But then, why hasn't he?'

The hurt was so plain that he felt it in his own breast. She was like an animal so accustomed to its cage that an open door did not signal escape. And in that moment, he hated the duke, and was sure that Dru's predictions were correct. The man would hate him in return for daring to ask for her hand, and his birth would have nothing to do with it. For whatever reason, Dru was not meant to marry and never had been.

So he took her in his arms, letting the anger and frustration leave him in a kiss that left her breathless with its force. 'I do not know, darling,' he said, when it was through. 'All I know is that I want you, and with all my heart. Despite what you may think, it is not a sign of desperation, or a weakness in my character to do so. If I have a fault, it is that I am prone to aspire far above my station. And now I have set myself the task of winning a woman of great wit and beauty. I will go to your father, whether it is wise or no, and I will ask for your hand. And we shall see what he has to say in the matter.'

'And when he refuses?'

He looked into her eyes, so that she would know he was serious. 'Then I suppose it will be up to you what happens next. I do not mean to be parted from you, until you send me away.'

Chapter Eighteen

I want you.

The words were still ringing in her ears as the carriage made its way the last miles of the road to London. The echo of them was almost loud enough to block the continual sighing of her sister, who had grown tired of the journey and was shifting restlessly in her seat and offering meaningless interjections that broke Dru's train of thought.

John had been very specific about that. And very insistent. She hid the smile on her face by turning to look out the window.

'I wish you had not come for me, Silly. It would have been better if it had been Father.'

Dru glared at her. 'And he would have raised such a fuss that the whole house would have known of your disgrace.'

Priss sighed. 'You will manage to hush it up and the whole trip will be for nought. Still, I suppose it is better that you found me when you did. I could not manage to drag my feet any longer. And if we'd have crossed the border, I might have ended up married.'

'I am glad that you are finally coming to your senses,' Dru said.

'But you need not worry. Mr Hendricks has got rid of Gervaise and he will never bother you again.'

'Nor I him,' Priss said emphatically.

'You must not take the blame for this upon yourself,' Dru said, trying for a change to be a comfort and not a scold. 'You could not have known, when he took you from the house, what he was planning.'

Priss laughed. 'You do not still have some ridiculous idea that he forced me into the carriage, do you? I worried at the poor man for ages to get him this far.'

Dru could feel the knot of nerves in her head tightening again, as they always did when she tried to reason with her sister. 'Did you not realise what such a decision could do to your reputation?'

'Destroy it utterly, I should think. Of course, if I had been forced to marry him, it would have been better in one sense. I would have been off the market and totally forgotten.' But she gave a little shudder as though there was nothing to like at all about the idea of wedded life with Gervaise. Then she brightened. 'Now I shall simply be thought loose.'

'You foolish girl,' Dru exploded. 'Marriage to Gervaise would have meant penury, isolation, hardship. You cannot think that Father would condone such a union, nor contribute in any way to your well-being if you made the match.'

Priss gave her a weary look. 'I suspected he would first try to undo it. And if he was not able, he'd have cut me off. But that was the only way I was likely to escape.'

'Escape? Whatever do you mean? You have everything you need, Priscilla, and have not known a moment's strife since the day you were born.'

'Nor have I known a moment's freedom,' her sister pointed out, and there was the smallest of frowns on her pretty face as she did it. 'You are wrong to think I can destroy my reputation over something so small as this.'

'I know you will not,' Dru said, with some bitterness. 'Because when we are properly home and Father is finished shouting, we will find a way to make it disappear.'

Priss gave her a strange smile. 'I hope not. Perhaps I am beyond redemption. Then we shall be spinsters and grow old together. Will that not be nice?'

Dru thought of Mr Hendricks and blurted, 'It most certainly will not.'

And she was surprised to see Priss falter. For a moment, there was a sparkle in her eyes that looked almost like the beginning of tears. Then her little sister regained control and smiled again. 'Well, never mind. You needn't worry that I will be a burden on you much longer. Father will pave it over, as smooth as glass. And when he has selected a husband for me, I will marry, and that will be that.' She sighed again. 'In the meantime, I suppose there shall be parties and picnics full of men to flirt with. And that will be some consolation.'

'When Father hears of what you have done, you will be lucky if he does not send you straight back to Scotland for an extended period of rustication.'

Priss looked at her speculatively. 'And you must come along with me. That might work well for one of us, now that I think of it.'

'I don't know what you mean.' But there had been that sudden, unavoidable image of making her own trip to Gretna Green.

'Of course you don't, Silly.' Priss rolled her eyes. 'But even if we are sent from town, within a year I shall be right back to London and married to the man of our father's choosing. It will be the sort of man who values the good opinion of Benbridge over mine, and is willing to overlook my unfortunate past. He will be more concerned with the advancement he might gain than the foolishness of his wife.'

'No matter who you marry, you will never know want,' Dru insisted. 'And it is not as if Father is likely to choose a cruel man to wed you.'

Priscilla laughed again. 'After three days with Gervaise?' She gave a little shudder of disgust. 'I think my only want is to remain unwed. And I shall be experiencing a permanent want of that shortly. As to whether or not my husband will be cruel? I doubt it matters one way or the other to Father. My husband will be rich and politically well placed.' She gave the coldest smile Dru had ever seen on that sweet face. 'But he is unlikely to be the heir to a dukedom, now that I have sullied myself. Father will have to settle for a second son, or perhaps an inferior.' She gave a short laugh. 'God forbid that he find nothing better than a baronet for me.'

Dru's already short temper snapped. 'And God forbid that you should settle for the man offered, when he will at least take the time to find you someone. There are others in the family that have even less freedom than you, and are just as unlikely to ever see a Season. Nor will we marry the man of our choosing.'

'Mr Hendricks,' Priss said with finality. 'Say the name, Silly. We are in the privacy of the carriage, with no one else to hear. You can admit to me that he is the one you want.'

'I...I have no idea what you are talking about,' Dru faltered.

Her sister gave her a sly smile. 'Mr Hendricks. Do not pretend that you have not thought of marriage with him. The man has been bedding you from London to Gretna and back. Oh, do not give me that look, Silly. I may be a sound sleeper, but not so sound as all that. I heard you creeping down the hall this morning, on your way back to your room. And I saw the look on your face when I kissed him. And his as well. He looked, for all the world, as though he had sucked a lemon.' She smiled. 'You need not worry. I have no intention of saying a word to anyone on the subject. And I applaud you for your good sense in this matter, taking advantage of my misbehaviour to have a little of your own for a change.'

'I did nothing of the kind,' Dru said, stomach roiling at the betrayal. It would be good, even for a moment, to tell someone the truth. To ask advice. Or to share the joy of it. But if she wished to defend her sister's honour, she could hardly admit to the cracks in her own.

Priss sighed again, sounding weary beyond her years. 'It would be easier between us if you trusted me, Silly. Just a little. Then we could talk as sisters, and it might not seem so…'

Priss was looking at her, as though waiting for some sign that she might lower her defences. It hurt to stay silent, almost as much as it had to lie about her feelings for John. But she had decided years ago that Priss needed a mother more than a sister. It was too late to retreat. And so she said nothing, giving her dear little sister the same stern look as she always did.

And Priss broke her gaze, staring in defeat at the floor of the carriage. 'Very well, then, Silly. Nothing has happened to either of us on this trip. We will remain in London, stifling in the heat. I will say nothing of the truth. Nor will you. Papa is likely to be very cross with you, for letting me run about so.'

And then Priss looked her in the eye, and her gaze was, for want of a better word, *knowing.* Now that Dru had experienced love herself, there was no missing the fact that Priss was as knowledgeable as she. 'And we both know he does not wish to know the answers to the questions he is most likely to ask. We will go home and live in silence and denial, just as we always have, until Father chooses an appropriate husband for me. Perhaps then I shall have you stay with me, to keep me company. You will have more freedom in my house than you will in his.' Priss thought for a moment. 'Considering the sort of man that Father is likely to pick, it would be quite useful to have someone to explain where I have got to, when I choose to be somewhere other than where I am expected.'

'You are planning alibis for your infidelities, even before you know the identity of your husband.'

Priss gave her a blank stare. 'It is better to be sensible and prepared, Silly. Have you not taught me that?'

'But that is not what I meant at all.'

Priss stared at her, as though she could not believe her sister's stupidity. 'Then you have been using your considerable organisational talents to no purpose. Our lives as I have described them are just as they are. Father means for me to be married. And for you? I doubt he thinks of it at all. I am his favourite. We both know it, although you will not admit it to yourself. With Mother gone, it has been your job to watch over me. Where I go, you will follow. Or you can stay in Father's house, play hostess and housekeeper, and grow old while he dangles the possibility of marriage until even you see how laughable it is.'

'No.' She was beyond speech now, beyond thought. With only that cold and very real future stretching before her.

Priss squeezed her hand, and said softly, 'It was not just my childish inability with Drusilla that lead me to call you Silly. You really are the most foolish girl. But it is all right, darling Dru. I will take care of you. If I can, I will force my husband to hire your Mr Hendricks. Then you shall visit me whenever you like.'

So that was to be the plan of the rest of her life: she was to be guardian of her sister's fragile reputation. And since Priss had no care for it herself, she was to be little better than an abbess, arranging liaisons, and making sure that the truth did not become too well known.

She looked back at Priss, disheartened. 'It was not until just now that I realised how aptly you have named me, Priss. I would need to be quite silly, to have such a life.'

She glanced out the window again, her fingers clasping the edge of the frame and praying for even a glimpse of John Hendricks.

And as though he could sense her desire, he rode even with the window and smiled in at her. Then he signalled to the driver to stop. It was not yet luncheon, and they hardly had need of it, for they had been on the road for only a few hours.

But Priss accepted it eagerly, and was out of the carriage as soon as the steps were down, as though she could not wait to be away from her sister. After the conversation they'd shared, Dru felt uneasy as well, and was glad for a respite.

And John came to her in the only way he could. He was polite, formal and distant, as though there was nothing more important between them than to discuss the condition of the roads. 'Lady Drusilla?'

'Yes, Mr Hendricks.' She waited until she was sure her sister was out of sight, and the grooms and coachmen were busy with the horses. Then, very deliberately, she smiled at him.

John returned her smile, looking more like a shy lover than a servant. He took a moment to fiddle with his spectacles, composing himself, until he was simply Mr Hendricks again. 'How is your sister faring, on the return?'

'She is resigned to it, I think.' Dru frowned. 'And less than happy with her lot in life. But there is very little I can do for her, in that respect.'

'Now that I am sure you are safely on your way, I will leave you to find your own way home.'

'No!' There was nothing proper or composed about her response. The single word came, so sudden and anguished, that the servants looked up, ready to come to her aid. Even Priss turned back to see what the matter was.

'It is all right,' John said back in his composed servant's voice. 'We will not be parted for long. Only a day or two. And I have a reason for it. If I am to see your father, I do not wish to arrive along with you, half-shaved and covered with muck. I am going on ahead to prepare myself for the visit, and to prepare the way for you, as well. It might be easier for you if I explain what has happened before you arrive.'

'And what, precisely, do you mean to say, Mr Hendricks?' Priss had returned to them, and was standing a little way away, looking daggers at him.

He looked back, bland, innocent and, as always, helpful. 'That I am unsure of the reasons for your departure. But that I happened to meet Lady Drusilla while travelling, and she was most distressed. I found you in the company of a Mr Gervaise, who was a base and unworthy fellow. I gave him a sound thrashing and made sure that he would bother you no further. Then I aided you in returning home. You are both shaken by the experience, but in good health. Does this meet with your satisfaction?'

'Well enough,' said Priss. 'It will cause the least trouble for Silly, at any rate.'

'But you will visit, when we have returned?' If nothing else, he could say goodbye. If Father sent him away, she was entitled to one last kiss.

'Of course I will visit. As soon after your arrival as is decent.'

Priss laughed. 'It does me good, Silly, to see you in such a state. With me, you act as though you are made of granite. But at the brief loss of Mr Hendricks, you are very nearly wringing your hands.'

'I am not,' Dru said defensively, knowing that she was. A day without him would seem like for ever.

'You have done her good, Mr Hendricks. In a week, you have made her human. Now kiss her and go.'

'Priscilla.' Dru barely had time to begin her outraged harangue, before he'd responded,

'As you wish, Lady Priscilla.'

And he seized her, quite capably, and pulled her off balance and into his arms. The kiss was the best one he had given her, deep and slow to make his claim on her in front of sister and servants and anyone else who might see it.

Dru flapped her hands in protest for a moment, before deciding that to struggle would be to waste an opportunity. So she stretched out her arms around his neck and kissed him back until she heard her wayward sister say, 'Really, Mr Hendricks. That is quite enough to prove your point.'

Then she felt Priss tugging her away and upright again. 'And you, Drusilla. You are near to eating the man alive on a public highway and making us all nauseous. There will be time enough for that later, when you are alone.'

'She is right, Dru.' John was straightening his coat and looking at her with a polite smile. 'Let me go and talk to your father. I will see you again, after.'

'After,' she said, holding on to the word and managing a wave of farewell. No matter what happened with her father, she would see him again, even if it was only to say goodbye.

Chapter Nineteen

John removed his hat and waited in the entry of the Folbroke town house for the butler to announce him. It was strange, after little more than a week, to be actively seeking the company of the very people he had run from. But in those few days much had changed, and he needed the advice of a friend. Now that he was not in the service of the Earl of Folbroke, he could think of no one in his life that better fit the position.

This particular house had been shut for so much of his tenure with the family that he hardly remembered it. On the few occasions he'd had to visit it, the Holland covers had been on what furniture remained, and the rooms eerily silent. It was quite different from Adrian's old digs, which were barely large enough for a bachelor and a small staff. They had been sufficient for the earl's reclusion from his wife, but unsuitable for a happily married man.

John smiled at the thought of Adrian's sudden eagerness to indulge his wife and probed his own heart for any hint of jealousy. He was relieved to find none. The care of Emily had been his sole concern for years. The idea that she somehow belonged to him had come on him slowly. But the madness had left quickly enough, when it was clear that she'd returned to her husband.

The reconciliation between husband and wife appeared to be a permanent thing, if Emily was setting up the London house, just as it always should have been. From his position in the foyer, John could see a steady stream of furniture going in and out of attics and box rooms. And he was sure that when Emily was happy with it, the composition would be both fashionable and easy for her husband to navigate.

From a door on his left, there came the familiar tap of the cane, and the call, 'Mr Hendricks. Back already? Do not hang about in the doorway, waiting for an invitation. My study is just to one side of the stairs. It is the only peace you will find in this house, until my wife is done arranging the chairs.'

He smiled in spite of himself, for as it always had, the 'Mistuh' before his name had the sharp call of a commander, and a tone that could cut through the chaos of a battlefield. 'Yes, my lord.'

'Or, at least, I think it is orderly and peaceful,' Adrian Longesley added. 'I barely know myself.' He had made his way into the hallway, his cane held casually in front of him so that he might feel for obstacles.

John resisted the desire to set his former employer on the right path. He knew, despite the man's blindness, that he would prefer to make his own errors than to be led about his own house like a wayward child. 'It presents a challenge for you, does it not, when you move from familiar surroundings?'

'The rooms in Jermyn Street were simple enough, but I'd grown far too comfortable in my misery there. Emily has seen to it that my study here was the first to be finished so that I might have sanctuary. The problems have been minimal.' He grinned at the thought of his wife. 'But she is always thinking of such things. I swear, Hendricks, it is quite miraculous the way she has adjusted to my quirks.'

'I am not the least surprised,' John replied. His only real surprise was the lack of trepidation he felt in meeting with Lady Folbroke again.

Adrian led him back to the study and gestured him to a chair, almost as if he could see the thing, then took a seat behind his own desk. 'But what brings you back again so soon, John? Not seeking your old job, are you? It has been barely a fortnight since you left me, you know.' There was a small amount of reproof there, and John wondered, should he be forced to ask for it again, if he would be welcome. Then the earl smiled. 'I had high hopes for you, when you stormed out of here. It was kindness that kept you at my side, after the war. But you are capable of more than the duties you performed for me.'

He hoped Adrian was not expecting him to give a polite insistence that the duties had suited him well, as had the pay. Perhaps they had, at the time. Instead, he said, 'I am beginning to suspect that you are right, Lord Folbroke. It is not that they did not please me while I worked for you. I left, planning to seek an equally satisfactory position. But I've recently come to the conclusion that I must aim higher. I doubt that my old salary will be sufficient, now that I am to be married.'

'Marriage!' Adrian laughed, and slammed his palm down upon the desk. 'I will help you to make your fortune, John, in any way that I can. But there must be quite a story attached to this and I will not lift a finger until I have heard it. Who is the girl?'

'Her identity is part of the problem,' Hendricks admitted. 'She is the daughter of a duke.'

'Better than the wife of an earl,' said Adrian. The blank eyes looked at him intently, but without animosity.

'If a certain member of the peerage did not have such a damned appealing countess, it would never have been a problem.' He glanced towards the hall, and said quietly, 'How is she?'

'As long as you mean to give your heart elsewhere, you must tell me for yourself.' Adrian called into the hall, 'Emily, come to the study. We have a visitor with a most interesting tale to tell.'

John stood to greet the Countess of Folbroke, giving his spectacles a nervous polish before she entered. It was not necessary. For even without them he could see that she was as beautiful as she had been. After only a moment's hesitation, she reached out her hands to him and he clasped them in greeting. 'Mr Hendricks.'

He dipped his head in a half-bow and said, 'Lady Folbroke.' There was the raised chin and the clear discerning gaze that he had found so attractive. But strangely, she seemed smaller, after his two weeks away. Everything about her was less than he remembered.

Then it struck him. The features that he had most admired in her, the strength, the forthright nature and the tenacity, were as flowers in bud, compared to the rose he had discovered on the way to Scotland. And Dru had the colouring to suit her temperament. He thought for a moment of that thick black hair, falling through his hands.

He fiddled with his glasses to hide his distraction, and his relief at being able to see the woman before him as clearly as he did. And then he turned to the earl and lied through his teeth. 'If it is possible, she is even lovelier than when I last saw her.'

'Perhaps our reconciliation has done me good,' she said, smiling at her husband. Without another thought for John, she released his hands and went behind the desk to perch herself on the arm of her husband's chair. In an equally unconscious gesture, the earl's hand came to her waist to steady her. Hendricks had to admit that, seeing them together this way, all was right with the world.

Adrian looked up at his wife fondly. 'Mr Hendricks is in need of our help. He has got himself affianced to some young thing that is quite above him.'

'Not affianced,' Hendricks insisted. 'It has not come to that yet, although I have asked and she has said yes. It is her father that is likely to be the problem.'

'And who might he be?' Folbroke asked.

'His Grace, the Duke of Benbridge.'

Adrian's mouth puckered as though he had been forced to taste something foul. And Emily nearly sprang from her chair. 'Do not say so, Mr Hendricks. I had thought that you had more sense than that. Why…the girl is quite unsuitable.'

'Now, Emily,' her husband cautioned. 'Mr Hendricks will think you have some unfair motive to reject his beloved out of hand in this way. The father is a pill, of course. But surely the girl—'

'Is someone you have not met,' Emily said firmly. 'And though she is pretty enough, Priscilla Rudney is a cloth-brained goose.'

Hendricks stifled a smile. 'Then I must assure you, it is not Priscilla at all that I mean to snare. It is the elder sister.'

'She has a sister?' For a moment, Emily seemed quite baffled. Then she said, 'A tall, dark girl, is she not? Or a woman, I should say. She must be almost four and twenty.'

'And still unmarried?' Adrian said in surprise.

'Her name is Drusilla,' Hendricks said, equally surprised at the protectiveness he felt for her.

'Her family calls her Silly,' Emily interjected.

'And I assure you, it is a most inappropriate nickname.'

Emily nodded in relief. 'That is some comfort to me then, for I would hate to think that the older daughter was any worse than the younger. Very well. You wish to marry above you, and it will be a challenge to present the suit to Benbridge. But, and you must forgive me for saying it, Mr Hendricks, at her age, the girl is on the shelf. He will not be so particular as he is for the younger one. If there is affection on both sides of this match—'

'There is,' John interposed. 'Very much so. And I have come to suspect that she is not on the shelf, so much as she has been placed there by her father. All his attention has been focused on Priscilla, at the expense of Dru.'

'And it has made her spoiled and wilful,' said Emily with conviction. 'But I will trust your judgement that Drusilla does not share those particular faults.'

All in the room grinned like fools at the thought of their own particular happinesses. Then John said, cautiously, 'It has all come on me rather suddenly. And as you can see, if I mean to have Dru, I have set myself a task. So I come to you, not so much seeking a position as seeking the advice…' he gave his spectacles another polish '…the advice of friends. I will go to meet Benbridge later in the day, to explain the circumstances in which I met his daughters, which are unusual. I am going with no family, no title, and not even a stable position. I have very little to offer but my love for his daughter, and her love for me.'

Adrian frowned. 'I am sorry, John, but while that might matter to another, that will mean less than nothing to Benbridge. The man is a miserable old sinner, with a heart like a flint. Still, tell us your story, and we will put our heads together so that you might present yourself in the most favourable light. I am sure that we will be throwing orange blossoms by spring.'

Chapter Twenty

'A Mr John Hendricks to see you, your Grace.' John had wondered, as he spoke to Adrian, whether it would be better to present himself as Captain Hendricks, and had been assured that a lowly captaincy would mean nothing, even if he were in command of a ship. But that it should not dissuade him, for it was nothing personal. Benbridge was so stiff that he was just as likely to wipe his feet upon a major as speak to him.

'It is in regards to their ladyships.' From the hall, John could hear the butler give a respectful pause.

'Bring him here, immediately.' *Sliced thin and served with mustard.* For all the warmth and concern in his voice, his Grace might as well have been ordering supper than expecting word of his daughters' safety.

John entered the study and stood in silence before the man, waiting his turn to speak.

'I left the city for barely a day,' the duke began, low and cold, 'and returned to find that all hell had broken loose, and there was nothing left of my family but a brief and inadequate note. My daughters had no plans to travel, nor did they have my permission to do so. What part did you play in their departure?'

He had not led with the question that John had expected. *Who are you?* But it seemed that the duke had reached a station in life where courtesy was neither required nor expected. He knew that John was a nobody, or he'd have known him already. Only his daughters mattered. 'I had no part at all in their departure, your Grace,' he answered with great relief. 'But I did my humble best to aid in their return.'

'From where, Mr Hendricks?' his Grace snapped.

'Kendal. A little south of the Scottish border.'

'I see. Which one was it, then, that caused the trouble? And how did you become involved in it?'

And please, sit. Though they would have been welcome, they were not words he was likely to hear, now that he had met Benbridge. Apparently, the length of the story or the comfort of the teller was of no concern to the audience. John took a well-measured breath to show that he was not the least bit ill at ease. 'These are the facts as I know them.' He proceeded to tell the most abbreviated version of them he could manage. He began with the carriage ride, omitting any mention of his drunkenness or the sleeping arrangements. He explained Dru's goal, while showing no particular interest in the scandal of it. He explained the problems with the carriage, while conveniently forgetting the trousers. And lastly, he explained the discovery of the runaways in the most deliberately vague way possible, eliding dates and ending with an assurance that the dancing master had decided it was in the best interest of his health to remain in Scotland.

When he finished, the Duke looked at him with a jaundiced eye. 'You say that before the journey, you were in the employ of Folbroke? He must be ruing the loss of you, for it is a rare talent you possess to spin a tale that is equally devoid of truth and untruth.'

'Thank you, my lord.' John was not completely sure that it was meant as a compliment, but he decided to accept it as one and let Benbridge make what he would of the irony.

'What is your opinion on the state of my daughters' reputations?'

'I cannot be positive that this will go unnoticed, my lord. I am more sure of Lady Drusilla, for I was with her from the first.' And knew exactly the risks that they had taken. 'Lady Priscilla was, perhaps, less careful.' And there was an understatement. 'But though the roads were beastly, the accommodations were crowded with people well below the level of the *ton*. It is quite possible that there will be no tales spread abroad at all.'

The Duke looked at him again, eyes sharp. 'No one will hear, unless you would choose to speak of it.'

'I find, even now, sir, that I have trouble remembering the particulars, or the name of the young women involved.'

The Duke gave a slight nod. 'I should have known as much. Silly would never have engaged you if she did not have total confidence in your discretion.'

There was the nickname again, delivered as offhandedly as breathing. And to a girl that was as unlike it as it was possible to be. He held his ground and remained emotionless.

'She promised you payment, did she not? It seems you have managed well. Knowing my girls, you will have worked to earn any reward. Many would not have taken the trouble with them, for they are high spirited, always getting up to some trouble or other.' He thought for a moment and then added, 'Priscilla, at least.'

John bit his tongue to keep from chiding the man that there was nothing of simple high spirits in the behaviour of the younger daughter, for he did not want to think that it was blackmail that brought him to thus.

The duke reached into his desk and produced a chequebook.

'About that, your Grace…'

The man stopped his hand on the way to the ink well, probably expecting John to haggle over the price.

'It is not that I am unappreciative of your offer. But I find that there is something I would value, more than reimbursement.'

'And what is that, then?' Benbridge seemed puzzled that there could be another reason for John to be still standing before the desk, other than the collection of a debt.

'In travelling with her for nearly a week, I found your daughter to be a most charming and agreeable young lady.'

'People often say that of Priss,' he said, as though another compliment meant nothing to him.

'Your elder daughter, my lord. Lady Drusilla.'

'Silly?' her father said, as though the idea had just occurred to him that there were two.

'Yes, my lord,' said Hendricks, trying not to wince. 'She is a lovely girl, with excellent manners, an even temperament and a quick wit. I have grown quite fond of her. And I have reason to suspect that she might return my feelings, given the chance.'

To this, the duke said nothing at all, as if he could not quite believe what he was hearing and was waiting for some word from Hendricks that would make it clear.

'I wish to pay my addresses to her, with your permission of

course, your Grace. Considering the delicate nature of our acquaintance, I would seek a proper introduction, here in London, so that there could be no question of our meeting in such inappropriate circumstances.' He waited for a response, assuming that the duke would question him about his prospects.

Instead, the man said, 'Oh, no. That will never do. I am sorry, of course. And glad that you have come to me first. But. No.' He did not seem without sympathy, but neither did he show any desire to continue the conversation.

'May I ask why, your Grace? If you have doubts, the Earl of Folbroke will assure you of my good character. I have sufficient funds to support Drusilla comfortably.' The last was a lie. But a small one, he was sure. 'And secure plans for the future.'

'Perhaps that is true,' Benbridge said, with a sad shake of his head. 'But you cannot claim a title, can you? Do you have family connections that might mitigate the fact? Are you a second son, perhaps? If so, is your brother in good health?'

John pitied his imaginary brother, to see him wished to death. 'No, sir. I am the natural son of a gentleman who saw fit to educate me, and place me properly, though he did not wish to make a formal acknowledgement.'

Benbridge drew away from him, as though the very air around him was contaminated by his parentage. 'Surely, you can see, now that you have been forced to admit it aloud, that such would never do for Drusilla. If you are as fond of her as you claim, you must wish something better for her, just as I do.'

'Of course, your Grace. But my feelings are strong and they moved me to speak.'

The duke smiled at him, relieved that the matter could be settled without fuss, since it involved nothing stronger than emotion.

'Well, then, if there is nothing else?' And then he snapped his fingers. 'But you needed reimbursement, did you not?'

'It is hardly necessary.' He said it a little coldly, for if the man thought that he had come begging for the price of a carriage ride, he was sorely mistaken.

'No, sir. I insist. For the kindness you have done for our family, if nothing else.' And the duke opened the chequebook and with a flourish signed over an amount that was equal to three years' wages. Heedless of the insult he had paid, he looked directly into John's eyes so that there could be no question of the reason for the payment and said, 'I trust this will be sufficient?'

He stared down at the duke without speaking, trying to see what Dru saw when she looked at the man that would make her care at all what he thought. Benbridge was every bit the image of his younger daughter, with blue eyes and hair that was almost ginger. But with the ruddy complexion and voice of a man who liked riding to the hounds in sun and wind, and following his exercise with a glass or two. Or perhaps three, judging by the thin veins that showed at the edge of his nose.

John had seen a portrait of the family in the front hall. If one measured the ages of the subjects, it had been painted some ten years past. From her mother, Priscilla had taken the delicate manner, the milky skin and the vivacious character.

And his Drusilla? It appeared that she had taken nothing from either parent, laid like a cuckoo's egg in the Benbridge nest. John suspected that, should he visit the house a quarter of a century past, he might meet another dancing master. Or perhaps an artist. Or a close family friend that could give him an easy explanation for how the duke could come to have a daughter so unlike himself.

And one for whom he seemed to care so little. In all his mentions of her so far, he had been respectful, pleasant and candid, but John could hardly call the man's actions loving. While he might dote on Priscilla, he looked at her sister rather as one might a distant cousin, who deserved better than she wanted, but should settle for what she was given.

You are like me, my darling. Even if you do not know it. We are natural children in an unnatural world. And we belong together. It gave John reason to hope.

Now, John stood there in front of the great dark wood desk, holding the bit of paper that the duke had given to him, feeling like a fool for ever having thought that the meeting would end in any other way.

'Of course, your Grace. You are most generous in your thanks.' The words were dry and bitter as ash. He forced his arm to bend and tucked the cheque into his pocket, swallowing bile until he could manage a tight smile of gratitude. And then, as if he was remembering the matter that had brought him here after all, he said, 'There is one other small thing. A nothing, really. Various personal items belonging to your daughters were left in my keeping, forgotten in the carriage when we parted. A ribbon. A book, a glove. A few small articles that slipped from a trunk when they were packing at an inn. I wish to return them, if it is not too much trouble.' And see his love again, to explain the difficulties and plot their next move.

The duke nodded. 'Very conscientious of you, sir. And careless of them for leaving the things. Bundle them up and have them sent to the house by mail, so that they can sort them out betwixt. You needn't trouble yourself with another call.' He looked at John in a flat, uninterested way, as though he had already forgotten why the man might want to visit, firm as a stone wall, and just as likely to be worn away by John's continued visits.

'Thank you.' John managed a nod, as though this suggestion had not just thwarted his plan. 'Tell Lady Drusilla to expect something in the afternoon post.'

Chapter Twenty-One

Dru entered the Benbridge house in London, pulled along in the wake of her sister. Now that Priss was resigned to the return, she took the lead, treating Dru as though she were nothing more than a servant, waiting to catch what scraps of affection remained after the tearful reunion with Father.

'Priscilla!' The duke had heard the commotion and came into the hall, hands outstretched, when they had barely crossed the threshold. 'I wondered at your absence. And all I had was your sister's cryptic notes.'

He glanced at Dru with a raised eyebrow. 'But your Mr Hendricks has been to explain already, and I am not quite so in the dark as I was before.'

'He was here already?' She hoped she did not sound as eager as she felt.

'You missed him by little more than an hour,' her father said.

Dru nodded, as though it were little more than a sign of his efficiency, and not a missed opportunity for another look at him. 'I am sorry, Father, that I was not able to explain further, nor to give you warning of his visit. But the situation was quite complicated. And speed seemed to be required.'

'You were in a great hurry. Yet you had time to engage Mr Hendricks.'

She wondered what John had said, on his visit, for it did seem that Father was unusually suspicious. 'That was a fortuitous happening, and nothing more. He protected me from the unwelcome attentions of another passenger. And I engaged him in case further aid was needed.'

'Next time, Silly, have the sense not to leave without a maid.' After one last glare, he turned his attention to Priss. 'And I suspect that you did not leave for Scotland unaccompanied?'

'No, Papa.'

'But that you returned alone.'

'Yes, Papa.'

'And does anyone else know of this trip that I am unaware of?'

'No, Papa.'

'Then we will speak of it no more.'

Even Priss seemed surprised at how quickly it was to be dismissed. 'I was gone for quite some time with Mr Gervaise, Papa.'

'According to my estimation, almost four days.'

'And in that time—'

'I said,' their father's booming voice cut the sentence short, 'we will speak of it no more.'

'Yes, Papa.' Whatever declaration Priss had been preparing was discarded and forgotten.

'And you, Drusilla, will speak with me, in my study.'

'It is hardly fair, Papa. For if you mean to lecture her for something that I...'

'I said, Priscilla, we...will...speak...no...more. Drusilla!'

Priss seemed to recede from the scene almost without moving, and Dru did not even have the time to cast a backward glance of thanks. The effort to defend her had been kind, even though it was ineffectual. It had been more than she'd expected to receive from Priss.

But it had failed, and she had no choice except to follow her father into the study, to give her side of events and accept punishment for her part in them.

Once behind the closed oak door, her father appeared almost warm to her, holding a hand out to her and gathering her into his arms to offer a fond kiss upon the cheek. 'It is so good to have you home, my dear, and that you have brought Priss back to me unaccompanied. I meant what I said before, although perhaps I should not have been so harsh with you. You cannot traipse across the country without so much as a groom.'

She gave a respectful nod. 'I would not have done it, your Grace, if I had been able to think of another way.'

'See that it does not happen again.'

Dru swallowed the confusion, for it did not seem that her father understood the gravity of the situation. 'Let us hope not. For Priss's behaviour tarnishes my reputation as well as her own. If she is so foolish as to breathe a word of what she has done, her supposed friends in town will use it to their advantage against us.'

He nodded. For a moment, she thought that he cared what might have happened to her. But then he said, 'It is better, if she ran at all, that she went without you. It was far more likely that she would have been recognised had the two of you been seen together. Next time, do not chase her. If I learned anything in the years your mother was alive, it was that when a woman realises that no one is in pursuit she will find her own way home.'

'Oh,' she said. For what more could she say to that? For it seemed that however it might seem, her father did not care any more for Priss than he did for her. Then she added, 'But it was good that I had Mr Hendricks to help us on this trip. Once he realised my dilemma, he was most eager to assist me.'

'Ah, yes. Your stalwart companion,' her father said, making a small face. 'I am sure, once he realised that you were my daughter, he smelled the money on you and could not keep away.'

'Not at all, sir,' she replied. 'He came to my aid before he so much as knew my name. It was only later, when I offered to retain him, that we discussed my family.'

'Well, he knows it now, for I have just had a visit from him.' Her father was laughing. 'If you could have seen the poor man, Silly, you would have been most amused.'

'Really,' she said faintly, listening to the blood ringing in her ears.

'He stood before me, all pomp and ceremony, polishing his little spectacles, and asked to pay you court.'

'He did?'

'He was quite effusive in his praise of you. Complimented your easy temper and your wit.' Her father gave a derisive snort. And then, as though he had forgotten, he added, 'And your looks. He seemed to favour them.'

John had wanted her, then. It had not been a mistake. Her heart leapt like a doe. Then it came crashing back to earth and she said, cautiously, 'How kind of him.' And added casually, not wanting to ruin the moment by seeming too eager. 'What did you tell him?'

Her father laughed again. 'I told him to go away, of course. Although he is well mannered for one of his sort, he is far too common for you, my dear.'

'I found him to be most gently bred,' she said, a little hopefully. 'And most pleasant company.'

'That is all well and good. But nice manners do not make a husband.'

Then what does? she was tempted to ask. But there was little point, for she knew what the answer would be. The man she wanted had no title and no money. If those two faults could be remedied, all others would be overlooked.

Unless Priss had been right. And then, no fortune or rank would be sufficient.

'I do not think I would mind so very much, if my husband was not a lord,' she said. 'And would it not be better for me to marry first, so that it would be quite clear to any potential suitors, that there is no impediment to courting Priss? I would hate to stand in the way of her happiness.'

He looked her over carefully, as though searching for the things that this strange man had seen in her, and then nodded to himself as though he had confirmed his first assessment of her. 'Do not worry, Silly, my dear. The men who court your sister are not bothered by your presence in the least. You will make a match yet. Perhaps next Season, when your sister has had time to cool her blood, I will send the pair of you on the rounds of Almack's and you shall have your pick of the young bucks there.'

The odds on there being a young buck that would notice her if she travelled with Priss were near to non-existent. That her own hunting should be put off for a year, while her foolish sister rusticated after this last embarrassment, or that hunting was even necessary, now that she had freely given her heart...

And her body...

She swallowed, not wishing to give away the sinking feeling inside at the risk she had taken while pretending that she would not be parted from him. 'It is really not necessary to give me another Season, Father. I fear, after all this time, there is little hope of success. And Mr Hendricks did seem quite capable and devoted to my happiness, even if he was not what you expected for me.'

'Nonsense, my dear. He was nothing more than a fortune hunter.' He stared at her.

Suddenly she was sure of a thing she had only suspected before. This was why there had been no shouting or threats over her lapse in allowing Priss to escape. This was to be her punishment. Her father knew she wanted John. And that was why she could not have him. 'No,' she said softly, so that there could be no misunderstanding. 'I am quite sure of it. He wished the best for me.'

'But you will need to fix your affections on a man that is more constant than that, if you wish my consent.'

'Not constant?' For that was the last word in the world she would have chosen, had she wished to insult him. John Hendricks was as constant as the rising and setting of the sun.

'He gave up the idea with barely a fight, I assure you. Left here with my cheque in his hand and his tail between his legs.'

'Your cheque?'

'You did not think that I would send an employee off from my service without paying him, did you? Considering the audacity of his interest in you, I think a reference is quite out of the question. But the ten thousand pounds I gave him covered the matter of his help, and there was more than enough extra there to make him forget his penchant for you.'

'You bought him off.' She would have sworn that it was not possible. The things he had said to her, the way he had sworn. And the way he had made her feel. All had counted for nothing, when compared with such a sum.

'The money was well earned if he managed to scare the dancing master away from your sister as handily as he claimed. The man is not all bad. But when all is said and done, he is no better than a servant. But he assured me he will be returning whatever love tokens you have pressed upon him with this afternoon's post. Then he was gone. That should tell you all you need to know about the focus of his affection. It had very little to do with you, and much more to finding a way into our family, and our fortune. He chose you because you are the weaker and more vulnerable sister. After this recent escapade with Gervaise, Priss would have seen through him and sent him packing. Now dry your eyes and go upstairs to see to your sister. I am sure she is most cross to have her plans so easily thwarted, and your hands will be full with placating her.'

As she walked from the room, Dru wiped absently at her face with the back of her hand, surprised to feel no tears.

Chapter Twenty-Two

She walked slowly, numbly, back to her room, as silent and polite as she ever was when in her father's house. And with each step, her brain screamed.

How could I have been so wrong?

Wrong about her life, which had seemed full, but was proven empty. And wrong about John, who had said he loved her. After the return from Scotland, she had been sure that she would see him again. Not positive he would go through with his plan to visit her father, but fairly confident that he could be persuaded to attempt it, if he faltered once he had seen the formidable Duke of Benbridge.

She had been much more confident of her father's response, which had been the dismissal she had expected. Of course he would say no, for he would see no further than the Mr at the beginning of her love's name. But she had assumed, after the initial disappointment, that John would come to her. She could have told him not to be put off by the first inevitable refusal, and when best to approach for another interview. Perhaps, with time and strategy, some progress would have been made.

If her father could not be moved, then at the very least they could have prolonged the parting so that he would have been allowed a proper goodbye to her. She had not thought that, with all the pride he had shown, he would simply take the money and leave. By doing so, he had proven all that her father had ever believed about the common men of England. And about her as well.

If he left so easily, what reason could he have had to attach himself to her, other than as a way to increase his paycheque? John had thought her gullible. He had forced himself into her rooms, taken advantage of her inexperience and her feelings for him. He had reduced her to a state where her virtue had seemed more of a disadvantage than a precious gift. Now he was ten thousand pounds richer. And he was gone. Lost for ever, for she had no clue how to contact him.

Though if she had, she did not know what she would say. She did not think herself likely to weep and beg him to return, for if she had nothing else, she had her pride as well. If she were a man, she would have called him out, for the embarrassment of being tricked and acting the fool for him was still stinging in her heart.

He was no better than Gervaise.

She lay down upon the bed, wishing that she had the abilities of her sister to throw a proper sulk. Priss would begin with tears, follow with the kicking of slippers and pounding of pillows, and finish by shrieking loud enough to bring the above-stairs servants to whisper at the door, and raise her father's anger at having his peace so disturbed. She would have a new gown out of it to stop her crying, and perhaps some ribbons as well.

And Dru would have a megrim. She sighed. There was little

room in the emotions of the house for another fuss. Even if she had attempted it, her tantrum would have been met with a simple, 'Do not be absurd, Silly. Now see to your sister, for she seems most unhappy.'

She lay still in the bright sunlight of the room, wishing that there were tears sliding slowly down her cheeks and into her ears and hair. What Priss had to cry about, she was not sure. Unless she had realised what Dru had: that they might both be in the very devil of a fix, in a month or so.

But was that anything to cry over? Father might be less particular of their choice of suitors, with less than nine months to make a decision.

She smiled a little in grim satisfaction at the thought, and felt the first angry tear burning her cheek. While it worried her that a child might be possible, it hurt far more to think that she had been so easily abandoned by its father. After all his high-and-mighty words about not caring for rank or wealth, he had taken her father's bribe and never looked back.

She wondered, as she always had, if it would have been different if he'd met Priss. Quite possibly Mr Hendricks would be howling outside the gates like a rabid wolf, eager to have the company of one who was not only rich and well born, but vivacious and pretty as well. For had she needed to protect her little sister from the likes of John, she doubted that she would have been so successful.

She blotted her tears with the edge of a pillowcase, surprised that they had not yet stopped, for she was rarely able to manage more than one or two of them, even with effort. But the thoughts of her sister and John—Mr Hendricks, she told herself firmly—had been so clear in her head, that for a time, it had consumed her. The sly smile he had given her when he had begun to take liberties, and the masterful way he had of touching just the right places on her body, were not things she wished him to share with any other woman in the world.

If her father was right, he had chosen her specifically because she was the weakest link in the family. While Priss was just as likely to have fallen from grace, she doubted that it would do the girl any permanent harm to be rid of Gervaise. While she might enjoy raising a fuss, Priss would not waste much time crying real tears over a man who was even tonight drowning his sorrows in expensive wine and a willing and experienced woman, laughing at the foolish heiress he had left behind.

Time had passed. Dru had a vague recollection of her maid poking a head into the room with offers of luncheon, and then tea. She had sent the girl away with a cross word, preferring the way the bitter emptiness of her stomach matched the sharp, empty feeling in her heart. This time, when the maid came again, she sat up and hitched up her skirts, grabbing a slipper and preparing to toss it at the head of the unsuspecting girl.

'My lady,' she said hurriedly, shielding her face against a blow. The poor thing had already been to see Priss and prepared herself for battle. 'There is a package for you, come with the afternoon's post. If you wish, I will take care of the contents.'

'No.' Dru took a deep breath, for even the one short word made her head sound stuffy and weak. Hadn't her father said something about John returning her possessions to her? Although what she had left with him, she'd no idea.

'Do not touch it. Bring it to me. I will open it here.' Perhaps it would be the letter of farewell that she hoped for. For if she was to be guilty of a horrible misalliance, she at least deserved a *billet doux* to hold against her quaking breast so that she could weep and swoon, cursing her father and the gods.

Priss had a box full of them, after all. And when she had nothing else to do, on a rainy day, she pored over them, reading choice lines and sighing. It was not too much to ask, was it, if Drusilla could have one such for herself?

But the package the maid brought to her looked more like forgotten laundry than it did anything else. Dear God, had she left some personal item in John's room that might indicate what they had been to each other? She was torn between the equally horrible ideas of him keeping a shift or a stocking as a trophy of her downfall, and the idea that it would mean so little to him that he would think she'd want it returned. The least he could have done was pined over the thing, whatever it was, to make her believe that he had trouble parting with it.

The girl was reaching for the strings to untie the bundle, and Dru said sharply, 'Leave it.' When the girl hesitated, hoping to get some glimpse of the contents, Dru dismissed her, then waited the few minutes it took until she was sure that she was alone.

Then she pulled on the string that held the brown paper in place.

There was but one item within. A pair of familiar leather breeches, and a single sheet of paper pinned to them.

Eight o'clock. Tonight. Hyde Park.

Chapter Twenty-Three

She waited at the gate, unsure of what it was that he'd meant her to do. It could not be safe for her to go, unescorted, into the darkness of the park. But it wasn't all that safe to wait alone on the street.

Suddenly, arms grabbed her from behind, pulling her into the shade before she could manage so much as a cry.

She was being kissed, and, Lord help her, handled. And before the fear could overtake the surprise of it, she realised that the taste of the mouth on hers was familiar, as was the way the hands gripped her. And so she relaxed, kissing back, and whispering, when he allowed her breath, 'Mr Hendricks?'

'Please, darling. After all we have been to each other, you must call me John.' And then he went back to kissing her, running his hands over her body, under her cloak. 'You disappoint me, love. You are not wearing the gift that I sent you.'

'Because there was no shirt or coat,' she said sensibly. 'I could not very well come to meet you in a public place wearing naught but the breeches under my cloak.'

The growl he made in response made her think that he would not have minded at all if she had.

'But I am wearing them, although they are hidden under my skirt. Mr Hendricks. Mr Hendricks! John.' For he had lifted the skirts, plunging his hands beneath to check for himself and was massaging her bottom in way that was most disconcerting.

'Just reassuring myself of the fact, darling,' he said. 'And there they are, you naughty little minx.'

There was certainly nothing little about her, nor did she think of herself as a temptress. 'If I am naughty,' she admitted, 'it is because I am most sorely tried by the company I have been keeping of late. I think you are a bad influence upon my character.'

'I only mean to care for you, my love,' he answered back. 'For if you stay in my company, you will be in for quite a bit of riding.' But the way he was touching her now, with the heel of his hand resting firmly between her legs, she wondered if he meant to be talking about horses, or something else entirely.

'Where might I be going?' she whispered back. And then gave a shudder, and thought, *I will be going over the moon, if you continue with what you are doing, John. And I wonder, do you know?*

'Scotland,' he answered back. 'The blacksmiths are most obliging, I hear, when met with thwarted lovers.' Then he proved that he knew exactly what he was doing to her. He was moving his hand over the leather, making firm tight circles with it, and she wrapped her arms about his neck to steady herself against the collapse that she was sure was coming.

'I thought that my father told you that your advances on my person were not welcome.'

'Not by him,' John agreed, and speeded the movement of his hand. 'But you have yet to tell me otherwise. And even if you do,

I mean to ignore you. Do not think that I will let you choose the sensible course and lead me back to your father for another go round in the study. It is quite plain to me that he will never change his mind on the subject.' He was kissing her throat now, running his tongue along the place, just at the back of her ear, until she shuddered and clung to him, almost forgetting her objections.

'You took his money to stay away from me.'

'I did nothing of the kind,' he answered. 'He wished to pretend that it was a reward for returning you safely. It would have been churlish of me to call it the bribe it was. But neither would it make sense to refuse payment for my services. I am not a gentleman of leisure, you know. I am a simple working man.' But there was nothing simple about the things he was doing to her now. With a final touch, he brought her easily over the edge, to leave her weak and trembling in his arms. And she clung to him, vulnerable and needy, and felt the old fear of being helpless in the face of another's plans for her.

Then his arms came around her, supporting her, but not trapping her. As an experiment, she relaxed her muscles, as though ready to fall into a swoon and drop from his arms. Other than a slight tightening to keep her upright and close, there was no change in him.

And she knew, for all his forceful words about taking her against her will, that he would release her if she struggled, or carry her if she collapsed. They were in tune with each other, as two parts of the same instrument.

'Do you truly think ill of me for the money?' he asked. 'Although the sum was generous, I did feel that I deserved recompense for enduring the company of your sister. I am sorry, Dru, but I find the girl tiresome in the extreme.'

She sighed, leaning a little harder against him. Although she did not wish to think ill of her sister, she had never expected to hear words so sweet. 'She is not so bad, once you get used to her. And much smarter than she first appears.'

'She would have to be. For I doubt that it would be possible...'

'John!' She was surprised at how easy the name came to her, now that she felt free to speak it.

'Darling.' He kissed her, smiling. 'You may scold me all you like, so long as you call me by name.'

'Then I will insist that you admit the truth. You know why my father gave you as much money as he did, John. He wanted you to stay away from me.'

'If he meant to imply that the cheque was contingent on my avoiding your company?' She could see his wicked smile, and the glint of the moonlight on his glasses as he dipped his head to her throat again. 'Then I am afraid we are at cross purposes. There is no sum that would keep me from you, now that I have experienced the delight of your body.'

'You vile man. Is that all you want from me?' she whispered as sternly as she could manage. Although if the answer was affirmative, she doubted she would mind so very much.

'Not at all,' he snarled. 'There must be some strange weakness in me that makes me long to feel the lash of your tongue, or the cold razor edge of your intellect.' He kissed her on the mouth again with such force that when he had finished with her, she could hardly string two thoughts together, much less wield a razor of them. Then he pulled her pliable body close inside the shelter of his heavy topcoat. 'Or perhaps it just sweetens the moment when I have such a strong woman completely in my power.'

And it was true. She was in his power, quite deliciously helpless for the first time in ages. She did not have to see to the running of her father's household, or watch over her scapegrace sister. Or wait for the chance to live her own life and find her own happiness after the futures of all around her were secure. Judging by the path of his fingers on the inside of her thigh, John Hendricks was about to force her to face her happy future right now, in a public park in the middle of London.

'In any case, the money your father gave me is already gone. I have no intention of giving the cheque or his daughter back to him.'

'Spent?' she gasped, trying to gather those wits that he claimed to find so attractive and push herself away from him.

'Invested,' he corrected, kissing her again. 'With a friend. I told him I meant to take a wife. He had suggestions for a man with some capital. When we return from our honeymoon, I will introduce you. The Earl of Folbroke and his lovely wife, Emily. My once and future employer. My ambition has grown beyond the menial tasks he required of me when I was his secretary.

'And fortunately for me, his interests have changed as well. He is in need of a steward for his philanthropic efforts, and was seeking a forward-thinking man who can be trusted to work independently. In the future, I will be more of a partner than a servant. We will be quite welcome in their house, which will give me the opportunity to make contacts...'

'Of what sort?' she asked, somewhat surprised.

'Political ones, I should think.' He grinned at her. 'What with the changes underway in the country right now, there will be a need for men with vision and an interest in reform.'

'Reform?' Dru smiled wickedly. 'My father will be horrified.'

'I expect he will be. But you needn't fear the damage to your reputation that such a poor marriage will likely make. A public servant will be better than a tradesman for you.'

'I am not giving my status in society two thoughts, John Hendricks,' she snapped. 'I have had quite enough of being Lady Drusilla if it means I am never to be a wife. And I will live in a haystack with you, if you wish.'

He laughed. 'That will not be necessary. Although I will instruct our driver to stop at one, if you wish. I have hired a coach for us, so that we may travel north in comfort.'

'You have thought of everything, haven't you?'

'I did not wish to marry you, until I was sure that I could provide for you,' he murmured between the kisses on her throat. 'I am not worthy of you, after all. And it will not be as you have lived. But if you come with me tonight, you need never doubt my loyalty to you. Or my love.' He groaned. 'Or my need. Oh God, Dru, do not deny me this. I swear, I will die without you. Come away with me. Marry me. Let me make you smile.'

She bit her lip, not wanting to seem too eager, or to admit aloud that the only thing that had really mattered in his last speech was the word marriage, and the thought that, wherever she would be, she would be spending her nights safe in the arms of John Hendricks. She moved against him, feeling her own arousal growing, again. 'Can we be in Scotland tonight?' she whispered.

He answered her in that calm and confident voice that made her believe he could dispense with any difficulties that stood between her and happiness, 'Gretna Green is over thirty hours away, even if we take the mail coach. But you should know by now, my Lady Drusilla, just how long it takes for me to get you to the border.'

And then he touched her.

HISTORICAL

Novels coming in June 2011

RAVISHED BY THE RAKE
Louise Allen

The dashing man Lady Perdita Brooke once knew is now a hardened rake, who does *not* remember their passionate night together…though Dita's determined to remind him! She's holding all the cards—until Alistair reveals the ace up his sleeve!

THE RAKE OF HOLLOWHURST CASTLE
Elizabeth Beacon

Sir Charles Afforde has purchased Hollowhurst Castle; all that's left to possess is its determined and beautiful chatelaine. Roxanne Courland would rather stay a spinster than enter a loveless marriage… But Charles' sensual onslaught is hard to resist!

BOUGHT FOR THE HAREM
Anne Herries

After her capture by corsairs, Lady Harriet Sefton-Jones thinks help has arrived in the form of Lord Kasim. But he has come to purchase Harriet for his master the Caliph! Must Harriet face a life of enslavement, or does Kasim have a plan of his own?

SLAVE PRINCESS
Juliet Landon

For ex-cavalry officer Quintus Tiberius duty *always* comes first. His task to escort the Roman emperor's latest captive should be easy. But one look at Princess Brighid and Quintus wants to put his own desires before everything else…

MILLS & BOON